"You don't need to do that, you know?" Angus said.

"What's that?"

"Be my cheerleader. I'm a big boy. I can take a hit."

"Yeah, you are," she said. "*Such* a big boy."

A slow smile spread across his face, even as his eyes narrowed. Even though he'd known more success than most men saw in a lifetime, that hunger still remained. It was a part of him. And when he switched it on, it always made Lucinda burn.

Then his gaze began to roam. Over her hair, over her cheeks, her jaw, pausing once more on her mouth, before traveling down the twist of a spaghetti strap, over the crisscross at her décolletage, her bare shoulders.

Lucinda's heart picked up pace and the hairs at the back of her neck prickled.

He shouldn't be looking at her that way.

And she shouldn't be relishing the fact that he was.

Dear Reader,

I've always been a big fan of "working together" romances.

Partly because it gives me the chance to "try out" occupations I'll never have the chance to enjoy.

As a kid, how adventurous an idea it seemed *not* to have a career, but to change jobs every year. I could be a taxi driver in Seville. Then a hairdresser in New York. A movie extra in Bollywood. A writer anywhere I pleased...

But I also love placing a hero and heroine into one another's work space day after day after day, as it gives us a glimpse into what life might be like beyond the happily-ever-after.

For if two people can endure working together, they can survive anything!

On that score, having watched Lucinda and Angus banter and support, cajole and bolster, and employ absolute honesty as they negotiate their working lives side by side, I have not a single doubt that their happily-ever-after will be a blast.

Happy reading!

Love,

Ally xxx

AllyBlake.com

Crazy About Her Impossible Boss

Ally Blake

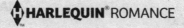

HARLEQUIN®ROMANCE

Recycling programs
for this product may
not exist in your area.

ISBN-13: 978-1-335-55612-7

Crazy About Her Impossible Boss

First North American publication 2019

Printed in U.S.A.

Australian author **Ally Blake** loves reading and strong coffee, porch swings and dappled sunshine, beautiful notebooks and soft, dark pencils. Her inquisitive, rambunctious, spectacular children are her exquisite delights. And she adores writing love stories so much she'd write them even if nobody else read them. No wonder, then, having sold over four million copies of her romance novels worldwide, Ally is living her bliss. Find out more about Ally's books at allyblake.com.

Books by Ally Blake

Harlequin Romance

The Royals of Vallemont

Rescuing the Royal Runaway Bride
Amber and the Rogue Prince

Billionaire on Her Doorstep
Millionaire to the Rescue
Falling for the Rebel Heir
Hired: The Boss's Bride
Dating the Rebel Tycoon
Millionaire Dad's SOS
Hired by the Mysterious Millionaire
A Week with the Best Man

Harlequin KISS

The Rules of Engagement
Faking It to Making It
The Dance Off
Her Hottest Summer Yet

Visit the Author Profile page
at Harlequin.com for more titles.

To Jamie, Merle and Ryan and the gorgeous staff at my "office," aka Café Bliss. They know me by name, point out excitedly when my favourite booth is free, let me rent a table anytime for the price of a latte and a piece of cake. True patrons of the arts!

Praise for
Ally Blake

"Now I'm used to being entertained by Ally Blake's wit, enjoying her young quirky heroines and drooling over her dark, brooding heroes. But this book stuck inside me somehow."
—*Goodreads* on *Millionaire Dad's SOS*

CHAPTER ONE

LUCINDA. PICK UP. Lucinda. Pick up. Lucinda. Pick up.

Lucinda's fingers hovered over the keyboard keys right as the voice stopped, their ends tingling from typing ninety-plus words a minute.

She cocked an ear but couldn't tell where the voice had come from.

From her desk—aka The Guard Tower Blocking All From Entrance Into Her Boss's Sacred Space—she could see all the way from his corner office, down the hall past Reception to the lifts at the end, and there was no one nearby.

She went back to typing and…

Lucinda. Pick up. Lucinda. Pick up. Lucinda. Pick up.

With a huff, she lifted her fingers from the keys and zeroed in on the sound.

It was coming from her phone, which was lit up beseechingly by her elbow. Someone had added a new ringtone. The picture smiling back at her gave her a fair idea who was behind the deep, gravelly voice.

Biting her lips to suppress a scowl—or possibly a smile—Lucinda pressed the little red "end call" dot on the screen, flicking the call to voicemail. She was a busy woman. The man could wait.

Straightening her shoulders, Lucinda found her spot on the screen once more, pressed a quick finger to her earbud and picked up the trail of the conversation in her ear as Dahlia—Executive Assistant to the Head of Advertising at the Melbourne Ballet Company—continued her story about the man who'd stood her up for drinks the night before.

As Lucinda listened, mmm-ing in all the right places, she continued to type a bullet-point list of the day's top business-related headlines—trending brands, celebrity gaffes and wins, as well as a few choice titbits she thought might be relevant to her boss—a ritual she'd begun when she'd first landed a job at the Big Picture Group six-and-a-half years earlier.

Then her mobile started ringing again, the tone deep, resonant and insistent. Male. *Lucinda. Pick up. Lucinda. Pick up. Lucinda. Pick up.*

Lucinda did not pick up. She opened a drawer, tossed the phone inside, covered it in a pile of miscellaneous paper and shut the drawer once more.

Then into her mouthpiece she said, "Dahlia, you are a rare gem. Find a man who sees your worth. One who looks you in the eye. Who listens when you speak. Who shows up when he says he will. Find a grown-up. Do not waste another moment settling for anything less. You'll thank me."

Dahlia thanked her profusely and rang off. But not before promising to send Lucinda a dozen A-circle tickets to opening night of the Melbourne Ballet's next show. Lucinda didn't bite back that smile. She already had a couple of clients lined up who'd love her for ever for those tickets.

Though she did wonder—if only briefly—whether she was, in fact, the best possible person Dahlia, or anyone, could turn to for dating advice. At least she hadn't given Dahlia any advice she wouldn't follow herself.

"Probably why you've been single for so long," she muttered, before getting back to work.

Until her phone started up again. *Lucinda. Pick up. Lucinda. Pick up. Lucinda. Pick up.* Only muffled. By paper. And a closed drawer.

Lucinda slowly typed the last bullet point, saved the file and sent it flying through the ether to her boss's computer, before turning on her chair to face the man himself.

Angus Wolfe, one of the top branding specialists in town, if not the country, sat on the other side of a wall of diffused, smoky glass that separated him from the rest of the world.

He leant back in his big leather chair, feet up on the decadently deep windowsill, face in profile as he looked out over the stunning view of the Melbourne skyline. The dying sun sparkled and glinted off the staggering shards of chrome and glass beyond but Lucinda only had eyes for the mobile phone pressed to his ear.

When the drawer began to vibrate a moment before her phone rang, she whipped it open, grabbed her phone and again pressed the little red "end call" dot. She then shoved back her chair, stalked to the discreet glass door that was hers and hers alone, opened it with a satisfying swish and strode across the acre of soft grey carpet to her boss's desk.

There was no way he wasn't fully aware she stood behind him. The man's ability to read a room was legendary. He noticed changes in temperature, pulse, breathing and tone of voice the way other people noticed being kicked in the shin.

Yet still she took a selfish moment to drink him in before officially making herself known.

For Angus Wolfe's profile was a study in staggering male beauty.

The man was all chiselled angles. Sharp jaw, close-shaven. Hair darkly curling and a mite overlong. The reading glasses he refused to admit he needed to wear did nothing to soften the impact of the most formidable pair of dark-hazel eyes that had ever been seen.

Even the tendons in his neck were a sight to behold.

Then he shifted. Slowly. Like a big cat stretching in the sun. The lines of his charcoal suit moved with him, cut as they were to make the most of his...everything. Each one cost more than she'd spent on her car. She knew. She paid his bills.

Then she spotted his socks. Peeking out from the top of his custom-made dress shoes was the merest hint of a wolf motif. She'd given him those socks for Christmas.

Her heart gave a little flutter, releasing a gossamer thread of lust that wafted from throat to belly to places less mentionable.

She squished the thing. Fast.

Angus Wolfe might be able to read a room, but if anyone dared claim that Lucinda Starling—his long-time executive assistant, his right-hand woman, his not-so-secret weapon—was a teeny, tiny little bit in love with him, he'd have laughed till he split a kidney.

Either she kept her cards closer to her chest than she realised or he had a blind spot when it came to her. The fact that he had no clue was a *gift*. And she planned to keep it that way.

For the sake of her job. Her self-respect. Her mental health.

When her phone went off in her hand—*Lucinda. Pick up*—she flinched.

Then she pulled herself together. She held her phone at arm's length and said, "Really?"

A beat slunk by before Angus turned in his

chair, mouth kicked to one side in the kind of half-smile that always meant trouble.

"When did you even get access to my phone?" she asked.

He tapped the side of his nose. "I have ways," he said, his voice deeper in person than in the recording, the words unhurried, the effect magnetic. "Ways and means."

"So they say," she sassed.

No one else would have noticed Angus's pause. The infinitesimal shift in his eyes. But Lucinda noticed it all. It was her job to do so. It was what made her so good at getting him what he needed before he even knew he needed it.

It was also why she mentally kicked herself for the flirty bass note in her voice.

Their relationship, as it was, was a finely tuned, perfectly balanced thing. There was sass, and plenty of it. And banter. There was also brutal honesty. And respect. A little flirtation was within the rules. Part of the game. For they worked really long hours and had to do what they had to do to keep it fun. It took work to keep the balance right. Work to make sure the guy had no clue how she felt about him.

Lucinda feigned resignation as she cocked a hip and waggled her phone in his general direction in order to deflect his attention. "Were you calling for a reason or were you just bored? Because I have plenty of admin I can sling your way if you're looking for something to do."

Angus blinked, breathed deeply through his nose and dragged his chair closer to his desk. "Thank you, but no. I wanted you."

"I was busy," she said, even while his words skipped and tripped through the unguarded parts of her subconscious.

"Doing what?"

She moved around behind his desk, turned the sleek monitor to face her and called up the screen that mirrored her own, where a bright-yellow computer-generated sticky note said, *Read me*.

Angus rubbed a single finger across the crease below his bottom lip. Lucinda tried not to stare at his mouth, she really did—but there she was, staring, as his face split into a grin. "Anyway, now I have you, sit."

His voice had dropped. A fraction. Enough.

She glanced up at his eyes. Imagined a bookshop full of self-help books taking her to task for allowing herself even a brief moment of fantasy.

Gritting her teeth, Lucinda walked back round his desk, taking the time to change her ringtone to something less likely to make the hairs on the back of her neck flutter and tickle. Where was a funeral dirge when you needed one?

She pulled up her chair, the rose-pink velvet tub chair he'd bought her for Christmas. The fact he let her keep it in *his* office, the absolute best part of the gift.

She sat then pulled out the notebook and pencil she'd grabbed without thinking when she'd picked up her phone. She scratched the pencil a few times to warm it up and settled in preparation for Angus's labyrinthine mind to shift, sway and touch on more bright ideas than any one person had the right to keep in their head.

"Ready?" he asked, that slight lift on one side of his mouth.

"Always."

Angus clapped and like that he was in work mode. One hundred and ten percent. "Right. The Remède account."

For the next ten minutes, Angus went on a wild and woolly stream of consciousness about the rebranding of the Remède cosmetics company, once upon a time a global force, now attempting a last-ditch about-turn in its fortunes before it sank.

It didn't matter if it was a lipstick maker, a political party or a department-store chain. Angus knew what made people connect with a product. What made them want.

Angus jumped from thought to idea, from grand plan to fine detail. Pausing rarely, never forewarning the shifts. Using Lucinda as a sounding board, a mental stress ball, a repository for the pyrotechnics that had built up inside his brilliant head throughout the long working day.

And Lucinda wrote. The adrenaline high of keeping up with Angus's mental gymnastics was cushioned by the tactile bliss of a dime-a-dozen 2B pencil tip gliding over quality note paper.

"And...?" she said, her voice a tad breathless, when he'd gone quiet for longer than a second.

"And we're done."

"Super."

She figured it would take about another half an hour to pour the notes from the page into the right files and to-do lists and then she could head home.

"Plans tonight?" Angus asked.

"Not much." Beyond the funny smell coming from the laundry that she'd promised herself she'd investigate.

Not that Angus would understand. His apartment was a sleek, temperature-controlled monument to earning big bucks.

While her cottage was...in need of a lot of TLC. But it was hers. Which made it wonderful.

"You?" she asked.

Again the small smile that tugged at the corner of his mouth. It told of fine dining, decadently expensive wine, all while looking across the table at a beautiful woman.

She rolled her eyes.

A well-timed reminder of the many ways in which she and Angus might as well have been different species.

He could survive on the barest amount sleep

per night, and often did, while if she didn't get a solid seven in a row she woke up looking and feeling part-witch.

He had a kitchen he never used and didn't need, considering he ate out every night, while she budgeted.

She could count on one hand the number of times he'd mentioned his family in six and a half years. While he knew everything there was to know about hers and they were more important to her than breath.

Her life was…slower. More structured. A daily routine of shopping lists stuck to the fridge door and juggling responsibilities. He said tomato, she said… Well, she said tomato as well.

The point was, at work they fit like custom-made kid gloves but their paths divided the moment they left the office.

On that note… When she reached the glass door at the boundary of his office, she stopped. Clicked her fingers. "Oh!" she said, as if she hadn't been trying to find a way to bring up something all day long. "I have some leave saved up. Enough that Fitz and his HR army are getting twitchy. I've checked the calendar, and there's nothing pressing, so I'm taking this weekend off."

"Off?" he asked. "Or *off*-off?"

She had weekends off anyway, but working for Angus ensured that meant very little. The man never stopped working. He was a hustler at heart and the hustle knew no clock. And, as she was basically his computer, his sounding board and his answering machine, if he needed to get it out, she was the one who caught it.

"Off-off," she said, taking a small step towards her door. "Friday through Sunday."

"Why?" he asked, pulling himself to standing and stretching his arms over his head. His white business shirt clung to the acres of muscle and might, one button straining so far she caught a glimpse of taut, tanned skin.

Her voice was only a little husky when she said, "Does 'none of your business' mean anything to you?"

"Can't say that it does."

"I have plans."

"What kind of plans?"

Come on, Lucinda. This is not a big deal. Stop prevaricating and tell him!

"Just…plans."

"Plans!" a voice boomed from the direction of Angus's main office doorway. Lucinda spun to find Fitz Beckett and Charlie Pullman, Angus's business partners in the Big Picture Group, amble on in.

"I love plans," said Fitz—broad, dashing, a total cad, the Big Picture Group's partner in charge of Recruitment, and Angus's cousin—as he hustled over to Lucinda, took hold of her and twirled her into a Hollywood dip. "Plans are my favourite. What are these plans of which you speak?"

Charlie—tall, lovely, an utter genius and the Big Picture partner in charge of Client Finance—followed in Fitz's wake, giving Lucinda a shy smile before heading over to Angus's desk and launching straight into a story about financial irregularities in one of their client's accounts.

The three of them in one room was a formidable thing. The three of them in one company made for one-stop business branding, recruitment and financial strategy.

From her upside-down vantage point she saw Angus raise a finger to his mouth to ask Charlie to shush.

"Lucinda was just telling me about this weekend's plans," said Angus, his voice a deep rumble.

"Exciting plans?" Fitz asked as Lucinda slapped him on the arm until he brought her back upright.

"Do any of you men know the meaning of the word 'boundaries'?"

Fitz shrugged. Charlie blinked. While Angus's intense hazel gaze remained locked onto her.

When Fitz cleared his throat, Lucinda realised the room had gone quiet. How long had she been staring back?

In a panic, she covered herself by crossing her eyes. When she uncrossed them, she found the corner of Angus's mouth had kicked into a half-smile.

Her heart fluttered like a baby bird in her chest.

"Look it up," said Lucinda, not giving them even an inch. "If I don't see you before I head off, have a good night."

Fitz shot her a grin. "Count on it."

Charlie lifted his hand in a wave.

Angus motioned the others over to the couches by the bookshelves and just like that he'd moved on to business. His one true love.

Lucinda turned and walked out of her boss's office, shutting the door behind her with a snick. She moved back to her desk where she sat and waited for the tremors in her hands to subside.

Why hadn't she just told him? Told all of them?

"Told them what, exactly?" she muttered as she put her notebook in her bag, deciding to type it up later that night, and closed up her desk for the day. "That you've been seeing a really fabulous man but you didn't tell anyone as you didn't want to jinx it? That, although he's absolutely perfect on paper, you know you've been holding back because of this hopeless crush you have on your unsuspecting boss that has kept you in an emotional wasteland for the past several years? So now, even though you haven't managed to light any real spark with Mr Perfect-on-Paper yet you've planned a dirty weekend with the guy because you're not getting any younger."

Yeah. She could just imagine their reaction.

Boundaries. Boundaries were a good thing.

Angus did not need to know every minor detail of her life.

Lucinda slipped into her jacket, whipped her scarf around her neck, grabbed her bag and strode down the hall towards the bank of lifts, lifting a hand to wave to any stragglers still at their desks.

Lucinda pressed the Down button and waited, recalling another "minor detail" she'd kept to herself; the phone call she'd received just that day with a job offer most executive assistants would kill for.

What was the point? It was hardly news. Recruiters attempted to headhunt her all the time.

But, whatever challenging conditions came with their working relationship, she'd never leave Angus. Their connection was rare. The repartee, the respect, the shorthand, the success they shared. Every other assistant she commiserated with over then phone made her realise how lucky she was.

While without her he'd fall apart.

Being the best assistant Angus Wolfe could ever ask for meant she'd come to know the man better than she knew herself—literally.

His favourite colour? Charcoal grey.

Hers? Who knew? Bluish? Periwinkle? Was that more purple? She did like her yellow kettle a great deal.

She also knew he was even more hopeless when it came to romance than she was.

Though he'd say otherwise. He called himself a dedicated bachelor. A strident holdout when it came to romantic entanglements. Too busy. Too set in his ways. That not imposing those constraints on any one woman was a public service.

All of which meant that even if by some strange twist of fate Angus ever saw Lucinda in the same light in which she saw him, he would still not be the man for her.

For Lucinda liked entanglements. She yearned for constraints.

So, she, Lucinda Starling, planned to put an end to her self-imposed emotional wasteland.

None of which Angus ever needed to know.

"Honey, I'm home!"

Voice echoing down the hallway of her small cottage in suburban Abbotsford, Lucinda took off her jacket and scarf, not bothering to disentangle either from the handle of her bag as she dumped the lot in a heap on the hall table.

"In the kitchen!" called Catriona, Lucinda's big sister, housemate and godsend.

Lucinda sniffed the air in the hope there might be a little leftover dinner she could snaffle and caught a whiff of chicken and potato wedges—the good ones she'd found on sale. She hoped Cat had added a little chopped carrot for colour and health. Maybe some baby spinach leaves.

Then she sighed as she kicked off her heels and padded down the hall.

Cat was in the kitchen, one foot tucked up against the other knee, chomping down on a piece of buttery toast.

Her sister had inherited their dad's lanky genes. Lucinda was shorter and curvier, like their mum. She grabbed a carrot stick in lieu of the toast.

Thinking of her parents gave Lucinda a sad little clutch behind her sternum, as it always did, even though it was over ten years since the crash that had taken them.

Then she looked past her sister to the small room beyond. Her heart swelled, her lungs tightened and her head cleared of any and all things that had seemed so important only a moment before.

For there sat Sonny. Her beautiful boy. Hunched over a book at the tiny round table tucked into the nook beside the small kitchen, distractedly polishing off the last potato wedge. His plate was wiped clean bar a few spinach stems. *Go Cat!*

"Hey, sweet pea!" Lucinda called.

Sonny looked up from the adventures of Captain Underpants, hair the same dark brown as Lucinda's hanging into his eyes. A blink later, his face broke into a smile filled with gappy baby teeth, one wobbly. "Hey, Mum!"

She edged around the bench and pressed back Sonny's hair to give him a kiss on the forehead, making a mental note to book in a haircut. She caught scents of sweat and sunshine. "Good day?"

"Yup."

"What's the newsy news?" she asked as she headed into the kitchen.

Cat tilted her head towards the microwave, where a plate sat covered in a little mound of cheap, easy goodness. Lucinda nodded her thanks then plonked onto a chair tucked under the kitchen bench.

Sonny looked off to the side, searching his data banks for whatever snippet he'd tucked away, knowing she'd ask. "Mr Fish, the fighting fish that lives in the library, is missing."

"*Missing*, you say? That *is* news."

Sonny nodded. "Jacob K and I went to the library at lunchtime and saw the tank was empty. Jacob K asked if it was dead. Mrs Seedsman said, 'Many believe they know what happens when a creature is no longer with us, but nobody knows for sure'."

"Did she, now?" Lucinda looked to Cat who was biting back a laugh. "Quite the progressive, Mrs Seedsman."

"I like her hair. It has purple bits on the ends."

"Then I like Mrs Seedsman's hair too."

Happy with that, Sonny gave her another flash of his gorgeous smile before easing back into his book.

Lucinda turned to Cat. "Jacob K?"

"New kid," said Cat. "Sonny was put in charge of him."

"Of course he was. He's the best. Anything else?"

Cat finished rinsing the plates and popping them in the dishwasher, before reaching for a glass of wine she'd clearly had airing in wait for Lucinda to get home and take over Sonny duties.

"All good. Came home chatty. Didn't touch his sandwich again."

Lucinda sighed. Once he was down, she'd be online searching for lunchbox ideas for kids who refused to eat sandwiches, as heaven forbid Sonny eat something she could prepare and freeze in advance.

She glanced at the clock on the wall. "Bath time, kiddo."

"Okay," said Sonny, not moving from his book.

Lucinda considered that her five-minute warning, knowing by now she'd have to ask at least three more times before he actually moved. It gave her time to unwind and settle into the different pace and sounds at home compared to the office.

Time to shed her work persona—proactive, sophisticated, tough, respected—put on her Mum skin—reactive, threadbare, fingers crossed she was making all the right choices, and a massive soft touch when it came to her boy—and remember that, whatever worries she dealt with at work, they always came second to this.

And always would.

* * *

A half-hour later, Sonny was bathed and dressed, his hair a little wet from being washed, his pyjamas soft from the two nights they'd already been worn. She could get another night out of them. He only had one other pair that fit. The joys of owning a growing boy.

Once he'd given Cat a goodnight hug, Sonny ran back into his room.

Lucinda carried him the last few metres, just because she could. It might not be an option for much longer. At eight years of age, the kid's feet were nearly dragging on the floor.

Once Sonny was settled, Lucinda tucked herself up on his bed, making sure not to block his bedside lamp so he had enough light to read. They took turns reading and listening. When she dozed off for the second time, Lucinda gently closed the book and went through the rest of the night-time routine: butterfly kiss, nose-tip kiss and kiss on both cheeks, followed by a seven-second cuddle.

Special toys were found and tucked into their respective nightly positions—Dashy the Dog behind Sonny's neck, Punky the Penguin behind his knees. Blankets were moved up to the chin, star-shaped night-light put on low.

This was the time of day when she felt so lucky to have this all to herself—this routine, this sweetness, this boy. Her heart filled her chest. She loved the kid so much.

Though give it ten more minutes and if he called her name needing a drink, or a trip to the toilet, she'd wish with all that same heart that she had a partner to shoulder the load.

Such were the swings and roundabouts of single motherhood.

Lucinda made it to the door before turning to blow one last kiss. "Goodnight, little man."

"Night, Mum."

"Love you."

Yawn. Then, "Love you more."

She went to close the door before she was stopped by a, "Hey, Mum?"

"Yeah, buddy."

"Did Angus ring you today?"

Lucinda narrowed her eyes. "We work about three metres from one another all day long. We can wave from where we sit. So why would he…? The ringtone!"

Sonny tucked his sheet up to his nose to smother his laughter.

"Did you have a hand in that, little man?"

"Angus messaged last night to ask me how. Cat had let me use the tablet to research planets for homework," he added quickly. "Not playing games."

"Hmm. You are a rascal."

Sonny grinned. The sweetest, most good-natured kid in the world, he was the least rascally kid ever. He made better choices than she ever would.

She was working on improving that score.

"Goodnight, little man."

"Goodnight, Mum."

She closed the door then notched it open just a sliver before padding back to the kitchen to stare inside the fridge in hope of healthy inspiration.

All the while thinking about Sonny. And Angus.

She knew they not so secretly messaged one another. She'd been the one to set up the private account when Sonny had worn her down with begging. And only after Angus had insisted it was fine with him so long as Lucinda had full access to the conversations.

Not that she checked much these days. It was mostly links to "try not to laugh" videos. But it had all started after a less innocent incident a few years back.

Sonny had woken up feeling sick one day, and none of Lucinda's usual methods of cajoling, encouraging and downright bribery had convinced him to get ready for kindergarten. So, with a huge, unwieldy backlist of things to do waiting for her at work, she'd taken Sonny to the office with her for the first time.

Angus—completely up to date on every small thing—had shocked the living heck out of Lucinda when he'd offered to let Sonny hang with him in his office. After a good two and a half seconds of consideration she'd handed over Sonny's tablet—a necessary evil of modern parenting—and left the men to their own devices.

Less than an hour in, over a mid-morning fruit snack, Angus had wangled from Sonny the real reason behind the "sore tummy". The kindy group had spent time that week making Father's Day cards.

Sonny—being Sonny—had put up his hand to ask his teacher what to do if he didn't have a father to give a card to.

Lucinda had made it her life's mission to make sure Sonny understood that, whether a child had a mum and a dad, or two mums or two dads, grandparents, siblings or a mum and a super-cool aunt, every type of family could be as rich with love as any other.

Unfortunately, other kids had pretty set opinions on what a "family" ought to look like and had made it their mission that day to make sure Sonny knew it too.

When Angus had pulled her aside that afternoon, while Sonny had been learning how to use the photocopier with one of the guys in accounts, Lucinda had felt sideswiped. Not only that Sonny had gone through such an ordeal but that he'd spilled to Angus. And not her.

Angus had taken her by both hands—something he'd never done before that day—had sat her down, made sure she was looking him in the eye and explained that he'd told Sonny how he'd grown up without a dad too.

She'd learned more about his childhood and his motivations for why he worked so hard in that one conversation than she had in all the time they'd known one another. And, when Angus had assured her that his imperfect mother's love had been his north star, the guiding light that had kept him on the right path, she'd been hard pressed not to sob.

Things had changed between them that day.

In trusting Angus with her son, she'd given him the impetus to step out from behind the figurative wall from behind which he engaged with the world, leading to a moment between them that had been honest, raw and real. And the tiny, innocent glint of a crush she'd happily harboured had erupted, splintering off into a thousand replicas, spiralling uncontrollably into all directions like fireworks, too much, too many for her to have a hope of reining back in.

While Angus, with his vintage chess set and killer AFL handball skills, fast became Sonny's hero. The strongest—maybe the only—male influence in his young life.

She'd never told Angus that Sonny had come home from kindy that week with a card made out to him. It was another of those "minor details" she figured best to keep to herself.

She heard the water cooler talk. She wasn't

alone in her crush. Every girl in the office was right there with her. Only, they talked about how infamously uncatchable he was. That he dated widely. And never for long. They called him the Lone Wolfe. If he knew how quickly Sonny had become attached to him it would have sent him back behind that wall.

As things stood, their friendship had grown. Evolved. Stretched. Become something important to them both. It was good. Just as it was.

Lucinda realised she was still holding open the fridge door. She let the door close, but not before taking out a small tub of chocolate custard.

Tossing the lid of the custard into the bin, Lucinda nabbed a spoon from the drying rack by the sink and went to find Cat in her usual spot, watching Netflix while typing away madly at the laptop balanced on a cushion on her lap.

A freelance journalist, Cat's life was a case of produce or starve. But it also meant that when Lucinda's husband had left, deciding marriage and parenthood was all too hard—while Lucinda had been cooking dinner and holding their toddler in her arms, no less—Cat had moved in the next day, more than filling the space Joe had left behind. Making Lucinda realise how little she'd asked of him. How little space she'd taken up herself.

Sonny had been thirteen months old. Earlier that day he'd walked for the first time.

That was nearly seven years ago now.

And it had taken that long for the regular routine, the comfort of home and the warm hum of work success to make room for other hopes and dreams that had begun to flicker at the corner of her mind's eye.

With a sigh, Lucinda sank into the lounge room chair.

"So," said Cat, *tap-tap-tap*. "Did you tell him?"

And, just like that, Lucinda's contented little bubble burst. "Hmm?"

"Angus. Did you finally tell him about this weekend?"

Lucinda wriggled on her seat, trying to get comfortable. "Yep."

Cat's fingers stopped tapping. "Really? Did you say the words, 'Mr Wolfe, sir, I am taking next weekend off because my man-friend, the estimable heart surgeon Dr Jameson Bancroft-Smythe, and I are going away to a fancy resort for some grown up time'?"

Lucinda's silence spoke volumes.

Cat snapped her laptop shut. "Seriously?"

"I said I was taking the weekend off. The reason why is *none of his business*."

Cat's nostrils flared. "You forced Angus to stay here, sleeping in your bed while you bunked in with Sonny after he had dental surgery, because the dentist said there was a chance of bleeding overnight. The two of you obsessively text one another through every new episode of that stupid Warlock school show. You both spend way too much time coming up with wilder and-or weirder gifts for one another, just because. Not to mention whatever went down at that crazy office Christmas party a couple of years back. You and I both know the lines are very much blurred between your boss's business and your own."

Lucinda's throat had gone dry at the mention of the office Christmas party. Cat must have been really agitated as she knew better than to bring it up. The events of that night had miraculously remained classified, locked in a vault ever since.

Moving on after a surreptitious swallow, Lucinda said, "What exactly do you want me to say?"

"I want you to admit to me why you didn't you tell him about Jameson. You didn't have a problem telling *me* all about it. If you and Angus are as tight as you claim to be, why not tell him?"

Cat was no idiot. Quite the contrary. She was a shark despite the fact that, modern journalism being what it was, she wrote as many stories about Instagram celebrities as she did about human rights violations. Which was why she said, "I need to hear you say the words."

Lucinda threw her hands in the air. "I don't know why! Maybe I've enjoyed keeping this part of my life just for me. Maybe it still feels precious, fragile and not quite real, and if I say it out loud it will pop. Maybe I'm slightly concerned if Angus knows then he'll come over here when Jameson is due to pick me up and answer the door with a shotgun in hand so Jameson knows not to mess with me. Maybe if I tell Angus he'll ask questions, and poke holes in my logic, and convince me I'm making a huge mistake."

Cat sighed. Dramatically. "Nobody but you can make you feel anything."

Lucinda dropped her hands and looked indulgently at her big sister. "I know that. I do. I'm just nervous, okay? I want this weekend to go as smoothly as possible. I *need* it to. I've already put so much effort into keeping things going this far, considering how often we've had to cancel our plans with his work and mine. And Angus is right in the middle of this huge account, working for a man he looks up to a great deal. It felt better not distracting him with things that don't matter."

Cat snorted, as if she didn't believe a word of it.

"He's sensitive," Lucinda attested. He really was. Highly attuned to people's needs and wants. It was what made him so good at his work. Judging from the little bits and pieces she'd picked up over the years about his childhood, staying hyper-aware had been the only way he'd survived.

"He's a man-child," Cat muttered.

"Cat!"

"He has a driver, a cleaner, someone else who answers his phone. No wonder *he* hasn't found his

own girl to take away for a serious weekend—
none of them could possibly live up to his contingent of carers. And, in that list, I include you."

"Thank goodness for that," Lucinda shot back.
"Without my part as a cog in the Angus Wolfe
wheel, we would never have been able to afford
this beautiful little house in which we now sit, all
cosy and warm."

What she didn't say to Cat was that she didn't
see herself as one of his "contingent of carers".
She was his outlet. His release. In the tough, hard-
working, driven life of Angus Wolfe, she was
unique.

"You really believe that, don't you?" Cat asked.
"You sell yourself short. And the great and wonderful Angus does too. He so takes you for
granted. I could…" Cat stopped. Shook her head.
"Tell him. Tomorrow. Or you'll burst from holding it all in."

Lucinda left Cat's comment be. It wasn't the
first time Cat had tried to convince her Angus
expected too much. She'd learned to agree to dis-
agree.

She'd been an exhausted, inexperienced mother
of a toddler who had no clue if she could do the
job, much less commit to the hours required, when
she'd interviewed to work for him. But he'd seen
something in her nevertheless. *Chutzpah*, he'd
said. A raging desire to pull herself up by the
bootstraps that he understood.

He expected her to work hard, but he worked harder. And he'd *never* made her feel as if he took her for granted. Despite all she'd given up in order to work with him—time with her family, romantic relationships...

She shook her head and settled deeper into the chair.

"What ifs" were never worth the time spent dwelling on them. Life was good. Her family was healthy and happy. She loved her job. She had the security that came with having a roof over her head. What more could she want?

A devilish little voice whispered into her ear. *Love. Intimacy. Romance. Someone who puts your needs first.*

Hence the dirty weekend.

When her phone buzzed in her pocket, she found herself unsurprised to find a message from Angus.

She glanced at Cat, only to find her back typing at her ancient laptop.

The message asked if she was keen to start watching the final season of *Warlock Academy* on Netflix—a decade-old schlocky, supernatural teen drama they were both obsessed with. Another part of her job description—find TV shows just soapy enough to engage Angus and brain-numbing enough to let his active mind slow down so he could fall asleep at a reasonable hour.

She messaged back.

You bet.

Then she grabbed the remote, changed the channel, poked her tongue out at Cat when her sister groaned and settled in to watch teenaged witches and demons battle it out at a high school football match.

Though she kept shifting in her seat, unable to find a comfy spot.

For there was no denying that if she had to choose between her upcoming weekend away, with a handsome, eligible doctor who'd made it all too clear how much he liked her, or snuggling at home watching TV with a man who wasn't even in the room, she'd choose the latter. Every time.

Worse, this was the first time admitting as much actually unnerved her.

Cat was right about one thing. Something had to give.

CHAPTER TWO

ANGUS LEANT BACK in his office chair, finger tapping against his lips as he looked over the impressive wall pinned with striking images, word clusters and thought clouds framing the penultimate drafts of the Remède rebranding that the graphics team had moved into his office earlier that morning.

Louis Fournier, the venerable president of the Remède cosmetics company, was just outside, leaning over Lucinda's desk.

Angus didn't need to see Lucinda's face. From the way she sat forward in her chair, chin resting on her palm, chair swinging from side to side, it was clear she was flirting her heart out.

Angus felt the smile start in his throat before it even reached his mouth. *Atta girl.*

Fitz's assistant—Velma—was built like a German tank with the accent to match. She was stern, efficient and ferociously protective of her charge. Fitz claimed he couldn't be trusted with anyone more tempting under his nose all day long. Everyone knew he adored Velma as much as Velma doted on him.

Charlie's new right hand—Kumar—was only slightly more human than Charlie. But, as work mates, they fit together like two pieces of a puzzle no one else understood.

In fact, there was not one single staff member at the Big Picture Group who was carried by someone else. Fitz for all his insouciance, was a ruthless recruiter. They ran a seriously tight ship.

And yet none of them held a candle to Lucinda.

The way she went about things was instinctive. And tenacious. She knew when to be brusque, when to be dulcet, when to be straight down the line and when to bewitch until she had even the most difficult clients eating out of her hand in a matter of minutes.

She was out there right now, wearing Remède's Someday perfume. He'd seen it on her desk about an hour earlier. There was a story there, about her parents, both gone long before he'd met her. Lucinda kept a bottle in a drawer as a reminder of them, but she only pulled it out when Louis was on his way.

As if she felt his thoughts, Lucinda turned to look over her shoulder, the floppy frills at her collar framing her face, her long, dark hair swinging, her red lips curled into a half-smile.

The crack of the glass door created a slight distortion. He shifted slightly so he could see her whole face. It was a good face. Candid, spirited, empirically lovely and as familiar to him as his own.

A pair of small lines criss-crossed above her nose. A rare indicator of indecision.

Perhaps *rare* was the wrong word, for the criss-cross of lines over her nose had shown up more and more over the past weeks. Then there was that new lipstick. Darker, glossier than usual. She'd cut sugar from her coffee. Added infinitesimal pauses before each sentence. All of which, in Angus's mind, spoke to restlessness. To a change in the air.

And he was not a man who liked change.

She lifted a single eyebrow in question. *Ready?*

It took him a moment to remember what he was meant to be ready for.

Louis Fournier. Remède. Saving his old friend's business. He nodded curtly.

The criss-cross above her nose flickered off and on before she turned back to finish up with Louis.

Angus breathed out hard and rolled his shoulders.

His instinct for branding came from the ability to tap into the greater collective human subconscious. To mine people's baser urges in order to encourage—no, *demand*—that they look to his clients to fulfil those needs.

Tapping into Lucinda's baser needs to find out what was going on in her subconscious was not something he had any intention of doing.

Whatever was going on with Lucinda did not impact on her work. It would pass. Everything did. Eventually. And, if not, he'd drag it out of her when he had the Remède account off his plate.

Angus pressed out of his chair and moved to look over the mood wall one last time to make sure nothing had been missed. For nothing was ever perfect. Not for him. There were always improvements to make.

A childhood spent being told that he was a mistake by the procession of men in his mother's life, a blight, in the way, had not been pleasant. But there was no doubt his burning need to prove them wrong was the root of his success. The reason he never stopped striving to do better, to be better, to reach for more.

Without them would he have been standing there in his huge corner office? Would he have had the gumption to land Louis Fournier as a client? As a mentor? As a friend?

He heard Lucinda's laughter from beyond the glass wall and he turned away from the mood board. She'd pinch him if she heard him speak that way about the business. Literally. She'd growl at him to "chillax". To appreciate all he'd accomplished. To enjoy the spoils.

His partners had no problem revelling in the benefits of their success. The highlight for Fitz had been when they'd been written up in *GQ*. Charlie's highlight had come when the university from which he'd graduated with his doctorate in mathematics had enlisted him to manage their financial matters.

Angus's one bright, shining moment?

It hadn't hit him yet. Or, more precisely, for him it wasn't about a moment. It was about moving forward. Stopping to look back, even for a moment, could halt the momentum he'd worked so hard to achieve. So he'd keep working. Keep striving. Keep kicking hard beneath the surface to make sure it continued.

Voices drifted through the glass door leading from Lucinda's desk to his as Lucinda waved Louis into the office. Angus moved to meet them halfway.

"Gus," said the older gentleman, a glint in his eye, and a goodly dose of French still in his accent despite his years spent in Australia. "Good of you to squeeze me in this morning."

Angus's gaze slid to Lucinda who was quietly shutting the door behind her. "Did you flirt him into calling me that?"

She opened her eyes wide and mouthed, *"Who me?"*

At which Louis scoffed. "You do not answer to Gus? I am an old man. Anything I can do to save the time I have left…"

"Fair enough," said Angus. "Then I'd suggest you call that one Cindy. Every lost syllable helps."

Louis looked over his shoulder in time to see

Lucinda scowl menacingly Angus's way. She tried to right herself, but only came across looking guiltier still.

Louis's resultant laughter was rich and deep, full of the smoke left by a lifetime of cigars. "You two. Even if I did not have a business to save, I would pay simply to watch you spar."

The guilt on Lucinda's face made way for chagrin as Louis reminded him of their Hail Mary attempt to right his company's ancient ship. For Remède, one of the world's most revered beauty brands, was on the verge of collapse.

It would not happen on Angus's watch. In fact, if he was on the hunt for a highlight, saving Remède from ruin would come close.

For, once upon a time, Louis Fournier had saved him.

Post-university, making waves as the youngest-ever junior partner in a whiz-bang upstart marketing firm, he'd met Louis at an industry night at which the older man had been a plus one.

They'd started up a conversation at the bar and found commonality in their disinterest in schmoozing and their love of French New Wave cinema.

The conversation had moved to the hotel lounge, leading to Angus missing the moment his team had won an award that night. Not that it had mattered. In the hour he'd spent with Louis he had already mentally moved on.

For Louis Fournier was the first man his senior who had seen straight through the cool veneer, the steely ambition, to the hunger beneath. The hunger to truly make a difference. And to show Angus that hunger had inherent value.

"Latte, Monsieur Fournier?" Lucinda asked, snapping Angus back to the present. "Milk, no sugar?"

"Oui. Merci."

Lucinda didn't need to ask for Angus's order. She knew how he liked his coffee, his steak, his calendar. She knew his shirt size, his in-seam measurements and his favourite underwear—having restocked the closet in his private bathroom many times over.

She also knew when to pass the team baton to Angus, to switch off the glamour and melt into the background.

When she returned a few minutes later, bringing the neat silver tray and comforting aroma of hot coffee into the room, Angus hid his smile behind his hand. He couldn't remember the last time Lucinda had brought him coffee rather than farming it out to an intern. The last time he'd asked if she'd be so kind, she'd laughed so hard he'd heard it even after she'd closed the door between them.

But Louis was old-school. The kind of gentlemen who would never enter a room before a woman, who smiled and nodded at every person who met his eye. And Lucinda had a huge soft spot for the man.

She placed Louis's elegant, heat-resistant, double-layered glass on the table at his elbow, alongside a plate of small French pastries.

"Ah," Louis said, eyes closing against the heavenly scent. *"Parfait."* Angus recognised his mug in an instant. She'd bought it for him for... Lent? The Queen's birthday? International Pirate Day? He'd lost track of the occasions once their gift-buying had become a blood sport.

He turned the mug. On one side it boasted his favourite Winston Churchill quote: *Success is not final, failure is not fatal; it is the courage to continue that counts.* The other side of the mug had a tacky photo of a penguin pushing another penguin off an ice shelf.

When he looked up, Lucinda was leaning over him, placing a smaller plate of pastries beside him. The frills trickling fussily down the front of her shirt weighed the fabric down, giving him a glimpse of white lace. The swell of female curves.

He tensed and looked up. Her eyes were on her work, a smile curving the glossy red of her lips. Definitely a new colour for her. It suited her. A great deal. So much so, he'd found himself staring. Considering.

Reminding himself this was Lucinda. His assistant. His right hand. His foundation. His conscience. The yin to his yang. The light to his dark. He could not do what he did without her.

Therefore, there was no staring at her lips. Or beyond the frills of her shirt. Or at any other part of her. No matter how inviting. No matter how lovely. Those were the rules he'd set himself from day one when he'd first seen her sitting outside Fitz's office waiting for an interview, foot tapping with nerves, the rest of her glowing with eagerness, charm and life.

Her eyes shifted to his.

"Appreciate it," he murmured.

"My pleasure," she replied, though the crisscross of creases over her nose were back.

Damn it.

Angus schooled his features until he knew he appeared cool, unmoved, the very picture of ambivalence—an expression learned over many years at the feet of those who'd enjoyed it when he flinched.

It was an expression that had once made an intern cry. Not a deliberate move, but there you go. Lucinda, on the other hand, raised a single eyebrow. Slowly. As if she was bemused he was trying such a move on her.

"Need anything else?" she asked, under her breath.

I need you to stand up, he thought, his eyes starting to water with the effort not to stray. He wondered for a brief moment if Fitz's tank-like assistant Velma had a twin sister he could hire instead.

Lucinda righted herself—thank everything good and holy—her glossy dark hair swinging past her shoulders and showering him in the scent of her shampoo; coconut and lime, making him think of cocktails. Of holidays. Of Christmas parties. One in particular that he did his very best *not* to think about. Especially in the middle of important business meetings.

"Shall I leave you boys to it?" she asked, hip cocking, swinging her pencil-skirt-clad backside right into his eyeline.

Angus's gaze shot to the ceiling. Was that a spider's web on the light fixture?

"*Merci*, Lucinda," Louis said, saving Angus from having to answer. "You are not only an utter delight and a great beauty, with excellent taste in perfume, you can now add coffee angel to your list of super powers."

"And I shall."

"In fact, have you ever considered cosmetic modelling?"

Lucinda un-cocked her hip. "What's that, now?"

"Your skin is like satin, *cherie*."

"My *skin*?"

"Louis," said Angus, his voice a little gruff. "Are you making a move on my girl?"

At that Lucinda twisted and pinned Angus with

a look he'd never seen before. Her eyes were wide, pink sweeping fast across her cheeks. Her mouth opened as if she was about to say something before she snapped it shut and turned slowly back to Louis.

"Monsieur Fournier, beneath the satiny veneer of my glorious Remède foundation is the lamentable skin of the mother of an eight-year-old who refuses to sleep past five in the morning."

Then she bent down and kissed the older man on the cheek.

"But you are sweet for pretending. Now, stop distracting me. I am an important person with important work to do." With that she stalked out of the room.

Both men followed with their eyes.

Louis broke the silence. "Never let that one go."

"Count on it," Angus promised, even if the amazing Velma did in fact have a nicer twin.

Then, putting all thoughts of red lips and white lace aside, Angus got to work.

For the next hour, and even after Louis had said his goodbyes, Lucinda sat at her desk and vacillated between fuming and telling herself to stop being so ridiculously reactive.

But the moment Angus had said the words *"Are you making a move on my girl?"* something had snapped inside her.

She wasn't usually so touchy. She knew it had

been a joke. One she'd usually have played along with if it got the job done.

It was as if the conversation with Cat the night before had pried something loose. Then her earlier chat with Louis, in which he'd constantly joked about her being far too good for the likes of Angus, had further shifted whatever it was that now shook inside her.

The fact was, she was rattled. If she'd been in a mood like this at home she'd have found a way to distract herself while she got her head on straight. But, here, she couldn't hide behind her desk all afternoon.

She was a grown-up who'd been through plenty worse. So, instead of sending an intern to clean away the cups, she did her best to shake it off and headed into Angus's office.

"How'd it go?" she asked as she placed plates and coffee cups back onto the silver tray.

"As well as can be expected," said Angus from his leaning spot, sitting on the wide shelf that ran under the long window, legs stretched out before him, gaze caught on some paperwork he held in one hand. "He kept reiterating that he has faith in us. In me."

Words that would usually be music to Angus's ears, but she could tell from his tone that they hadn't been.

This, she thought, *is what I need to find my equilibrium again.*

Work talk. Pure, clear cut. Uncomplicated.

"But?" Lucinda said.

"He spent far more time talking about you. About how his perfume has never suited a woman more."

And with that his eyes lifted to hers.

With the sun behind him he was little more than a silhouette, but she felt the glance all the same. Felt it hit her eyes, before tracing the line of her cheek and landing on her mouth.

She wished she hadn't reapplied her lipstick as it suddenly felt too red. Too slick. And yet, conversely, as his gaze remained, she was also glad that she had.

Then he seemed to shake himself before he looked back down at the papers, lifted himself away from the window and tossed the papers onto his desk. "He also made it clear he believes that whatever I'm paying you it's not enough."

"He's right, of course."

"No doubt." Hands sliding into the pockets of his suit pants, he rounded the desk towards her, those long legs eating up the distance between them in three short strides. "But it was a distraction. I get the feeling things are worse than he's letting on."

And there she was, caught up in some throwaway line, while Louis was in actual trouble. Gripping the tray harder, Lucinda said, "Could you convince him to let Charlie weigh in on his financials? Say it's part of the service? No extra fee?"

Angus shook his head. "It was hard enough for him to come to me at all, and he could only do that by convincing himself he was doing me a favour."

"Would you like me to put it to him?"

She saw Angus allow himself a moment to consider the offer. She wished Cat could see him in such a moment. For all his genius, and his self-belief, he was always open to her opinion.

But then he shook his head. Which was wasn't uncommon either.

Yet, while any other time she'd have moved on, it turned out the rattle had not gone away. It trembled as she huffed out a breath filled with sudden frustration. "Seriously, I can sweet talk him into a meeting at least. I know I can."

"I'll handle it."

"Louis respects me. And likes me. But he also doesn't have to worry about keeping up appearances where I'm concerned. He won't fear that I will no longer look at him like he's my hero."

Angus shifted uncomfortably. "Leave it, Lucinda."

"But—"

"Enough." Angus ran a hand through his hair, giving the ends a tug.

Lucinda stilled. The only parts of her that moved were her shoulders, inching back, and her nostrils, flaring gently as she put the brakes on her temper. Barely.

Until his eyes once more snagged on hers.

"Was there something else?" he asked, slowly leaning back against his desk and folding his arms over his chest.

While he acted as if he hadn't just shut her down, as if they were in the middle of a regular conversation, the rattle inside her began to shiver and shake until it bumped against her ribs like a drumbeat. Like a call to arms.

"Actually, yes," she said before she even felt the words coming. "It's about this weekend."

"What about it?"

"My plans. I am going away with…" She stopped there. As if her words had smacked up against a stone wall. She ran her tongue over her bottom lip in an attempt to loosen them.

"Is this a guessing game?" Angus asked, his voice now edged with impatience. "You're going with… Catriona? The Easter Bunny? Elvis?"

And just like that the rattle stopped rattling. As if a storm inside her had stilled. And her voice was calm, even, as she looked her boss in the eye and said, "I'm going away with a man."

She watched Angus closely. As closely as one person could watch another. She noticed the flare of his nostrils. The tightening of his jaw. The way the rest of his body went preternaturally still.

Then she did her very best not to read anything

into it. To pretend she was simply an employee passing on a titbit of little interest to her boss.

"A man," Angus finally managed.

"Yes, *a man*. Not just any man," said Lucinda, the floodgates now wide open. "The man I've been seeing. For a few weeks now." Off and on. When he hadn't been called away to surgery. Or to phone calls with doctors in developing countries needing his advice *stat*. He was a doctor. Had she mentioned that?

"Sonny?" Angus asked, his voice a mite strained. But that part she understood. That part made her shoulders relax down away from her ears. Raised by a single mother himself, Angus took Sonny's welfare nearly as seriously as she did.

"Hasn't met him yet," she assured him. "But if this weekend goes well..."

Her boss blinked at her and said nothing. And now she couldn't get a read on him at all. Only the fact that he looked so utterly disinterested told her that he was trying too hard.

Which, in turn, brought the rattle back to life. With a vengeance.

"Would you like to know where we're going?" There, a flicker below his right eye.

"A resort. Near Daylesford. Called Hanover House. It's gorgeous. Well, Cat says it's gorgeous. She did an article on it for a travel blog last year. Super-romantic."

His Adam's apple bobbed lightly before he said, "Sounds nice."

Nice. This from a man who put words together that took businesses from the verge of ruin to stratospheric.

From the outside, Lucinda was certain their conversation seemed reasonable. Polite, even. But she felt as if she was watching it unfold from another dimension. The air crackled between them, voices rippling, words they were steadfastly refusing to utter buffeting against them in steadily increasing waves.

"How about the man himself? Don't you want to ask who he is? What he does for a living? School grades? Parking tickets? How he votes? You're usually all over that kind of thing. Figuring people out. Putting them into neat boxes so you know how to deal with them."

A muscle twitched beneath his right eye.

What are you doing? a voice cried in the furthest recesses of her mind. *What do you want from him? Are you looking for a reaction? Are you baiting him to tell you, "no, you can't go"?*

Angus lifted a hand and ran it over his chin, then around behind his neck. "Lucinda," he said, "If you're thinking ahead to letting Sonny meet him, then he is no doubt the kind of man both Sonny *and* I should hero worship. Now, are we done?"

He glanced pointedly at the coffee cups on the

tray. His eyebrows rose, as if to remind her what she should be doing with her time rather than nattering with him about her private life.

Wow. Harsh.

They clashed all the time. Telling it like it was was their dynamic. And it worked. In fact, they fed off it. She knew if she walked away things could settle. They always did after such electric, static-fuelled dust-ups.

But, rather than feeling invigorated, she felt twitchy, discomfited and strangely hollow.

She turned and walked towards the door, her feet numb, her face burning.

But when she reached the door she stopped, turned and gave Angus one last look. "One more thing," she said.

Angus breathed out hard. As if he was clinging to control by a fingernail. His voice was deep and tight as he said, "I think we've covered everything. You're going away. HR has signed off on it. It's done."

"Not about the weekend," she managed, even while storm clouds gathered about her head, lightning flashing with the darkness. "It's about today. When I asked if I might be given the chance to try to convince Louis to talk to Charlie about Remède's finances…"

She closed her eyes, shook her head and started afresh. "I get that you have the final word, that as your assistant it's my job to grease the wheels, keep you fed and watered so that you're able to perform at your best. But Angus?"

She waited, squeezing a breath into her tight lungs, as it took for ever for him to respond.

"Yes, Lucinda?"

"I'm not *your girl*."

With that she took his dirty plates and left.

CHAPTER THREE

I'M NOT YOUR GIRL.

Lucinda's words from earlier that day bounced off the inside of Angus's skull like echoes inside a bell tower.

He hadn't meant anything by it. She knew it, too. It wasn't like her to be so pedantic.

A voice that had emerged from the swampier parts of Angus's subconscious since he'd sat down at the bar around the corner from work said, *It's also not like her to go on a dirty weekend with some guy you've never heard of.*

A hand slapped down hard on Angus's shoulder, followed by Fitz's voice. "You look like hell."

Angus grabbed his cousin's fingers and pried them off his shoulder. "Appreciate it."

"I, on the other hand, am not sure how anyone survives a single day without getting a load of my handsome mug."

As he dragged out the stool next to Angus, Fitz caught the eye of the bartender, tapping Angus's drink and asking for one of the same. "So, what's the haps?"

"Does a man need a reason to have a drink with his favourite cousin?"

Fitz snorted. "Only cousin. And, yes, I don't think you've wasted a single minute in your entire adult life. Then there's the dark cloud hovering ominously over your head, and the fact your leg looks ready to take off…"

Angus looked down. His left leg was shaking so hard it all but crackled with excess energy. He stopped, only to find he couldn't, so gave up and let it jiggle for all it was worth.

"Did someone have a better idea than you at work?" Fitz asked.

Angus shot him a look.

"You're right. What was I thinking? So what? Designers no longer making suits? The cobblers of Spain all out of shoes? Lucinda mad at you?"

Before he could stop it, Angus felt a tightening around his left eye.

Fitz let go a long, high whistle between his teeth. "So, it's the lovely Lucinda who has you hunched melancholically over your scotch. Interesting. What did you do?"

"I didn't *do* anything."

Fitz snorted. "So what didn't you do? I know you didn't miss her birthday, what with the charming gift-a-palooza thing you have going between you. So what?" Fitz slammed a hand against his chest. "Was there another...*event*? Dare I say, Christmas party?"

A muscle flickered in Angus's jaw, while every other muscle in his body clenched. Hard. His glass paused before it hit his lips. When the liquid finally spilled down his throat, he relished the burn. "Nothing happened at that damn Christmas party, as I've told you a thousand times."

Yet, every time that night came up, something slippery and uncontrolled uncoiled within him.

"I could say the suspense is killing me, but the truth is I'm actually beginning to bore of—"

"Lucinda's gone and got herself a new man and they are going away together this weekend."

Fitz stilled, then burst into laughter. "That's it? That's why you look like your doctor just gave you bad news? Because Lucinda has a *boyfriend*?"

Angus shook his head. He had no better answer.

"Come on, mate. She's bright, bold and knows more dirty jokes than any man I know. It's more of a mystery why she hasn't been snapped up already."

Angus gripped more tightly to his glass.

He'd thought about this—about why he was reacting the way he was. It wasn't the fact that she was seeing someone. Or even that she hadn't told him about it till now. He felt as if his tendons had frozen solid because she had never come close to introducing any man in her life to her son.

Well, his subconscious perked up and responded, *apart from you*.

That was different, he shot back.

The day he'd met Sonny he'd felt as if he'd been hit with a lightning bolt: this was his opportunity to be, for another kid, the kind of man he'd desperately needed in his own life at the same age. A man to encourage his curiosity, to welcome his boisterous side, teach him how to stand up for himself in the playground and to appreciate his mother.

When the day came that Lucinda introduced Sonny to a man in her life, the kid would be smart enough to understand what that meant. And, once that door was opened for Sonny, it could never fully be closed again.

It was his duty to make sure she realised how formative such a moment would be. To make sure, before she did anything she couldn't take back, that she was sure.

"The real question is," Fitz intoned, "why hasn't she nabbed herself a long-term fella? All she'd have to do is snap her fingers. The woman is smoking hot. Hair like a dark-chocolate waterfall. Skin like Italian marble. Those big, brown cow eyes that can see right into the depths of your deeply charred soul."

"You might want to tone it down."

"What? The smoking hot thing?" Fitz was clearly on a roll. "I'm not trying it on. It's an empirical fact. You must be aware that your assistant is as good as it gets. Say it out loud so I know you are a human man: *Lucinda Starling is a glorious, gumptious, gorgeous specimen of womanhood.*"

Angus took a long, slow sip of his drink, only to find he could no longer taste it.

Fitz tapped a finger against his lips. "No? Too busy drinking? Well, I'll say it—for a woman like that, every weekend ought to be a dirty weekend."

Angus turned to Fitz. Everything in him clenched, as if readying to take a swing.

By the glint in Fitz's eye, he knew it. Hell, he'd have welcomed it. As if it would prove a point. A point Angus had no intention of helping him make.

"Enough," Angus managed through gritted teeth. "You're talking about someone's mother."

At that, Fitz burst out laughing. He laughed until he had to grip the bar so as not to fall off his stool. "Man, you kill me. I gifted you so many other ways to defend her and *that's* where your mind went? I guess if a guy is in need of a bucket of iced water to toss over himself, that'll do it. Though, if the first thing you think of when you look at Lucinda is 'mother', then I worry for you and the future of our bloodline."

Angus flinched. As if their bloodline was anything to write home about.

His father had left when he'd been around Sonny's age. He still remembered the fight. The smash of glass. His mother's scream. The roar of the car engine and the squeal of tyres. And the relief, short-lived as it was…until the procession of men his mother had let into their lives as she'd searched for a way out of the poverty cycle in which she'd grown up. So she could give her son a different life. In the hope he'd be a better kind of man.

Fitz slid his phone out of the inner pocket of his jacket. "This guy of hers, who is he? Give me a name."

"I didn't ask."

Fitz blinked at Angus. "Your precious assistant told you she has a new man in her life and you didn't ask who he was? What he did for a living? What he ate for breakfast? How he voted? You, who creates mental portfolios of every person he ever meets in case the day comes you need to beat them in battle." Fitz clicked his fingers at the bartender. "Excuse me, good sir, did this gentleman ask you a slew of questions the moment he caught your eye?"

The bartender gave Angus a look. "No. I mean, kind of. We talked about uni. And which hospital I was born in. And that time I saw a UFO."

The bartender looked between them, suddenly rethinking his recent choices. Then he moved stealthily to the other end of the bar.

"What are you doing now?" Angus asked as Fitz continued typing madly into his phone.

"Messaging Cat."

"Lucinda's *sister*?" That was enough to snap Angus out of his funk, his senses coming back online with a crack. "How the hell do *you* have her number?"

Fitz shrugged. "We met at the work Christmas party we're not allowed to talk about. You drank your feelings. Lucinda wore that insanely hot green dress. Ring a bell?"

Too many.

Such as the large boardroom emptied of furniture. Cocktail tables laden with buckets of champagne. Walls dripping in sparkling lights and silver stars. Loud chatter and laughter.

In his mind's eye the crowd parted, which surely had not happened. And there, in the breach, Lucinda. A bare-armed, long-legged vision in a spring-green dress. Dark hair down and curled seductively over one creamy shoulder. Lips a slippery red.

He remembered blinking, as if the view had been too bright to believe. That dress, made from some witch-designed material that shifted and shimmered over her waist, her hips, her…everything as she walked. As she breathed.

Until she'd caught his eye, a smile like no other stretching across her lovely face.

Fitz broke in. "Turns out Cat had just written an article about female Viagra for some women's magazine. One thing led to another and…we hooked up. Before you go all Hulk on me, it was one time. She decided pretty quickly that, while I'm a tiger in the sack, I'm not nearly good enough for her. We've been friendly ever since."

Angus sank his head into his hand. His scoundrel of a cousin and Lucinda's terrifying sister had been "friendly" for over a year. Did Lucinda know? Did he want to be the one to tell her?

Fitz clicked his fingers at his phone. "Here we go. Cat said she's met him and he's awesome."

"Met who?"

"Lucinda's fella," said Fitz. Slowly. "Jameson BancroftSmythe."

"That's his name?"

"Every bit of it. Now, let the cyber-stalking begin. Okay, we have a skateboarder from Sydney. Looks about fourteen. A guy with about a hundred great-grandchildren. And…whoa. You need to see this."

I really don't, Angus thought, training his gaze to stare into the melting ice in his glass.

"Man, I'm sorry to tell you this, but the dude looks like Robert Redford."

"Now?"

"Uh…no. I'm thinking circa *The Way We Were*. Maybe even *Barefoot in the Park*."

Fitz held out his phone and Angus looked. *Whoa*.

"*Dr* Jameson Bancroft-Smythe," Fitz read. "Born in The Netherlands. Educated in London. Worked for Doctors Without Borders. Now head of Paediatric Surgery at Princess Elizabeth Hospital. And…there!"

Fitz held the phone under Angus's nose so he had no choice but to look.

And there he was—Robert Redford's doppelganger—decked out in a well-cut tux, surrounded by people in benefit black, including one Lucinda Starling who stood at his side, grinning from ear to ear, champagne flute clutched in both hands, Dr Jameson Bancroft-Smythe's hand resting possessively on her lower back.

Angus must have made a noise, as Fitz murmured, "Hmm?"

Though Fitz was already distracted by a pretty blonde making eyes at him at the end of the bar. His barstool scraped against the floor as he pushed it away. "Now, I've gotta go see a blonde about a phone number. Promise you won't do anything exciting till I get back?"

"Exciting?" Angus mumbled.

"Change company by-laws to insist upon seven-day working weeks. Dance on the bar. Track the good doctor down and declare pistols at dawn. Call Luc and make up some excuse as to why she has to work this weekend with you instead."

"Promise."

Fitz grinned then headed off.

While Angus leant his head into his palms, pressing hard into his eye sockets.

Because this slippery feeling in his belly, this

discontent, wasn't him. Not since he'd been a scared kid who had no idea where he'd be sleeping or who he and his mum might be living with from one week to the next. Controlling his environment, or how he responded to it at the very least, was at the core of how he interacted with the world.

He was so good at it he'd made it his living, controlling how people responded to a brand by how it was packaged.

Maybe there is something in that, he thought as he lifted his head out of his hands.

In honing, in his own mind, the core promise of the Lucinda Starling brand.

He started at the beginning—the day they'd met.

Several years back she, along with a couple of dozen men and women, had come into the Big Picture Group offices to interview for a spot in the office pool.

The place had smelled like fresh paint. Half the furniture had yet to arrive. He, Fitz and Charlie had been up to their eyeballs in debt and they'd just had their first big win—a client whose rebrand had gone beyond viral. In order to keep the momentum going they'd decided to recruit: hungry, sharp, lateral thinkers who could help them take their business intergalactic.

Fitz had sent his assistant Velma to eyeball the line-up of hopefuls and weed out the chaff. Not that it had stopped Angus and Fitz from taking a peek, putting down bets as to which had faked their résumés, which would keep up with Fitz's famously twisty interviews, which would flounder and which might become a part of the Big Picture family.

To a one the interviewees had been a study in edgy, sleek, über-cool university graduates in a range of grey, white and black, prepared to claw one another's eyes out for a place in the booming start-up.

And then there'd been Lucinda.

She'd been wearing a whimsical floral dress, her dark waves of hair tumbling over her shoulders, her big, brown eyes wide with excitement, her toes wriggling in the ends of her summery high heels as she chatted brightly to a severe-looking girl who looked part-Dementor sitting beside her. She'd been like a sunflower among a field of thistles.

"Check out Snow White," Fitz had said. "A blue bird might land on her finger at any moment, right before she breaks into song."

Angus had laughed, as he'd been meant to do, but all the while he hadn't been able to take his eyes off her. The way she'd charmed the people either side of her, making them relax, sit back in their chairs and laugh—even as they were all going for the same job.

For all that he'd been dubbed a wunderkind,

the "people" side of things let Angus down. He struggled with levity. Small talk. Building client relationships. If his job had entailed no human interaction, it would have been perfect.

As such he had little need for someone with an honours degree and a well-curated LinkedIn profile. What he needed was softness. Laughter. Light. Warmth. What he needed was a sidekick who could make the clients loosen up and agree to do as they were told.

Very few times in his life had a clench in his gut meant something good. But this was one of them.

His message to Velma had read: *Dibs on Snow White*.

They hadn't had the easiest of starts. He wasn't proud of the moment he'd found out she was a single mum with a toddler at home. He'd reconsidered. For a week or two. Before giving her something his mother had rarely had—a real chance.

And, without the education or experience to fall back on, she'd made mistakes. Plenty of them. But she'd owned up to them. And had always endeavoured to do better next time. In Angus's book, when it came to people, that was about as good as it got.

For several years now, in his mind, Lucinda's "brand" had been his not-so-secret weapon. His counterpoint. The best decision he'd made as far back as he cared to remember.

But she was right. She wasn't *his girl*.

She was, by the look of things, someone else's. Some stranger by the name of Jameson Something-Or-Other-Smythe. The man taking her away to some romantic resort he'd never heard of.

Hand moving of its own accord, it reached into his jacket pocket and pulled out his phone. With the barest sense of masochism, Angus said the words *Hanover House*—the name of the place Lucinda said she'd be staying.

Like a man slowing at the site of a car crash, he squinted as he flicked through the pictures—all misty vistas, glittery cocktails and flickering fireplaces, award-winning spa, business centre…

His thumb hovered over the screen as he processed the information looking back at him.

Then he looked up, into the middle distance, a tingly feeling at the back of his head telling him to swipe the page away and forget about what he'd just seen.

Another feeling—deeper, grittier, louder—told him to follow his gut.

Lucinda was as key to the future growth of the business as she had been to its past. The business that was now so tightly intertwined with Angus's very identity they could no longer be separated.

If Lucinda was considering introducing this man to Sonny, it had to be serious. Meaning everything was about to change.

And, for Angus, change was a four letter word.

He'd worked too hard, sacrificed too much—time, relationships—to create the life he lived. To ensure the success of the business. To show those who'd told him he'd never amount to anything how wrong they were.

He was about to find out just how far he'd go to protect that.

He glanced back at the phone and drilled in.

A few minutes later, Angus slowly slipped the phone back into his pocket then pushed his stool away from the bar.

He slammed a hand down on Fitz's shoulder as he passed, smiling for the first time in hours as Fitz flinched. "I'm off."

Fitz blinked. "And looking far more like yourself, I must say."

He had an actionable strategy now. So round and whole and complete in his head, he was shocked he hadn't thought of it sooner.

"Crisis over?" Fitz asked.

"No crisis," Angus said, offering the blonde a polite smile. "I don't do crises."

"He's kidding," Fitz demurred. "Crises are his bread and butter. Superhero complex, this one." Then to Angus he said, "Fun and games aside, if any one of us poor slobs deserves love and valentine hearts and eternal happiness, it's Lucinda. Am I right?"

"Rarely," Angus allowed, even as his mind was already ticking away in other directions. Then to the blonde he said, "Be gentle with this one. He's my favourite cousin."

"Only cousin," Fitz called as Angus strode purposefully out of the bar.

That Thursday, Lucinda wriggled her toes in her shoes as she stood waiting for the lift to take her back up to the office, the final minutes of her long-overdue lunch break ticking down.

It had been a huge working week.

The day after Lucinda had told Angus about her upcoming weekend, he'd come into work like a man possessed: snapping up three huge new clients and committing to insane deadlines on top of the Remède rebrand, which was due to be pitched to Louis Fournier and his board early the next week.

Lucinda felt breathless and stretched, like she couldn't stop, even for a second, or it would all collapse on top of her. It was the best natural high she knew.

The lift doors opened and she slipped inside.

Work had been great, but things between her and Angus? They'd been...odd.

Fitz often lamented she and Angus were like four-year-olds on the playground the way they kissed and made up after their feisty skirmishes as if nothing had happened.

Not that they *kissed*. Ever. Not even close. Well, there was that one time something *might* have happened. But it hadn't.

Lucinda shook her head. Hard. The point was, Angus had been weirdly polite. She'd even caught him whistling.

"What did you expect?" she muttered to her wavering reflection in the lift doors.

Well, her subconscious muttered back, *you expected him to be grumpy. Like a bear with a sore tooth. As if the fact that you were heading off on a weekend away with another man might matter. Might burn.*

The lift binged and she pressed the button for the Big Picture Group offices, waving to the receptionists, who happily waved back.

She took a left and strode down the long hall to her desk, which sat like a castle keep protecting Angus's office which took up the entire far corner of the second-to-top floor of the city building.

Once there, she tucked her shopping bag under her desk so that no one could see the distinctive label before she sat in her chair. Then she gave the bag an extra little shove with her toe.

She'd hadn't gone out with the express decision to shop, but when she'd walked past the slinky, black negligée in the store window a little voice in the back of her mind had told her that perhaps she ought to be making a bit more of an effort for bedtime than packing an old T-shirt, stretched-out yoga tights and her ancient tasselled pashmina.

A surreptitious glance through the smoky glass

into Angus's office found him in the exact same position in which she'd left him—sitting back in his big, cushy office chair, easy smile on his face, hands moving elegantly through the air as he wooed some client on the phone.

Lucinda shifted on her seat as she felt the low-level hum that came to life inside her whenever she focussed on Angus for too long.

Her phone rang and she reached for it gladly, answering, "Jameson. Hi."

"Hey."

A busy man, he wasn't one to bother with endless small talk. It was one of the things she liked about him. His directness. The way he said what he meant and meant what he said. Not the fact that he was busy. Though, as a working mum, the fact that he didn't put much of a claim on her time *was* a bonus.

"All good to go?" she asked. As one of the top doctors in the city he was constantly on call. They'd barely made it through a whole date without him having to dash off to save an organ. Or a village.

"Good to go. You? Packed and ready?"

"Not even close! But I will be by seven tomorrow morning."

"I'll pick you up then." A pause, then, "I'm glad the fates have aligned and we are finally able to do this, Cindy."

Her nose twitched at the nickname. Not a favourite. Which was why Angus had told Louis Fournier to use it. The cad. She'd tell Jameson another time, when they knew one another a little better. And how they'd laugh!

She meant it when she said, "Me too."

"Until tomorrow," he said.

"Tomorrow."

When he hung up, Lucinda slid her phone back onto her desk with a sigh.

Jameson Bancroft-Smythe really was one of the good ones. He was kind, considerate, attentive—when he wasn't rushing off to tend to some major medical emergency or another.

He'd never once pushed her to go any faster than she was ready for, which she appreciated. Most of the time. Other times she wished he'd look at her in a way that told her he'd like to tear her clothes off and have his way with her then and there.

It had been a long time since a man had looked at her that way. In fact, she could count back to the actual day. It had happened at a certain Christmas party a year and a bit ago.

Lucinda closed her eyes tight, shoving the memory deep down into her memory banks.

Her smart watch buzzed against her wrist. Another gift from Angus—for her birthday this time. The leather band was her exact favourite tone of spring-green.

It was an hour till she was clocking off. A rare

early mark on a Thursday afternoon. Her desk was tidy. Angus's calendar was up to date. Every one of her favourite 2B pencils was sharpened to a weapon-grade point.

"Lucinda."

Lucinda all but leapt out of her skin at the sound of Angus's voice. She was usually far more attuned to his movements. Not hard when the air all but shifted to make way for him as he moved.

When she turned to him, she found him staring under her desk, his gaze caught on the shopping bag.

Turned out, in attempting to poke it deeper under her desk, she'd knocked it over. The *Foxy Lady* logo was all too obvious on the sparkly hot-pink bag, its slippery black contents having spilled out of the tissue wrap and onto the floor.

"Oh, good Thor," Lucinda muttered, leaning down to shove the lot back in the bag.

When she looked up, she expected to see Angus smiling beatifically as he had been all week. But his jaw was tight, his eyes unusually dark. When his gaze lifted to hers, her heart knocked about behind her ribs.

His voice was no more than a rumble as he said, "I have some bad news."

"Oh?"

"It's about this weekend."

Angus's words took a moment to register, said

as they were in a deep, rough voice that sent trickles of heat down her spine.

"I'm sorry, what?"

"This weekend. I know its last minute, but a conference opportunity has come into play. I need you and your 2B pencils there with me."

And just like that the trickle of heat turned into an inferno, sliding into her belly and radiating out to the ends of her extremities. No, no, no, no, no!

With tingling fingertips, Lucinda pushed back her chair, shoved her handbag over her arm, rummaged under her desk for the *Foxy Lady* bag and gripped the handle tightly in her fist. "Not happening. I'm on holiday. As of right now." Well, an hour from now, but a girl had to do what a girl had to do. "Take someone else. They can even use my pencils."

Lucinda looked at the jar filled with freshly sharpened nibs and felt a small jolt of disloyalty.

Until Angus said, "It's for Remède."

And just like that the raging inferno of self-will turned to ash.

Any other account and she'd have told him to suck it. But Remède?

For, just as Louis Fournier meant a great deal to Angus, the Remède brand meant so much to Lucinda. Her father had bought her mother a bottle of Remède's Someday perfume every year for Christmas.

She continued to keep a bottle nearby, rarely

wearing it but liking the fact that she could open it up every now and then, dip her toes into the past and bring up so many more lovely memories of her parents long after they were gone.

And now that she'd met Louis Fournier her love for the brand was even more personal.

She knew how precarious things were with Remède. She'd been in the room that morning when Angus, Fitz and Charlie had called a special partners-only meeting to address the fact that even a successful rebrand might not be enough to save the company.

"Where is it? The conference?" she asked through gritted teeth.

Angus glanced past her a moment. "You won't believe me if I tell you."

She barely believed him as it was.

"It's at Hanover House."

Her eyes whooshed to his so fast they nearly rolled back in her head. "You have to be kidding me."

Angus shook his head. Slowly. Hypnotically. And she'd never before felt a stronger urge to smack him.

She barely managed to grit out the word, "How…?"

"Curious as to where you were heading, I looked up the place online. When I stumbled onto the business centre page, there it was. A conference the likes of which we've never attended before. A conference that may be just the thing we need."

Lucinda hardly heard the last words over the sound of her heart rattling around in her chest. All week long he'd acted as if he hadn't even remembered her telling him she was going away, yet he'd remembered the name of the resort. And he'd looked it up.

"You were there, Luc. In the Remède meeting. Things aren't looking good."

"With the company, yes. But that's why he came to us. Your rebrand, the social media, the print ads, the website—Angus, it's all gorgeous." The campaign was lush, elegant and aspirational while using hip, young influencers in an attempt to draw a younger, fresher audience to the brand. "It's some of the best work you've ever done. And it's launching next week. Surely there's nothing more that can be done."

He held her gaze a moment, then a few more, till she found herself drowning in the dark hazel depths. Then his gaze dropped to the bag in her hand. The bag they both knew contained a sexy black negligée.

Angus cleared his throat. "Forget it. I shouldn't have asked. I'll be fine. I can function without you."

She felt every strand of the cord handle in her tight palm, hoping her bravado covered up the fact that Angus had unwittingly just poked her greatest fear: that she was inherently dispensable. Her ex had certainly thought so. Not even their beautiful boy enough to keep him around.

Angus said, "Velma can organise a temp."

Before she even felt the words welling up in her throat, Lucinda countered with, "No. Don't."

And for a second, a flash, a smile lit up his face, one that made her knees turn to jelly and her head come over all woozy. She shook her head. Cleared the cobwebs. Made plans.

Okay. With the Remède relaunch imminent she'd never forgive herself if she didn't do all she could to help.

But this weekend was important. If it went well, if she and Jameson had the time and space to see if there was a spark amongst the rapport, it could change everything. For her and for Sonny.

Despite the little glitch in self-confidence as Angus had blithely claimed he could function without her, she knew she was not defined by the moment her ex-husband had left without a second glance. She was defined by decisions she had made since—raising a fantastic, healthy, loving kid and being the best damn executive assistant in town.

"I can do both," she said.

"Hmm?"

"I can have my weekend and I can help you out when you need me at the conference. That's it. That's the deal I'm willing to make."

While Angus considered, Lucinda held her ground. She imagined running from Jameson to Angus, Angus to Jameson, and felt a little ill. But it was what it was. She only hoped he didn't come back with a counter offer, as deep down in places she preferred not to visit she knew if he asked her to choose there was a good chance she'd choose him.

Then Angus nodded once. And Lucinda turned on her heels and walked away before he could change his mind. Or she changed hers.

Over her shoulder she called, "Have someone flip me the conference details."

"Will do," he called back. Then, "Until tomorrow," mirroring Jameson's exact words.

Until tomorrow, Lucinda repeated in her head. Wondering if two such innocent words had ever felt so ominous.

CHAPTER FOUR

WHAT THE HELL were you thinking?

Angus stood at the edge of the foyer of Hanover House's business centre, peering into its conference room to find women as far as the eye could see.

But no Lucinda.

He'd asked an unimpressed Velma to forward her the itinerary. And had heard nothing since. Forcing him to wonder if she was still on her way to the hotel, or if she'd arrived the night before. Alone. Or with Jameson Whatsit-Whatever...

"Hey, honey. You looking for your wife?"

Angus turned to find an older woman with a gravity-defying silver coif, a skirt suit so pink it burned his retinas and a name badge boasting a bright yellow gerbera and the words *South Victorian Regional Beauticians' Organisation* written thereon.

A conference dedicated to cosmetics happening in *this* hotel, *this* weekend, had felt like a sign, right when he was struggling with the Remède account and Lucinda's announcement. Now faced with the reality—booths draped in gauze and lace and velvet, tables covered with bottles and tubs and tubes, signs promising a life of no frizz, spot-free skin and youthful nails—he wondered what the hell he'd been thinking.

For a moment he considered going along with the woman's assumption, jumping in his car, heading back to Melbourne and leaving the future to fate. But in his experience fate was a mischievous, interfering dirt bag who made a habit of putting hardship in the way of good people.

Angus held out his hand. "Angus Wolfe, conference attendee."

The woman's eyes widened to the size of ten-cent pieces before she gathered herself ably. "Elena Zager, conference organiser."

She held out her hand for a shake. Or a kiss. Angus went with a shake and a slight bow, which went down just fine.

"Well, aren't you going to be a cat amongst the pigeons? Shake things up a little. Just what this conference of ours needs."

Soon, two other women approached. One had long, red dreadlocks down to her waist and what looked like henna tattoos winding from her neck to her wrists. The other was small—even in her sharp-as-a-blade black heels—and bone-thin with straight black hair that stopped a knife's edge before her chin.

Each wore badges showcasing their business names and how many years they'd attended the conference. Both looked him at him as if he was a hot lunch.

"Ladies," said Elena. "This here is Angus Wolfe. He's here to attend our little shindig."

"Happy day," said Ms Henna.

"Amen," purred Ms Black Heels.

Angus gave them each a smile, wondering how long it might take for Lucinda to swoop in and do the peopling for him so he could get to work. For, if they were going to save Remède, they would need more than the best branding revamp he'd ever pulled off—they would need a miracle.

Yet he had quipped that he could function without her so…"Not sure if you can tell," he said, "But I'm a first timer. I'd be grateful if someone could show me the ropes."

Elena muscled her way forward when it looked as though Ms Black Heels was about to leap in. "Mr Wolfe, I'm the president of this fine organisation, so I will make it my mission to take care of you this weekend. Let's go find your name tag and a map and then you can tell me what brings a tall drink of water like yourself into our oestrogen-laden midst."

After one last glance over his shoulder in the hope Lucinda would appear, Angus held out an elbow and Elena sneaked a possessive hand into the crook. "Let's do it."

* * *

Lucinda lay back on the sumptuous bed in her king suite with its glorious mound of velvety soft pillows on luxurious sheets.

Only problem was, she lay there alone.

For, when she'd rung Jameson late the night before to explain the turn of events, he'd been… fine. So fine he'd suggested they simply postpone. And, while she'd told him he was a saint and a gentleman and a star, in the back of her head she felt more than a little wounded.

She hadn't expected Sir Galahad but she'd have liked him to put up a little fight.

Maybe he was purloining mood-suppressors from the pharmacy at work.

Or maybe… She closed her eyes and shook her head but it wasn't enough to stop the little doubt demon from finding a way in.

Maybe she was effortlessly dispensable after all. As always, the sentiment made her flinch like the fast, shallow bite of a paper cut.

But maybe it was simpler than all that. Maybe she'd built this weekend up into something bigger than it was.

She *liked* Jameson. He was good and kind and handsome and successful. He didn't press claims on her time. He was easy to be around. He was comfortable.

He was the kind of man she'd be happy to have in her son's life. Sonny was of an age where he noticed how many people in his life loved him. Where he needed a father figure.

He has Angus, a little voice piped up in the back of her head.

And he did. Sonny adored Angus. And Angus adored Sonny. They wrestled. They had a secret handshake Sonny flat out refused to share with her. And Angus always got Sonny the wildest presents for his birthday and Christmas. And just because. Volcano kits, Nerf guns, two hours with a reptile handler—things Lucinda would never consider as they were too messy or dangerous.

But, for all that she allowed herself the occasional fantasy of imagining how it might be if that was her life—for real, every day, every night—it was just that. A fantasy.

She and Angus were friends. Real friends. They bickered, they forgave, they had in jokes, they felt comfortable in their silences. They'd developed a shorthand, a trust.

But a romance? No.

Not least of all because it would change everything at work. Unlike the wild west that was single parenting, and the absolute quagmire of dating, work was the one part of her life in which she felt secure, in control.

But also because Angus wasn't a "for ever" kind of guy. Too many ghosts. Too many walls. If they tried and failed Sonny would never understand. Sonny loved Angus so much she quietly worried that he'd take Angus's side.

So for all that Angus had the ability to make her shimmer, writhe and yearn with a simple look—more than any other man, including the good doctor, had ever come close to—she had to shove it all down deep, deep, deep inside.

Growling out loud, she dragged herself to sitting, the bed so big she had to wriggle her way to the end before she landed on her feet.

Either way, no romance for her this weekend. Just work. She'd do it and she'd do it well.

Still, the thought of having to go out there, find Angus and tell him Jameson had happily told her to go ahead without him was crushing.

She glanced at her watch.

Assuming Angus had made it inside the business centre doors for the Market Stall Day, he'd have been there a good hour by now. On *his* own. At the South Victorian Regional Beauticians' Organisation Bi-Annual Conference. Without her to run interference. To look after the small talk. To be his bodyguard.

Meaning he'd have to talk, listen and engage with what she imagined would be a couple of hundred women in excitable first-day-of-conference mode as they talked about make-up.

Let him see how it felt to function without her.

The thought of it made her feel a little bit better.

* * *

Based on the bones of a one-hundred-and-fifty-year-old mansion, Hanover House's sprawling extensions touted a perfect mix of country comfort and purposeful elegance.

After getting lost—twice—in search of the meeting place Angus had texted to her, she was in desperate need of a strong coffee when she saw the gilt sign reading Bean and Brew Bistro.

The cosy booths were already taken and a bunch of boisterously loud women sat huddled around a few tables that had been pressed together.

Lucinda moved to the counter to order as she waited for Angus.

A voice—an all too familiar male voice—rumbled behind her. "And then Fitz tried to convince us it was his date's stay-fast lipstick. But, as any who visited Maude's booth this morning will know, the only way it would be on his mouth was if he put it there himself!"

A cacophony of feminine laughter followed.

Slowly, so slowly she could all but see the dust motes floating around her head, Lucinda turned as someone, presumably Maude, said, "Exactly! It's the lack of wax that makes all the difference."

And, as if a ray of sun had poured through a gap in a cloud, Lucinda spotted a head of curly dark hair amongst the flock of female heads. Shoulders of Adonis. A blue suit she herself had made sure was back from the cleaners the day before because he'd needed it for that weekend. And it hit her. That meant he'd known about the conference days ago.

Before she even felt her feet moving, Lucinda was at the table. "Angus?"

As one, the women looked her way, each of them sporting a look somewhere between curiosity and suspicion.

Then her boss turned, his gaze landing lazily on hers. "Lucinda, hi. Nice of you to join us."

Don't you "Lucinda, hi" me, you self-serving, stubborn, interfering...

When Angus realised that she was struggling to speak, he glanced back at his flock of fans. "Everyone, this is Lucinda, my executive assistant extraordinaire."

She gave them a group smile, even as her skin felt as if it was stretched so tight over her face it was about to snap.

As one, the group exhaled. And then the questions came her way, thick and fast. "Oh, she does look smart. You never said she was so pretty! Is that your natural hair colour? It's gorgeous. Maybe a little dry. Have you tried a deep condition? Maxhydration would help too. Here's my card. But your skin! It's like a baby's bottom. What do you use?"

The talking suddenly stopped, the entire group waiting for answers.

"Oh. Uh…" she said. "Yes, it's my natural hair

colour. Um…sure. Max-hydration sounds smart."
Once she found out what max-hydration entailed.
"And…goat's milk soap and water."

A collective gasp went around the table like a
Mexican wave. Was that good? Bad? Ought she
to be concerned?

Before anyone had the chance to tug her deeper
down the rabbit hole, Lucinda planted a hand on
Angus's shoulder, her thumb digging into the
tendon between neck and shoulder, the place she
knew he sent all his tension when the ideas didn't
flow as fast as usual.

"Sorry ladies," she said. "Do you mind if I bor-
row him for a second? Boring work stuff."

Angus slowly pushed back his chair and sent
the table a smile that had them all melting into
puddles before holding out an arm and ushering
Lucinda out of the café with a subtle roll of his
shoulder as he went.

Finding they couldn't go ten feet without someone saying, "Hi Angus." "Having fun, Angus?"
"See you soon, Angus.", Lucinda grabbed Angus
by the arm of his suit and dragged him out of the
bistro, around the corner and behind a lush, eight-
foot-tall, fiddle-leaf fig tree that had been planted
in a pot big enough to hide in.

He looked at a big broad leaf curling over his
shoulder, then at her, one eyebrow lifting.

"Put that eyebrow back down. I'm the one who
should be giving you the single-eyebrow-lift treat-

ment. Angus, I am so angry with you right now I can't even… How long ago did you know about this conference? Days, right? It didn't occur to you it might have made my life easier if you'd let me know earlier? Or were you afraid if you gave me too much time I'd organise that temp for you after all?"

"The short answer: yes."

Oh. Okay then.

"Right. Next time you might want to give me a little more credit. Okay?"

When Angus had no response, she looked up to find him staring at her poodle sweater. Not a sweater made of poodles but black, knit, fitted, with a silver poodle motif on the front.

That plus skinny jeans and knee-high boots was miles from her usual uniform of pencil skirts and fancy tops, sleek hair that took far too long to do in the mornings and high heels that made the balls of her feet ache by the end of the day. The pains of looking professional. Indomitable. Indispensable.

But when Jameson had blithely agreed to postpone it hadn't occurred to her to repack until it had been too late, leaving her with a choice of outfits she'd now spend the weekend regretting. Especially if Angus kept looking at her the way he was now.

When Angus still hadn't blinked, she glanced down to realise he *wasn't*, in fact, looking at her poodle sweater —his gaze had snagged on the small, gold ladybird charm resting warm against the dip in her collarbone.

The one Angus had gifted her the first Christmas they'd begun working together.

Not long before, she'd told him the story of how Sonny's first sighting of a ladybird—the delight, the wonder, the utter joy—had been a turning point for her after her husband had left. How that day she'd known she could do it. Be a single mum. Raise a happy, kind, curious boy.

It was the gift that had started it all.

It hadn't occurred to her to leave it behind this weekend. To replace it with something less...*his*.

Feeling like Alice about to fall through the rabbit hole, she shook herself back to the present.

Then clicked her fingers in front of Angus's face to snag his full attention. "Angus. Eyes up."

He blinked, his jaw clenching for half a second before his expression cooled. His hands slid into the pockets of his suit pants, all ease and nonchalance.

"Where were you this morning?" he asked. His voice came out low, with the intimacy demanded of being shuttered behind the fronds of an oversized house plant.

"Checking in," she said. "Settling in. As one would normally do when on holiday. Which I am. I checked the itinerary and figured you wouldn't need me for this morning's market stalls." She glanced in the direction of the bistro. "Seems I was right."

Not rising to the bait, Angus instead asked, "Where's what's-his-name?"

And her gaze slid right back to his. Still not settled on the least embarrassing way to tell him that what's-his-name had stayed home, she said, "You know what his name is."

The jaw clench was back. So maybe he wasn't as cool and nonchalant as he was making out.

But maybe it had nothing to do with her situation. Angus wasn't overly fond of crowds. Or people in general. Situations such as these were when he needed her most.

And, if the fact that that made her feel all warm and fuzzy wasn't a sign that she needed to be hit over the head with a frying pan, she didn't know what was.

This was her moment to let him know he could relax, that she was at his beck and call for the weekend. But some small part of her, possibly the part that had been rattling around in her chest the past few days, stopped her.

"Don't worry about Jameson, okay? He's a big boy. He can take care of himself."

At that, Angus's jaw clenched so hard he looked as if he might break a tooth. Meaning it wasn't the crowds that had made him so tense. Lucinda slowed her breathing and tried not to spin stories in her head.

"How did this morning go?" she asked, moving carefully into work mode.

"Good. How's your room?" he asked, his voice a little rough.

"Lovely. Yours?"

"Adequate."

"Just adequate? Who booked it? Velma?" Lucinda's mouth twitched at the thought of Velma muttering away at having do work for anyone but Fitz, thus booking a broom closet when he'd be expecting a suite. "Look at you, making friends all over the place this week."

"Mmm. Look, can we find somewhere private? Quiet? I need to unload everything I saw this morning. And there's a lot to unload."

Angus ran a hand up the back of his head and shifted from foot to foot, bringing him deeper into her personal space. There wasn't all that much room behind the plant, as it turned out.

Lucinda pressed her back against the wall. "Can't get much more private than this."

"And yet, it's not what I had in mind." His eyes snagged on hers, all hazel and gorgeous, before sliding off to the side, allowing her the chance to breathe out.

"Okay. I'm fairly sure the French doors in my room lead to a small balcony, table and chairs." She remembered a moment too late he was expecting her to have her lover hiding in there. "But no. Not there. It's…um…too cold to work outdoors."

"Lucinda," Angus said, his voice deep, low, raw. "I know this is awkward. But I didn't come here to cramp your style."

"Whatever," she said, holding out a hand, only to find it hovering mighty close to his chest. Close enough she could feel the shift in the air as he breathed. "If it can help Louis, then it's fine."

It wasn't even close to fine.

Angus nodded. She could see the question in his eyes. But she found herself in a rare moment of having no clue what it meant or what to do with it. She only hoped he couldn't see the prevarication in hers.

"Good," he said, deciding to take her words at face value. "Because, while I had hoped that coming here might reiterate that our rebranding was right on track, after this morning I'm more confused than ever."

"How so?"

"I don't know," he said, his voice dropping, the sound scraping against her insides like sandpaper. "It's just… I've got this itch between my shoulder blades. Like we're close, but one wrong step and it will implode faster than we can clean it up."

Lucinda swallowed.

Angus noticed. His gaze on her throat, he said, "It was the strangest thing. When the conference appeared on the hotel website, it felt like I had to be here. Like I'd regret it if I didn't come. It felt like fate."

"First you asked Velma to book you into a conference, then you admitted you're not perfect. And now you're talking about fate? Who are you and what have you done with my Angus?"

Angus's eyes lifted back to hers.

What? Wait! No. My *boss*. She'd meant to say *my boss*.

Too late now. The air around them seemed to shift and shimmer as the words vibrated between them like a plucked wire. It put his "my girl" quip from the other day in the shade.

Feeling as if the small space behind the plant was about to run out of air, Lucinda said, "Anyway, let's go. We can do this. We'll find a room somewhere. I've got my notebook and pencils. You can give it to me there. Your ideas, I mean. Thoughts from this morning."

Stop talking now and get the heck out of here!

When Angus made no move to follow, Lucinda gave him a little shove, the feel of him—all hard, warm planes beneath his suit shirt—searing her palms. "Move."

He stepped away a smidge. Holding her breath, she slipped past the warmth of his body, ignoring as best she could the tingle of goose bumps popping up like burn blisters all over her body.

We'll find a room—and you can give it to me there? her subconscious mocked.

If only she'd had her actual weekend date with

her, the one with whom she'd been hoping to summon up a spark, that line could have gone down a treat!

Angus decided to stay for a moment, hand against the wall, eyes closed as he packed away myriad conflicting thoughts, revelations and sensations that had bombarded him as he'd found himself sharing four square feet of space behind a plant with Lucinda.

What the hell had just happened?

From the moment he'd seen his ladybird charm nestled in the V of her top, the air around them had crackled with electricity, with history, with possibility.

And now, despite his protestations to the contrary, seeing her in that playful little sweater, jeans that fit way too well for comfort, her hair held back by a ribbon that looked as if it would fall open with the slightest tug, in rare flat shoes that brought the top of her head just to his chin, the perfect height to tuck her in tight, his reasons for being there at all felt decidedly muddied.

Was he there to work, making the most of a rare grass-roots insight into the beauty business to shore up the Remède rebrand?

Was he there to protect Sonny? To make sure Lucinda didn't jump the gun on bringing him into any new relationship?

Was he there to protect his business? To do

what had to be done to secure the life he'd worked hard to build?

Or had the "superhero complex" Fitz insisted he harboured sent him there to look out for Lucinda? To make sure this man of hers was good enough? Though any man would be hard pressed to live up to that claim.

He knew why Lucinda was there, of course. In her *lovely* room with French doors and a balcony. She was there for *Jameson*—a big boy who could take care of himself.

As a primal growl built up at the base of his throat, Angus shook his head, his brain taking longer than he liked to stop banging against the side of his skull.

"Angus?" Lucinda's voice called from the other side of the plant.

"Mmm...?" he said. "I've lost...something. Just a second."

Lost something? Lost his mind, more like.

"I'll find us a room, shall I? So we can get your thoughts down before the next session?"

"Yep. Do that."

She was right. Whatever the reasons for coming, from this moment on it had to be about Remède. All he had to do was focus.

But all he could focus on was how, if he breathed through his nose, he could almost still gather the scent of her—apple and cinnamon and soft female skin.

Like Christmas. All that egg nog…all that bloody cheer. And don't even mention the mistletoe…

Angus groaned and ran a hand over his face. *Enough. All right? Enough.*

It wasn't the first time they'd had such a moment. And chances were it wouldn't be the last. The important thing was they were always able to move through it. To work together despite it. Hell, maybe that constant tension was one of the reasons they got so much done.

But it could never…be anything.

They needed one another too much to mess with what they had.

She needed his constancy with Sonny, something he knew would crumble if anything ever happened between them. He'd been there, in Sonny's shoes. And when she realised she deserved more than he was able to give it would fall apart all too fast.

And he needed her to play her part in the business he and Charlie and Fitz had worked their downtrodden, working class asses off to build.

Feeling better—or at the very least as if he had a clearer vision of what came next—Angus gave his head one last shake before leaving the safety of the plant, hoping he'd never set eyes on the thing again.

CHAPTER FIVE

ANGUS SAT IN the back of the generous yet only half-full auditorium as a speaker talked animatedly about the "curly girl movement", losing him when the lingo headed down the lines of "squish to condish" and "scrunch out the crunch".

He turned to his right, ready with a joke for Lucinda, only to still when he remembered she wasn't there. She'd gone to another talk, one about the science of cruelty-free cosmetics, something he'd have been far more interested in than "deep conditioning".

It made him wonder if she'd ordered him to sit in on this one as some kind of punishment for making her come at all.

The woman three seats up blushed and gave him an encouraging smile.

He gave one back—though less encouraging—before grabbing his suit jacket from the back of the empty seat beside him and shuffling along the empty row to his left.

"Everything okay?" It was Elena Zager, conference organiser, exit gatekeeper.

"All good. Great speaker. Lots of personality. Your attendees are lapping it up."

"Curls are a booming industry right now. Hugely energised, grass roots, engaged social media community. Making big waves. So to speak."

Angus wondered briefly if Remède had any products that might be swept up by a grass-roots campaign but knew it wouldn't be enough.

Elena motioned to his own head of curls. "Do you oil?"

Angus blinked. "Wash and wear."

"Mmm…"

Before she began to dole out advice, Angus crossed his arms and leaned against the door, positioning himself as her partner in the line of defence against room-leavers. "How are things going? With the conference."

"Brilliantly!" Elena looked around. "Though it would have been nice to have a few more attendees. Our speakers are world class. Those who come rave about the events in the feedback sheets. Time was we'd fill a room like this, but our numbers are slipping, especially as we struggle to drum up fresh faces. Present company excluded, of course."

Angus smiled, his eyes roving over the stage set-up, the banners, the promotional signage. It all looked a little tired, no doubt due to funding restrictions that came from diminishing numbers. A vicious cycle he and Lucinda saw time and again when clients came to him, feeling at the end of their rope.

"Have you ever had professional help, branding-wise?" he asked.

Elena leaned away. "Whatever do you mean?"

"Logo refresh, colour choice, website SEO audit, advertising buy-ins, social media spreads, creating viral headlines..."

When her eyes began to glaze over, Angus swallowed the lingo and thought about how Lucinda might put it. "Uh...how do people know about the conference?"

"My nephew made our website, and this year he started a Facebook page. It's quite good. We advertise in trade magazines, but that gets more and more cost-prohibitive each year. And we do a mail-out to our list. I think that's all."

Before he even felt the words forming, Angus heard himself say, "If you'd like me to put together some ideas, ways to invigorate interest, I'd be happy to offer up some thoughts."

Elena blinked, splotches of colour rising beneath the thick layer of make-up she wore. Damn it. He'd offended her. When he'd only been trying to help.

This was why he needed Lucinda. She was the one who usually drew the client in, for she was honest and real. You felt it the moment you looked into her eyes.

But she wasn't around, so he had no choice but to fend for himself.

Angus lowered his voice, found what he hoped was a warm smile and said, "Just between you and me, I'm not actually in the beauty industry."

"Oh?"

He leaned in conspiratorially. "Updating business brands, helping companies connect with the people who need them, is what I do for a crust. And I'm quite a big deal in my field, if I do say so myself."

"Oh! Well, then, I guess if you have any advice, I'd be amenable to hearing it."

Angus gave her a smile. A real smile. Clearly, he'd picked up some of Lucinda's skills after having watched her in action over the years.

Elena patted him on the hand before heading back down into the auditorium.

Angus leaned back against the door, the realisation of what he'd just offered to do slowly sinking in. He didn't have the time for this. Or the head space. The answer to Remède's very big, very real problem was the only thing he ought to focus on.

Especially when it felt so close. As if the answer was right under his nose.

Where *was* Lucinda when he needed her?

With her discount-store pencils and fancy notebooks in hand, she'd have the idea out of his head and into a user-friendly plan in no time at all.

It was a hell of a thing, the way she did that. Head cocked so her dark hair swung over one shoulder, soft brown eyes narrowed as she pierced him with a laser look. It was as if she could see right inside his head, to his very core.

A place few people had ever seen.

Client relationships never went beyond the professional. Other friendships—neighbours, work acquaintances, old uni friends—were peripheral. The women he dated remained at arm's length. Allowing them any closer would mean giving them the power to move him. Affect him. It would mean risking loss of control.

Having watched his mother let man after man into her home, into her heart, he'd also had to watch them leave, every one of them taking a piece of her with them until by the end he'd barely been able to recognise the woman who'd promised she'd give him a better life no matter what.

Of all the life lessons she'd tried to impart, the most lasting was one she'd never said out loud. She'd lived her life wide open and it had changed her. So, he lived his as a closed book. Invulnerable.

To everyone…except one.

Pressing himself away from the door, he slipped through. His steps ate up the miles to the small single room Velma had booked to grab a stash of hotel stationery.

Needing to keep his mind busy, to keep his thoughts from straying, he chose the accoutrements necessary to whip this organisation into the best shape of its life.

It would be like sorbet for his creative brain, leaving a clean slate on which a moment of clarity might shine, lighting the way to bring the Remède rebranding together.

After the Science of Cruelty-Free Cosmetics session, Lucinda had sent Angus a message to say she'd meet up with him later in the afternoon for a debrief.

If he took that to mean she was spending time with Jameson, then surely that was on him?

Instead, she spent an hour wandering the grounds of Hanover House, breathing in the fresh air, literally smelling the roses. Grateful to have some time to herself. Time on her own was at a premium, what with her long work hours and her beautiful boy to take care of.

When she found herself wandering aimlessly in and out of a series of tall conifers, her first thought was that they were the perfect size for a man to tug his woman behind and kiss her till her knees gave out. Taller than a fiddle-leaf fig, in any case. Denser. More private.

Thought what did a fiddle-leaf fig have to do

with anything? It was Jameson who should be dragging her behind a bush and kissing her senseless, not...anyone else.

And he would. When they rebooked their weekend away. She'd make sure of it! Though the handful of kisses they'd shared so far hadn't boded all that well for the promise of swooning and watery knees.

Suddenly, the thought of lining up a weekend when they were both free, booking the time off and getting Sonny used to the idea of another weekend without her felt all too hard.

Her phone vibrated silently in her pocket.

She stopped walking and made a deal with herself. If it was Jameson checking in, calling to whisper sweet nothings and tell her how much he wished he was there with her, alone, she'd make it happen. And soon. But if it was anyone else...

She lifted the phone from her bag, her shoulders slumping. In disappointment? Or relief?

Phone at her ear she said, "Hey, Kitty Cat."

"Loosey-Lu," her sister sing-songed. "You free to talk? Not handcuffed to the bed? Swinging from a chandelier?"

"I'm free."

"How's the good doctor?"

Okay, so she might not have told her sister her weekend plans had changed either. She'd have to do a lot of nice things for a lot of people to balance out the karma her recent decisions might unleash.

Eyes closed, she tore off the proverbial Band-Aid. "Don't know. He's not here."

Silence.

"Didn't I mention? Turned out I had to work this weekend. A conference. At Hanover House, of all places. But when I told Jameson that I could do both—weekend with him and work a little—he blew me off."

"The villain," was Cat's flavourless response. Then, "So you're at the resort. Only not with Jameson. With instead, I'm presuming, your dashing boss?"

"Mmm-hmm."

Speaking of Angus, Lucinda took the phone away from her ear to check the time. Time to head back. She was joining said dashing boss in fifteen minutes in the small meeting room they'd nabbed within the business centre.

"You sound out of breath," said Cat. "Are you certain you're alone?"

"I'm walking. Fast."

"Right. Sure."

"Okay, I have to go. You know Angus—work, work, work. Remind Sonny when he gets home from school that he can call me any time."

"Are you sure? I know you no longer have hanky-panky as your primary mission this weekend, but you don't want a blackout period? A metaphorical tie hanging from the hotel door? Just in case?"

"He can call me any time."

"Okay, then. Bye."

Lucinda hung up without saying goodbye, threw her phone into her hand bag with a little more force than necessary and grumbled and muttered all the way back to the hotel.

She was getting a little sick of her sister's passive-aggressive commentary on her relationship with Angus.

Though for a moment or ten, behind the fiddle-leaf fig, it had felt…new. Hot. Breathless. The way he'd looked at her. Holy-moly. His body had vibrated with a level of tension that was quite something, even for him. As if it was taking Angus as much effort not to touch her as it was for her not to touch him.

To run a hand up the back of his neck and another up the front of his business shirt, sliding a finger beneath a button until it popped free of the hole. To press herself against him until she felt the hard press of his…

"Argh!" she cried when she realised where her mind was going, scaring a pair of topknot pigeons who leapt squawking from the lawn into the air.

She pressed her hands against her eyes as if that might wipe away the vision now burned into her retinas. "Okay. Pull yourself together. You just need to get through this weekend, do all you can for Remède and, come Monday, everything will be back to normal."

As pep talks went it was a bit of a fizzer. For the first time "normal" didn't sound like everything she'd ever wanted.

But it got her feet moving again. So, by the time she found her way back to the meeting room she was ready to work. Or ready to fake it, at the very least.

She lifted a hand to knock, then shook her head and opened the door. Angus was already there, sitting at a small round table which was covered in pens and paper.

His curls showed signs of having been raked with frustrated fingers. His left cheek was a little pink, as if he'd been leaning on his fist. His tie was missing, as was his jacket. His shirt was wrinkled and rolled up to the elbows. His right leg jiggled like crazy under the table. He looked raw, ravaged. Like a boardroom warrior.

When he realised he was no longer alone and looked up at her, his eyes a little wild, intense, glinting behind his reading glasses, Lucinda had to shake her head in order to stop staring.

"Hey," she said, moving to dump her bag and jacket on a spare chair before grabbing a notebook and pencil and carefully shoving papers aside to claim a small corner of the table.

He blinked, a small measure of the heat in his eyes dimming as he said, "Where's Dr Whatsit?"

She waved a hand in the direction of the door. Or Melbourne. "Probably on a call."

There was a good chance. When they were together he was always on the phone. Which, come to think of it, was actually pretty frustrating.

She'd brushed it off, putting it down to the fact he was an important man who did important work. But would she be happy to be second fiddle to a man's work all the time? If she ever opened her heart truly, all the way open, it would be because she trusted the man in her life would be there for ever. For her. For Sonny. For them.

Angus cleared his throat again. Probably because she was staring at him. Again.

She shook her head. "Sorry. A million miles away."

Angus did not look impressed. In fact, he looked mighty uncomfortable. As if he imagined she'd been daydreaming about Dr Whatsit and what they might have been up to together behind the conifers.

Finding herself rather enjoying seeing Angus flummoxed, Lucinda opened her mouth to fan the flames with some carefully chosen words then snapped it shut.

Enough. Really, enough.

She brought her notebook onto her lap. "Before we get to work, I have a confession."

He frowned. "I prefer the 'get to work' part of that sentence."

"And yet I'm telling you anyway. It's about Jameson."

Angus sat back and held up a hand, the column of his throat turning patchy. "Lucinda——"

"He's not here. In the hotel. He was never here."

He stilled, his hand still hovering in mid-air. "I don't understand."

"He was *meant* to be here. This weekend was a real thing for us. A big thing, or so I thought. But, when I rang and told him I had to work a little while we were here, he bailed."

Angus slowly sat forward and ran a hand over his chin. After a few long beats, in which the only sound was the ticking of a clock on the wall overhead, he said, "Luc, I'm sorry. Truly. I didn't mean for that to happen."

Didn't you? a small voice piped up in the back of her head. Thankfully she stopped it from escaping through her lips.

"You led me to believe he was here."

Lucinda held up a finger. "If you think back, you'll find I never once said he was here, I simply didn't let on that he was elsewhere."

Don't ask why. Don't ask why. Don't ask...

"Why?"

Ah, the eternal question. There were many reasons. She chose one. "I was embarrassed. After making such a big deal about this weekend and the thing that spilled out of the shopping bag. The ease with which he took the news was less than flattering."

The look in Angus's eyes was telling. But telling of what? There was a quiet intensity about him, a sense that all kinds of big emotions rippled beneath the surface.

His voice was so quiet when he said, "He's a surgeon," that Lucinda jumped.

"Yes."

"Meaning he is on call a fair bit."

"Yes. Often."

"Having your time together cut short is one of the joys of dating a doctor."

Snort. "Like you'd know."

"I did, in point of fact, date a doctor once."

"A doctor of what? Astrology?"

The intensity in Angus's eyes changed. Shifted. Warmed. "No," he said, his voice dropping to a purr. "Vivian was an actual medical doctor."

Lucinda opened her mouth with a qualifier, but Angus got there first, "Who doctored on humans. From memory, I quite liked the fact she was constantly on call. It meant she had so little claim on my time. I wonder what happened to her?"

"I bet you do."

His smile was wide. With teeth. And, oh, the things it did to her insides. And outsides. All over.

Lucinda frowned down at her notebook to find she hadn't made a single note.

Then Angus asked, "Do you want to talk about it? About him?"

"With you?"

He looked over his shoulder as if checking to see who might be lined up behind him.

"Funny," she deadpanned. "We don't do this. You and I. We don't talk about the people we... date." She might as well have used a number of other terms, given how the temperature in the room seemed to rise.

"We don't, do we?"

She shook her head. Slowly. Feeling more than a little mesmerised by the look in his eyes. "Best we keep it that way, don't you think? I know we don't have much in the way of boundaries but the people we date...maybe that should be one of them."

"Maybe. But, while we're considering that, tell me this: is there anything I can do to make it up to you both, if you imagine you'll be...dating him again any time soon?"

A second or three went by before Lucinda realised she was still shaking her head.

"No, I can't help, or no, you're done with him?"

Her voice cracked a very little as she said, "Both." And she meant it. For, if he'd let her go all too easily, the truth was she was glad he wasn't there.

"Good," Angus said, the edge of his mouth kicking into a slow-burn kind of smile that made Lucinda's insides melt.

"Good?"

"You deserve the kind of man who'd stand up and tell you no."

"Ah, what now?"

"Along the lines of no, you can't work this weekend, as I have plans. Plans that won't work if I don't have you all to myself. All weekend long."

Lucinda tried not to swallow. She really did. But if she wanted to get the words out she had no choice.

"I'll keep that in mind. Now, what's going on here?" She flapped a hand at the table to distract him. "Did a stationery shop crash-land on your table?"

She was gifted a slight tilt of the head—the equivalent of giving her a C+ for her distraction efforts—before he nudged his glasses higher on his nose and his attention slid back to his work.

"I'm helping the committee rebrand before their next event."

"What committee?"

A muscle ticked in his jaw. "The, ah, committee who organised the conference. That we are attending."

"Elena and her lot? They *hired* you?"

"I volunteered."

"You volunteered. To help them. For nothing." This from a man who let his underlings deal with small-fry accounts such as cinema chains and TV stations as he was too busy catering to airlines and media conglomerates. This man who equated success with the number of multinational clients on his waiting list.

She popped out of her chair and placed the back of her hand on his forehead. "Are you okay?"

Feeling warmth, feeling her skin tingling where it had met his, she curled her fingers away and sat back down. "Do they have something on you? Please tell me you won a free makeover and there are photos to prove it!"

Angus slowly leant back in his chair, long legs sliding deeper under the table until one of his feet brushed against hers. She quickly crossed her ankles and tucked her feet back as far as they would go.

"Can't a guy just do something nice for a bunch of beauticians with it not having to mean something?"

"Not you."

Something flashed behind his eyes.

"Angus, I didn't mean…" Lucinda leant forward. "Remède, Angus. You're here, rather than having a much-deserved weekend off, because of Remède. Right?"

It took a few beats longer than it should have for him to nod.

"Then do you even have time for this?"

"Probably not. But I was looking for a win."

Oh? *Oh.*

Lucinda's heart gave a little kick.

The guy was the most winning person she'd

ever met. Some campaigns were more successful than others, but they were always baseline
successful. For him to be *that* worried about
Remède's account? For him not to have complete
faith in himself? Boy, that must be messing with
his head.

And she felt more than a little silly for har-
bouring a teeny, tiny thread of hope in the back
of her head that the reason he was here was for
her.

Agreeing to a quickie pro bono for a non-profit,
that was way out there for him. And it was her
job to go there with him, to make sure he made
it back to safe ground. Meaning it was time to
go to work.

"Okay. Let's do this. A genius fix, but on a low
budget. Feels like how it used to be back in the
beginning. Remember?"

The moment she said *okay,* Angus looked
slightly less haunted. "It was the Wild West—
scrounging for time, pulling in favours, like digging for diamonds in the back yard. Bloody hard
work, but fun, right?"

She couldn't help but grin. "The *funnest.* Now,
while it's terribly cute that you tried to do this
without me, let me sort out the crazy you have
going on here."

It took Lucinda about a minute and a half to
have Angus's scattered notes in neat piles. Another ten—during which she kept shushing him

when he tried to interject—to read through the piles, pick out the thread tying it all together and annotate.

Once done, she sat back with a happy sigh, flush with the sense of accomplishment.

When she caught Angus's eye, she found him watching her with a darkly indulgent smile.

She glowered. "Now what?"

"You made the noise."

"What noise?"

"The happy 'humph' you make whenever you're feeling particularly pleased with yourself. You make it a lot."

"I do?" She licked her lips which suddenly felt preternaturally dry.

He nodded, his gaze dropping to her mouth. And suddenly it felt as if they were back behind the fiddle-leaf fig again. As if there wasn't enough air. As if they were saying more without words than with.

"Then I must be pleased with myself a lot. Which makes sense. Because I'm awesome."

Angus's smile stretched. "And no matter how busy we are, how tight the deadlines, how much work I pile on your plate, that noise always tells me you're happy where you are."

"Where I am?" she said, her voice light.

"Working with me."

Her chest tightened pleasurably.

With him, he'd said. Not *for* him. Whenever she

found herself particularly frustrated, when he was grumpy or stubborn or locked away in the impenetrable mental cave in which he lived much of the time, it was moments like this, when he treated her not just as another employee but as his partner, that turned it all around.

That made her tingle. And sparkle. And wonder. And hope.

And yearn.

Look away! her subconscious cried, and for once she did as she was told, picking up a piece of paper from the table and staring at it as if it was the most interesting thing she'd seen in a long time.

"'South Victorian Regional Beauticians' Organisation'," she said, reading the conference package he'd scribbled all over. "*That* has to go."

"Right there with you." Angus pulled out a sheet of paper he had tucked up inside the conference folder, on which he'd sketched out a new business name and logo.

"When did you come up with this?" she asked.

"Five minutes before you stormed in and I let you pretend you'd taken over."

She shot him a look before her gaze was pulled back to his sketch.

It was simple, elegant, aspirational, feminine, strong and dead on target. The colour was not the usual cosmetic pink, but a sweet, wistful spring-green. Extremely close, in fact, to the colour of her watch band. Her reusable takeaway coffee mug. Her favourite dress.

Another woman might have imagined that was because he'd been thinking about her as he'd worked. Lucinda steadfastly refused to imagine any such thing.

"Are you sure you're not a woman?" she asked.

The curl of his smile, the gleam in his eye, the roll of his shoulder, were all so very male that Lucinda's ovaries hiccupped.

"So, what about…? Where's that bit with the membership restructuring…?"

They both leaned forward to reach for a piece of paper at the same time. Lucinda grabbed it, Angus's hand closing over hers.

She glanced up, finding herself close enough to see all the colours in his magnetic eyes. To see stubble darkening the edges of his hard jaw. To watch him attempt to control the measure of his next breath.

She ought to have pulled some ninja move and unglued her hand from his before he even knew she was on the move.

But, while she was considering, he lifted her hand to have a closer look. Sonny had drawn on the back of her hand before she'd left, so she'd "remember him" while she was away. It was a now faded lopsided heart.

Angus sniffed out a breath, his eyes creasing into a smile as he ran this thumb over the drawing. Then, as if he was in some kind of trance, he turned her hand over, distractedly watching his thumb as it traced her lifeline. Or was it her heartline?

Lucinda could not breathe. She could barely think. Every nerve, cell and emotion centred on the gentle swipe of Angus's grazing touch.

When he reached the tender underside of her wrist, it became too much and she jerked her hand away.

Hope, confusion and years of pressing her feelings deep down inside mixed into a tempest inside her, pushing her to her feet so fast her chair scraped sharply against the floor before teetering and tipping over.

She spun and crouched to pick it up, right at the same moment that Angus came round the table to do the same. Her eyes snapped to his to find them dark and bottomless.

Lucinda slowly pulled herself to her feet, her legs shaking with the adrenaline coursing through her body.

Angus stood by her, the chair in one hand. He gently placed it back down. And stayed where he was, breathing hard enough that she could see the shape of him beneath the constraint of his shirt.

"The next session starts soon," Lucinda somehow managed to croak out.

"Right."

"I think I'll go freshen up before heading to… whatever it is I'm heading to."

"Okay. I need to track down some coffee and then I'll come back here. Keep working on this. Can I grab you a cup? To take with you?"

Now he was asking if he could get her a coffee? Lucinda really needed him to say something smug. Or arrogant. To restore balance to the galaxy.

She shook her head then leaned around him to reach her bag, holding her breath so as not to swoon as she brushed so close to him she could feel his body heat.

Somehow her feet remembered how to walk, admirably carrying her to the door. Where she stopped. Turned. She couldn't leave with that kind of tension pulling between them or she'd not hear a word of the next session.

"Will you be okay? Doing this on your own? Because I can stick around…"

"I'm fine. This feels…good." The warmth that lit the edges of his smile made her wonder if he was fully aware of the butterflies smacking into her ribcage. Then he said, "I'm sorry about Dr Whatsit. Truly."

"Yeah," she said. "Me too." For she was. It should have been so easy to fall for him. To fit him into their lives. Then, "And, should you have a Dr Whatsit in your life one day, you can talk to me about it, you know. Any time. Boundaries, schmoundaries."

Something dark swirled behind his eyes. "There'll be no Dr Whatsits for me, Luc. You know better than anyone that my mother taught me the benefits of a life of solitude. Which either makes me a very lucky man, or it's the great tragedy of my life."

Lucinda gave him a smile, as was expected.

All the while, as she headed back out into the hotel and walked unseeingly towards the conference rooms, her heart twisted so hard it hurt.

She'd lost loving parents while still relatively young. Her husband had left her when they'd had a beautiful thirteen-month-old boy.

And yet, Lucinda thought with a heaviness settling over her like a rain cloud, the fact that this man flat out refused to move beyond the ghosts of his boyhood might yet turn out to be the great tragedy of her life as well.

CHAPTER SIX

"WHAT THE HELL are you doing at a beauty conference in the same hotel in which your assistant is meant to be having her dirty weekend but now isn't because she's stuck working with you?"

Fitz's voice rattled through the phone pressed to Angus's ear as he leant against the cold concrete balustrade outside the Bean and Brew Bistro, watching the trees below sway in the moonlight.

He nursed the end of a strong, post-dinner coffee, one he'd begun just before Lucinda had given a good impression of a fake yawn before claiming exhaustion and heading to her room. Alone.

"Who told you?" Angus growled.

"Who *hasn't* told me? I had questions. About things. And you're not here to answer them. To stop me whinging about it, Velma informed me where I could find you. Then the lovely Cat, in a scratchy mood I must say, called to demand I do something about it. About you."

"Me?"

"Apparently everything in the world is your fault."

"I see. What was so important you had to track me down?"

A pause. "Can't remember. But, now I have you, anything you need to get off your chest? About the amenities, perhaps? The chamber maids? How you and the lovely Lucinda are getting along out in the blustery wilds?"

"It's Daylesford, not the Outback. And, like the many conferences we've been on together over the years, we're getting along just fine. And trying to get a deeper insight into the industry in the hope it gives us another angle to add to the Remède rebrand."

"Fair enough. Any highlights thus far?"

When it came to Remède? No.

As for the weekend, so far it had all the hallmarks of a roller coaster.

Dinner had been...polite. Lucinda had met him after the conference day was done. Had kept her eyes on her notes as she'd talked through a series of neatly written bullet points. Had recited a phone conversation she'd had with Sonny that afternoon, word for word. Then bolted.

Whereas in the meeting room, earlier that day...

Angus closed his eyes against the memory of Lucinda sitting before him, her brown eyes huge as she watched him trace his thumb down the soft skin of her palm, her throat working, her cheeks pinking. He'd all but seen her light up from the inside out.

He shook his head. He couldn't possibly say what he'd been thinking. He'd seen the drawing on the back of her hand and had pulled it closer to find the endearing love stamp from her son.

As for the rest? Something had come over him when he'd felt the warmth of her hand curled beneath his. The erratic pulse beneath the skin. Something primal and deep.

But Lucinda was out of bounds.

No. She was the one person in his life with whom there were no "bounds". She called him out when he was too demanding. Rolled her eyes when he refused to budge. She knew when to give him space. She had even more faith in him than he had in himself.

She knew him. The good bits and the bad. And she stuck around anyway.

Then there was the fact she'd let him into her family. Gifted him the friendship with her son. No limits. No rules. She trusted him to have Sonny's best interests at heart.

For a guy like him, who pushed back against anyone who tried to get close, that was exceedingly rare.

Never in his life had a person been as important to him, to his success, to his self-worth, to his mental health.

Messing with that would be self-defeating. And Angus was no masochist.

As such, he recapped all he'd seen and heard in case Fitz saw something he didn't.

Apparently, Fitz saw no such lightbulbs, as he said, "So, nothing to hang your hat on so far. Bar scaring Lucinda's guy away. Probably a good thing there, right? Last thing any of us need is for Luc to turn into a love-sick muppet. The woman runs the whole ship. We'd be dead in the water without her."

"Dead," Charlie's voice agreed amiably. "In the water."

"I'm on speakerphone?" Angus asked, coming to a halt.

"Always. Now, why did I call you again?" Fitz asked.

"Heaven only knows."

"Is Lucinda there?" Charlie's disembodied voice asked in the background. "Can you get her? I wanted to ask her something."

"She's not with me," Angus answered.

"Why not?"

Fitz piped up. "Probably avoiding him."

"What am I missing?" Charlie asked.

"The twenty-first century," Fitz answered. Then, with exaggerated patience, he went on. "Okay, here's the sordid tale in a nutshell. Angus, pipe in if I miss something. Lucinda was all set for a dirty weekend with some hot doctor. Until

Angus found out and went all superhero and figured out a way to be there to save her from herself. So, though they are there together, the lovely Lucinda is not *with* Angus. And that, dear friends, is the issue of the day. Now, if our erstwhile hero would only man up and admit that he and our gorgeous girl are—"

Angus didn't bother saying goodbye. He simply hung up.

Lucinda stood in her hotel bathroom, hands gripping the edge of the sink. Not feeling anywhere near as tired as she'd made out.

In fact, she felt wired. Too much cheap conference coffee? Too much Angus.

Which was ridiculous, considering the time they spent in one another's company at work. And yet somehow this weekend she'd found the usual methods she employed to keep her feelings at bay just weren't cutting it.

During the afternoon's laugh-out-loud session spent guessing famous perfumes while blindfolded, then shouting out the scent ingredients that stayed with them the most, she'd managed not to think about Angus's thumb grazing her hand. Much.

But the moment she'd walked into the bistro, seen him sitting by the large picture windows, the dusk light playing over the angles of his face, her heart had raced so hard she'd felt as if she was about to go into full-blown panic.

She'd never eaten dinner faster.

Glancing up, she caught her reflection in the mirror. The slinky black negligée she'd slipped on after the cool shower she'd taken gleamed in the down-lights. She'd also touched up her make-up. Even dabbed on a spritz of perfume in unmentionable places.

For nothing. For no one. Just because.

She turned her face this way and that. Not yet thirty, her skin was pretty good. She liked her nose. And her crooked smile. She'd always thought her eyes a little dark, but it was a good face.

She stood, turned side-on. Lifted onto her toes to see as much of herself in the bathroom mirror as she could. Having had Sonny young, there were few signs on her body that she'd ever given birth. A little roundness in the belly. A couple of stretch marks that gleamed in the right light.

She was attractive enough. Funny. She liked talking. She was a great listener. Good at reading between the lines. Working for Angus as long as she had, it was a skill that came in handy on a daily basis.

So, with all that going for her, what about her had made it so easy for Jameson to say, "No worries. Weekend away postponed. Easy-peasy"?

What made not one of the men she met at work

gatherings, parties or those she passed in the fruit and vegetable aisles at the supermarket fall madly, irreversibly in love with her?

What about her had made her husband able simply to walk into the kitchen one day and say, "I can't do this any more"?

True, she and Joe had not had an easy time of things. She'd met him not long after her parents had died suddenly. He was a man with itchy feet and little to hold him down. Everything her regular suburban life had not been up to that point. She'd fallen hard. Followed wherever he'd led. They'd married fast, a baby already on the way.

But it hadn't taken long for him to tire of their life after she'd made them stop and put down roots. For at heart she was that kind of girl. A home girl. A stayer. A believer in for ever.

Would she ever find someone—not Jameson but someone better? A stayer, like her? Someone who made her heart race, her toes curl, her cheeks hurt from laughing, someone who made her tell Angus *no*?

Angus. A man to whom it was nearly impossible to say no. Whom it was nearly impossible to sway. Nearly impossible to resist.

But there was still an inner wall she'd never made it beyond.

It was that wall that made it easy for her to harbour her secret crush. She could never truly lose her heart to the man as his wasn't up for grabs.

Realising her hands were sliding over the slinky fabric while she thought of Angus, she lifted them away, curled them into fists and walked away from the mirror, turning the bathroom light off behind her.

She climbed from the end to the head of the bed before falling in a heap on the right-hand side. She'd never migrated to the middle of the bed by habit as, after Joe had left, Sonny occasionally made his way into her room when he was sick or had bad dreams.

She lay on her back and flung an arm over her eyes. Hoped sleep might take her so the dangerous thoughts still swirling behind her closed lids could be excused as dreams.

Her phone buzzed on the bedside table.

This time she knew who it was before she even checked. When Angus's face showed above the message he'd sent, her limbs came over all warm and her breath released on a sigh:

They have Netflix. Should I keep going with Warlock Academy or wait for you?

Knowing sleep wasn't coming any time soon, she sent back her response.

She put her phone aside, grabbed her fluffy old pashmina and dragged it with her under the covers, pulling the blankets up to her chin and stretching out her arm for the remote.

* * *

Lucinda was in reception the next morning, struggling not to yawn as she made sure she and Angus had access to their small meeting room for the next two days, when a familiar voice rent the air.

"Mum!"

Lucinda spun nearly a full circle before she saw her boy rushing her like a whirling dervish. He leapt into her arms and she twirled him around. "Hey, baby boy! What on earth are you doing here?"

"Cat brought me. As a surprise. She said your friend couldn't come any more so you'd be really sad. And lonely. So we came to keep you company!"

Lucinda scanned the foyer to find her sister swanning across the floor, dragging two small battered suitcases behind her. "How wonderful," she said, while she glared at Cat for all she was worth.

"Really? You don't sound like it's wonderful."

Snapping her gaze back to her son, she let him drop to the ground then took his adorable face in her hands, knowing that only this face would save her from strangling her sister. "Really. Every moment I have with you is my best moment ever."

Sonny grinned. "Mine too."

Lucinda held Sonny tight to her front as she straightened and faced her sister. "Kitty Cat."

"Loosey-Lu. Sleep well?"

"Very well." At the thought of sleep, Lucinda's yawn could no longer be denied. Her nostrils flared from the effort at swallowing it down. She'd asked for dreams and she'd got them. Racy, lusty, hot, sweaty ones.

Cat's smile was all too knowing.

"Go look out that window," Lucinda said, pointing to a window seat near the front doors. "They have the most beautiful, fluffy white clouds out here. Come back and tell me what shapes you can see in them."

Sonny bolted for the window, leaving Lucinda to turn to Cat with hands on her hips. "What on earth are you doing here?"

"Sonny already hit the high notes."

"I'm working, Cat. I can't hang with you guys. Does Sonny understand that?"

"We've made plans. Marco Polo in the heated pool. Skimming stones by the lake. Jurassic Park marathon."

All things they could have done in and around home. So why were they…?

"Are you *babysitting* me?" Lucinda asked, her voice rising enough that the guy behind reception gave her a look.

"Something's different," Cat said. "I can smell it. I'm here to make sure you don't do something you can't take back."

Lucinda's mind went instantly to the hand-holding incident the day before. Put like that, it sounded so innocent. But it wasn't. It hadn't been. It was out there now. Woven into the fabric of their story.

"I am a grown-up person, Cat, if you hadn't noticed. I've managed to survive thus far without an overseer."

Cat glanced towards Sonny. Making the point that he was the result of a time in Lucinda's life when her decision-making had been less than stellar. Falling for Joe, sticking with Joe, marrying Joe. Not that she'd have changed a single moment. Not when it had brought her her beautiful boy.

But she got it.

"Do you have a room?" Lucinda asked. Her mind went to her beautiful big suite, with its huge bed, lounge, desk and balcony. They could make it work. Before buying her cottage, they'd lived together in smaller digs.

"All good," said Cat. "After I wrote that article on the place, they offered me a room for a night, so this is my chance to take them up on it. And I know you're working, so Sonny will stay with me." Cat moved a little closer, her eyes downcast, her foot nudging against the wheel of a suitcase. "Look, I probably shouldn't have sprung this on you, but I felt like I had to. When I moved in after Joe left, you asked me to help make sure you never fell for someone so wholly wrong for you again. So this is me. Helping."

Cat moved to the desk to check in, while Sonny's footsteps slapped against the floor as he came bolting back from the window. "A chicken. A flamingo. And a pair of yellow gumboots."

"Yellow?" Lucinda asked, her skin feeling as if it was burning at Cat's insinuation that she was in danger of falling for Angus. Who was, according to her sister, wholly wrong for her. "How could you tell?"

Sonny shrugged. "Just could."

"How was the drive? What's the newsy news?" Lucinda asked.

"Traffic was bad. Cat thinks it's going to rain, but I told her there are no cumulonimbus clouds so it won't. And she said the S-word."

"Did she, now?"

"She said it was okay because you can use that word in the car. When drivers are being…you know. Because they can't hear you. And because it's true."

"Stupid," Cat called out. "The S-word was 'stupid'. And that driver was stupid. Right, Sonny?"

Eyes wide, Sonny nodded. "He really was, Mum."

Then suddenly Sonny tugged his hand from hers and bolted, right as Angus's deep voice boomed across the lofty space, "Hey! Kid!"

"Uncle Angus!" Sonny cried as he threw himself at Angus's suit-clad leg.

"Speak of the devil," Cat murmured as she sauntered up to stand by Lucinda, arms crossed.

Freshly shaven and in a dark charcoal suit, the man did look as if he could charm anyone out of anything. Then, with a growl, he leant over, grabbed Sonny by the waist and flipped him upside down till Sonny's laughter bounced off the walls.

If Cat's intention had been to use Sonny as a prophylactic, it wasn't working, as Lucinda's heart clutched so hard she winced. But it was a good kind of pain. As it always was watching her two favourite guys together.

Sonny was so thirsty for a good man to look up to and Angus, though he'd never admit it, more in need of a family than anyone she'd ever met.

Then Angus looked up, searching the vast lobby till his gaze landed on hers. And caught. All hooded dark eyes and simmering charisma.

Then Angus ambled her way, slowly tipping Sonny the right way up. And Lucinda felt herself catapulted right back to the night before, standing in the bathroom, hands running over her sexy negligée, thinking about him.

"You need a tissue? To wipe up the drool," Cat said, right in her ear.

"Oh, shut up."

"Morning, Catriona," Angus said as he came to a halt before their little tableau.

"Angus," she said with a nod.

"This is a nice surprise."

"Is it?"

Angus had the good grace to grin. Then he turned to Lucinda. The impact of those deep, clever eyes of his made her come over all fluttery. "I found this pet monkey roaming the lobby. Any clue who it belongs to? Or should I give it to lost property?"

"I'm her son!" said Sonny, jumping up and down, trying to catch Angus's eye.

"Her son?" Angus asked. "Well, hello, Her Son."

Sonny laughed so hard he clutched his side. "It's *Sonny.*"

"Sonny, you say? Well, that's a far better name." Angus held out a hand. "I'm Angus Wolfe."

Sonny flopped a hand into Angus's.

"This way, remember?" said Angus, catching Sonny's eye. Then he shifted the limp hand into the proper grip, waited for Sonny to grip harder and they shook three times.

Angus smiled at Sonny. Lucinda smiled at Angus. And Cat groaned as if she was in physical pain.

"Look, Angus and I have about half an hour before we need to get to work." She could grab a pastry from the conference coffee-cart. "Would you like me to help you guys find your room first?"

"Yes!" Sonny yelled.

"Okay, then. Let's get this show on the road."

Lucinda held out her hand to Sonny. He took it, then held out his other hand to Angus.

S-word, S-word, S-word.

When she looked up at Angus he was watching her, his face inscrutable, before he took a subtle step back. "Go on, kiddo. I'll catch you later, okay?"

"Okay," said Sonny, his shoulders rounding tragically.

"Oh, good gravy," Cat muttered. "We were up with the sparrows this morning. I need a lie down. And a coffee. Let's check out our fabulous room, hey kid? Goodbye Angus."

"Catriona. Lucinda."

"I'll make it quick," Lucinda promised.

Angus nodded and Lucinda felt the burn of his eyes in the middle of her back until they turned the corner leading to the lifts.

"Do *you* think it's going to rain, Mum?" Sonny asked.

Lucinda smiled down at him. "Not a chance."

CHAPTER SEVEN

BY SIX O'CLOCK that evening, Lucinda's nerves were shot.

Not from the conference, which was fantastic, and they'd really hit their straps. By then most of the attendees knew who they were—who Angus was, at any rate—had heard that he'd volunteered to help them update their brand and someone had researched him enough to know he was doing the same for Remède.

As big fans of the venerable label, so many came forward with thoughts, advice and stories about the times Remède products had marked different periods of their lives.

Angus had insisted they stick together for the day—take the same sessions, sit in on the same conversations, two heads being better than one. Meaning she'd had to cope with his hand at her back as they'd all snuggled into a lift, the brush of his arm as he'd reached for a pen, the constant hum of his body heat simmering away beside her.

Add the fact that Sonny kept messaging from Cat's phone asking when she'd be done.

She'd originally booked dinner for two: romantic corner booth in the resort's premier restaurant. The chef was famous. He'd been on TV. Now, with the conference awards dinner later that night, and her little boy to consider, she'd changed to a table for three at six pm, at the family restaurant with the kids' play room. That phone call to change the booking had physically hurt.

But she'd long since chosen places to eat according to what Sonny might like on the menu. Turned out, that night it didn't much help. He was not in an amiable mood.

Sonny was tired of wandering around the hotel. Bored. He didn't want to answer questions about school the day before. Or how his junior AFL team might have gone without him—probably quite well, as he still preferred making shadow puppets to actually getting his hands on the ball.

By the time they finished dinner, Lucinda had bribed him with promises of hide-and-seek. Later, in her hotel suite. And only if he used his real voice, not the one that came with a pouting bottom lip.

No doubt keen on a break herself, Cat had taken off to the powder room about ten minutes before and was taking her time returning.

It was a blessed relief when Angus appeared in the restaurant.

It was short-lived, though, as a dark-haired woman came walking in beside him. Laughing, touching him on the sleeve.

Lucinda readjusted herself on her seat, tugging on the neckline of her spring-green dress, feeling more than a little over-dressed for a date night at a family restaurant with her son, but her suitcase boasted limited options.

Sonny said, "You feel sick, Mum?"

"Hmm?"

"You're frowning. Is it food poisoning?" Currently, one of his favourite books was about the human digestive system. "Or gastro?"

"What? No. I'm fine," she lied as her gaze tugged back to the bar.

To Angus. And his mystery companion. Was she someone from the conference? A random hotel guest, perhaps? She'd been with him once when a random gorgeous woman had walked up to him in the middle of the street and given him her card, saying, "Call me."

No wonder. He was a gorgeous man. All broad shoulders, strong jaw and dark curls. His hand waved elegantly as he spoke and he had one foot hooked on the small ledge beneath the bar, his body turned towards the woman, who looked at him as if her bones were slowly melting in his presence.

"Uncle Angus!" Sonny cried, leaping from the chair and bolting around the tables.

"Sonny!" Lucinda called, but it was too late.

Angus turned, smiling in genuine joy when he saw Sonny rocketing up to him. He caught the kid mid-fly and held him at eye height to ask him a question. Sonny pointed. Angus lowered the boy to the ground, his gaze searching the restaurant.

Lucinda held her breath until his eyes found hers. They were dark in the low light, his face more familiar to her than her own.

Then something in his expression changed, hardened, smouldered. Even from that distance she felt it like a sunburn across her cheeks, her bare shoulders, the backs of her knees.

He said something to his lady friend. She nodded, grabbed their drinks and headed towards the other end of the restaurant, away from the kids' room. While Angus wound his way through the tables to Lucinda.

She was standing before she even realised she'd moved.

"Sorry," she called when he was close. "I see you're busy. I tried to stop him."

He shrugged, just the one shoulder, until his eyes landed on her dress. After a beat or two he looked away, to anywhere but at her. She felt like jumping to catch his eye.

"Enjoying your dinner?" he asked.

"Yes," said Lucinda, right as Sonny said, "No."

Lucinda waggled her hand towards Sonny, who was gripping Angus around the middle, trying to drag him away. "Sonny. Sit. Leave Angus be. He has company."

"Company?" Angus's gaze narrowed and finally connected with hers, before gliding over her face, no doubt taking in her warm cheeks, her tight jaw, the flicker of a pulse at her throat. "Ah. Griselda is on the conference committee, just arrived this evening. Elena asked if I could catch her up, so I talked her through what we had so far on the way here, as the committee are meeting for drinks."

"Oh!" Probably best not to sound quite so relieved. "How did she like the sound of it?"

"As expected," he said with a smile and a quick half-wink to surreptitiously thank her for her help.

"So, they're talking sainthood?"

He chuckled, the sound low and deep and intimate. She could feel it travel over her bare shoulders before diving into her belly.

Then his gaze dropped back to her dress and a muscle ticked in his jaw. His eyes seemed to darken a few degrees. And then…

"When they say it's a small world, they really have no idea," said Cat as she appeared from nowhere, arms crossed, eyes alight with malevolence.

While Angus came over cool as a cucumber.

Chance were, she'd been projecting anyway. With a jaw like that, muscles were sure to tic. And his eyes were always smoky and dark. It was no wonder she felt constant hot flushes.

"Don't let us keep you, Angus," said Cat.

Lucinda shot her a telling glare, but Cat just poked out her tongue.

"No!" Sonny said. "He's playing hide-and-seek."

Sonny reached out and slid his hand into Angus's. Without even seeming to realise it, Angus closed his fingers around Sonny's.

"You promised," Sonny said, as if knowing a no was on its way. "You've finished dinner. It's nearly bed time. Hide-and-seek."

Officially out of the energy to deny him, Lucinda lifted her eyes to Angus.

"He's wilful," said Angus.

"He's eight."

"He's you."

If Lucinda hadn't already had feelings for the man she might have fallen head over heels for him right then and there. As it was, it took every ounce of that wilfulness of hers not to melt into a puddle at the sight of the big man holding her son's hand. Not to imagine giving in, telling Angus how she felt, him smiling at her and saying he'd been waiting to hear those words since the day they'd met.

But Angus began bouncing on the balls of his feet and stretching his arms over his head. "Haven't played in years but I was neighbourhood champ when I was the kid's age. Keen to find out if I've still got it."

And Lucinda breathed again.

"Okay, then," she said. "The rules. We team up. That way nobody gets lost for good. We'll have time limits to each 'hide'. Grown-ups keep phones on. No hiding outside. No getting in people's way. This floor only. Once you hide, there's no moving. It's not a race. Sonny and I can be on one team—"

"No," said Sonny. "I want Auntie Cat on my team."

"Oh."

If Lucinda sounded a little rebuffed, Angus looked it. She caught Sonny's eye only to find his jaw was set. "Are you sure? You can go with Angus, if you'd like?

"You always tell me what a good team you and Angus make, when we go through that list you have of what makes a good friend."

Cat laughed, though there was no humour in it. Then she reached out and took Sonny by the shoulders, moving him into her corner. "Well, I give up. Let's get this show on the road, shall we?"

"Fine," Lucinda gritted out. She looked at her watch. "So, who's it?"

Sonny stuck his hand in the air. "Us. We're counting to one hundred. Go! Mum, hurry, hurry, hurry."

"Right. Um…okay." Lucinda grabbed her bag and her phone and checked the table to make sure she'd left nothing behind. She checked her memory to make sure they'd paid.

"Come on, *Mum*," said Angus, his voice low, his hand held her way. "Hurry."

Competitive spirit lit, Lucinda took it and together they fled.

"Excuse me. Sorry. Excuse us." Lucinda was near breathless with laughter by the time they'd squeezed through the tightly packed tables of the family-friendly restaurant and burst out into the hall.

"Which way?" she asked, turning back to Angus. When she realised she was still holding his hand, she let go and made as if she needed that hand to hitch up her bag. "What do you reckon?"

"I've got an idea," he said, taking her by the hand once more.

It would have been impolite to pull away a second time.

"Where are you taking me?" she asked, her high heels tap-tap-tapping as she jogged to keep up with his long, loping strides.

"Our tree."

"*Our* tree?" she asked. Only to pull up short when they rounded a corner to find themselves facing the humungous fiddle-leaf fig behind which she'd dragged him the morning before.

Before she could demur, Angus grabbed her by the hips, spun her about and pressed her behind the big, fat leaves of the fiddle-leaf fig.

She turned at the corner to complain about the manhandling only to have him place a hand flush over her open mouth while he held a finger to his own.

Then she heard it: Sonny barking orders, his voice growing in volume as it neared. "This way!"

"Slow down, mate."

"Come on!"

When the voices neared, instinct had Lucinda grabbing Angus by the shirtfront to pull him closer, using him and his big, dark form to shield her. She pressed her head into his chest and locked her knees to stop them from jiggling away the excess of adrenaline pouring through her body.

"Run, Auntie Cat!" cried Sonny, close by now. "Angus is really fast."

"How would you even know that?" That was Cat.

"He told me. It doesn't matter if you're wearing the wrong bra, you have to run!"

When Sonny's voice faded into the distance, Lucinda began to laugh.

Angus removed his hand from her mouth and rubbed his thumb against his palm as if rubbing away a tingle. Her head still against his chest, his deep voice rumbled right through her as he said, "That was close."

Lucinda looked up. The fact that she still had a handful of shirt and was using it to pull him to her was clearly not lost on either of them—Angus's eyes were pitch-black, his jaw as hard as granite, his heart thunderous beneath her hand.

"Too close," she said, waggling her eyebrows in an attempt at levity, but the huskiness of her voice gave her away.

Slowly, she unpeeled her fingers, one by one, before leaning back into the corner, as far as she could go, until none of her was touching any of him.

His usually perfect shirt was all squished and messed up, so she gave it a tug, lining up the buttons before ironing the crushed sections with her hand. She could feel the bumps of his chest, his ribs, his abs...

Swallowing hard, she carefully lifted her hand away.

"So," he said. "What now?"

On any other man that deep, devilish tone would have made her sure it was an invitation. Lucinda looked anywhere but at Angus, lest he see it in her eyes.

"Should we move? It's pretty tight back here."

"Can't. You made the rules. No moving."

Right. She and her rules had a lot to answer for this weekend. "Then we wait."

But not like this. Not face to face.

So, she sat, sliding ungracefully down the wall, knees bent up to her chin, dress tucked discreetly behind her thighs.

After a beat, Angus turned his back to the wall and did the same.

"Lift," he said.

She let out a little whoop when he grabbed her by the ankles. Then, realising what he was trying to do, she held onto the feathery layers of her skirt as he stretched out his long legs beneath hers before gently lowering her legs on top of his. He held her ankles a moment before sliding his hands away.

Then he closed his eyes and let the back of his head hit the wall behind him.

"You okay over there?" she said, her voice sounding strangely intimate in their little tree cave.

"Big day."

"Was."

"This is the first time I've been able to catch my breath."

"Comes from being a wanted man."

Eyes still closed, Angus's smile grew. Slowly. Enticingly. "It is nice to be wanted."

"I'm sure." She'd meant it as a joke, but even she heard the caustic edge.

She regretted it the moment Angus opened his eyes and tilted his head her way. Shadows poured over his strong features, creating hollows beneath his jaw, his bottom lip. Their faces were so close, she breathed in the air that he breathed out.

"Don't tell me you're still smarting about Dr Whatsit?"

"Nope," she said, shaking her head. "Last night I got to thinking. There's a pattern. With the men in my life."

She caught his eye, waited for him to say the word "boundaries", but he simply waited for her to go on. And, shrouded by the intimacy of their strange, leafy hidey hole, she found herself saying, "I can't seem to keep them. The men in my life. They seem to find it all too easy to leave."

A tempestuous expression came over Angus's face as he imagined the men who might have slighted her. He grew bigger, like a bear about to attack. But he never came close to the brink.

The man pained himself to be civilised, never burdened others with his emotions. But his emotions were big. Deep. Raw. If he ever let them free, boy that would be something to see.

"Luc, come on."

"I mean it. Look at Joe. I put that down to the fact the man was as deep as a puddle. Cute—sure. Swaggering—you bet. But vapid. I should have seen that coming. I've dated since. Chosen better. And still I'm single. Then Dr What's—*Jameson*. He had all the hallmarks of the kind of man who'd stick. Yet here I am."

"Stuck with me instead."

Lucinda coughed out a laugh, even while her belly flip-flopped at the multi-layered truth behind those words.

"What's wrong with me?" she asked, letting

her face fall into her hands with a comic whimper, even while she didn't feel much like laughing.

"Not a single thing."

Lucinda stilled. Not only at Angus's words, but the ragged tone in which they'd been said. Little spot fires burst into life all over her body, making her face burn, and she wondered how hard it might be to live the rest of her life with her face in her hands.

Too hard, she thought, taking a deep breath before lifting her face. Lifting her eyes to his.

Angus's mouth lifted gently at one corner. Then he said, "You, Lucinda May Starling, are good and clever and brave and adventurous and charming and honest and lovely, and for a man to have had the chance to be with you and not do everything in his power to make it work makes him a schmuck."

Lucinda wished she'd been recording all that on her phone. It could keep her warm through many a future winter. "Even Dr Whatsit? He once saved several boys who got lost hiking by rappelling down a cliff to pluck them off a ledge."

"Not even Dr Whatsit. You hold yourself to a higher standard than most. That's not something to feel ashamed about. It's admirable. You do it because you know your worth. And you do it for Sonny."

"I do it for Sonny."

"He sounded just like you right now," Angus said, his hand dropping to rest on her knee.

"Hmm?" she said, having forgotten what it was they were talking about as every cell focussed on his hand.

"Sonny."

"Oh. Right. We do sound a little alike."

"I meant the fact that he's a total bossy-boots who has no qualms about telling his betters exactly what to do."

Lucinda narrowed her eyes. "If the kid knows best, why hide his light behind a bushel?"

"Why indeed?" he said, his voice low in the shadows. "For the world would be a far darker place without the Starlings in it."

Lucinda swallowed as Angus's words washed over her like a balm.

He never baulked at showing his appreciation—with thanks, with praise, with the thoughtful gifts he'd given her over the years in their nutty contest to one-up one another.

But this felt different.

This whole week had felt different. From the moment she'd told him she wasn't "his girl". As if by looking him in the eye and saying out loud to his face that the flirtation that added sparkle to their work-laden days wasn't serious—the game-playing and the gift-giving—she'd peeled back one extra layer, pressing one step closer to the heart of him.

And that step closer made her yearn so badly to go one step more. And another and the next.

Until she alone was allowed to see all the way to his broken, beating, beautiful core.

"Rest assured, Angus," she said, her voice soft, light as a cloud, "we Starlings count ourselves ever so lucky to have a Wolfe in our midst too."

His smile kicked up at one side, his gaze locked on to hers for a few long beats before it dropped slowly, achingly slowly, to her mouth.

What was he thinking when he looked at her that way? Did he have a single clue what that look did to her? Could he hear the revving of her heart? Was it even possible he was imagining stripping *her* layers back?

She heard the double entendre inside her head and her imagination ran with it. She pictured him shifting his hand, just an inch, until his little finger tucked beneath her skirt. Then a second finger. And a third.

She squirmed, shifting so that the back of her knees rubbed against the pants of his suit. Nerves now on high alert, the friction sent a shiver through her from tip to toe.

"Need me to move?" he asked.

She shook her head. The only thing that could fix how she felt in that moment was for him not to exist.

"Then what now?"

"Shall we talk about work?"

Angus shook his head. "Worked enough today."

"Okay. Then shall we talk about why you feel like you're struggling with Remède?"

A grimace came over Angus's face before his expression cleared, as if the grimace had never been. "I think you'll find that's work."

Lucinda shifted and turned, her knees brushing higher against Angus's thighs. But, now she had something concrete to focus on, she was sticking with it. "I don't believe you."

"You don't believe me."

"I've never seen you like this. Erratic. Doubting. It's as if your very foundations have been given a good shake. This isn't just about work. So what's wrong?"

Angus breathed in deeply, breathed out hard, his face a study in broody suspense. Then he said, "You know that Louis is more to me than a client."

"Of course. He's the one who convinced you to leave your marketing job and go out on your own."

"He was also the first person who looked at me and didn't see a punk kid."

"Angus," she chided. "I don't believe that."

The first time Lucinda ever set eyes on Angus had been only a few months after his infamous meeting with Monsieur Fournier. She'd been sitting in Reception on the top floor, waiting to be interviewed by the head of HR, one Fitzgerald Beckett. The business was so new, the place had smelled of fresh paint.

She'd been surrounded by smart-looking people, most of them younger than her and far more savvy, many of them tapping away on their phones as if they were already running the world. The only reason she'd been given a shot at an interview at all was because Sonny and Fitz had the same dentist. Fitz had mentioned to his dentist they were hiring the same week she'd joked that she needed a better job to pay her dental bill.

Fitz had made an entrance as Fitz was wont to do—welcoming them all and warning them the process was about to be brutal and only the toughest among them dared stay. Angus had slipped quietly into the room, leaning unobtrusively against a wall near the door.

He'd been no "punk kid" even back then. He'd seemed nerveless, riveting, hungry, his laser focus taking them in one by one, as if weeding them out before any of them had uttered a word.

"You might have been a little incorrigible back then, but only because you had ambitions. You were hungry. But you were never a 'punk kid'. I know. I was married to one."

Angus's gaze landed back on hers. "Then you were one of the only ones to see that. Not that you'd have ever had the chance to come to that conclusion without Louis Fournier's interference. If not for him, I'd have likely been a marketing cowboy at some slick, soulless firm. And I'd be going home at the end of the day feeling…empty. Whereas now…" He sighed. "This isn't a game to me. Or a puzzle to figure out. We change people's lives. I am so very grateful to be able to do what we do, Luc. Right, deep down inside."

Lucinda smiled and nodded, struggling not to burst into tears. For she felt moved. Moved that this man could admit such things to her.

To think of all the things that had to align to get her to that moment. To get them both to that moment. Joe and Sonny. Fitz and his dentist. Angus and Louis. Without every piece of that puzzle she'd not be sitting on the floor behind a humongous plant, her legs draped over Angus's while his finger traced gentle circles over her knee.

"Have you heard of a thing called *kintsukuroi*?" she asked.

Angus shook his head.

"It's a Japanese art of repairing broken bowls, plates, vases, whereby they use lacquer mixed with powdered gold so that when the pottery is fixed the repairs are obvious, like veins of gold. The breakage is seen as part of the history of an object, rather than something to hide."

Angus watched her, saying nothing.

"That's what Louis saw in you, Angus," she said, her voice husky. "Not just your potential, but the breaks along the way, and the determination to get back up, to repair."

Angus sat forward and lifted his hand from her knee to rub both hands over his face before letting out a primal growl. "A man like that should not have to step over the crumbled remains of his once great company on his way to forced retirement."

Lucinda reached out, peeled his hand from his face and held it in both of hers, battling to hold in her feelings as she sat witness to a rare tumult of emotions Angus could no longer hold in.

"And that's why," she said, "He came to you."

Angus's gaze cleared. Slowly. Until he was more like the man she was used to. But the shadow of his shaken confidence remained.

"You don't need to do that, you know," he said.

"What's that?"

"Be my cheerleader. I'm a big boy. I can take a hit."

"Yeah, you are," she said. "*Such* a big boy."

A slow smile spread across his face, even as his eyes narrowed. Even though he'd known more success than most men saw in a lifetime, that hunger still remained. It was a part of him. And when he switched it on it always made Lucinda burn.

Then his gaze began to roam. Over her hair, snagging on the swathe that never stayed put. Over her cheeks, her jaw, pausing once more on her mouth, before travelling down the twist of a spaghetti strap, over the criss-cross at her décolletage, her bare shoulders.

Lucinda's heart picked up pace and the hairs at the back of her neck prickled. She'd seen the same predatory gleam light his eyes as clients had signed contracts. Well, not exactly the same look. For there was heat here, ferocious and deep, that would send most clients running for the hills.

He shouldn't be looking at her that way.

And she shouldn't be relishing the fact that he was.

"Were you really going to introduce Dr Whatsit to Sonny after this weekend?"

The change of subject nearly gave her whiplash. "Yes. But what does that have to do with—?"

"I didn't only sign up to the conference for Remède. I couldn't stand the thought of you being here, with him."

Oh, help. "Angus…"

She didn't even realise she still had hold of his hand until he used it to pull her closer, wrapping his other hand over hers. Enveloping her in his warmth. His strength. His fingers sliding over hers, making her belly quiver. Her heart squeeze. Her lips part.

"When you told me you were hoping to introduce him to Sonny, I saw red."

Lucinda blinked.

What the…? Was he really looking at her like that, her hands in his, telling her his only concern was for her *son*?

Anger, mortification and heartache —deep, haunting heartache—rose in a maelstrom inside her. Her voice rose with it, getting louder and higher with each word as she nearly shouted, "Are you flipping kidding me?"

"Luc, you know my background. I can't say strongly enough what a game changer that will be for the kid."

Lucinda yanked her hands away from his so fast he nearly fell on top of her. Scrambling to her feet was no mean feat, with the tangling of limbs, the shortness of her dress and the fact she felt so close to tears she could taste them.

"Why am I so surprised? For such a smart guy, you really are the dumbest man I know. Seriously. Of all the conceited, idiotic, selfish—"

Then, close enough to have Lucinda flinch, Sonny's voice split the silence. "I'm gonna check the café! Mum's always saying she needs a coffee, they're totally in there!"

"Sure thing, bud," Cat's voice followed. Then, "I'll wait right here so don't go where I can't see you." Then, to empty air, "Jeez that kid can run."

"I'm calling time," Lucinda said, just above a whisper. "This game has gone on long enough."

Angus pulled himself to standing far more gracefully than she had.

When Sonny's voice called, "Auntie Cat," Lucinda grabbed the trunk of the plant and shook it for all she was worth.

"Wait a second," said Sonny, before he peered through the leaves, then, "Found them!"

Lucinda reached through the leaves and roared. Sonny jumped out of his skin before bursting into tears. And Lucinda's shoulders slumped.

Seemed she couldn't do anything right tonight.

"Lucinda..." Angus said, tracing a hand down her arm.

"Goodnight, Angus. I'll see you in the morning."

"But the awards dinner..."

"No one will miss me. You'll do just fine without me. I'll be there tomorrow, for the keynote at nine."

He stood back, an inch at most, and waved his hand for her to go first. She slid past him, brushing against his side, feeling too big a fool to get any kind of kick out of it at all.

Then she wrapped Sonny up tightly in her arms, holding him close, wiping his tears as she walked Cat and her boy back to their room without once looking back.

CHAPTER EIGHT

WHEN LUCINDA TOOK a right, Angus took a left, heading back towards Reception. Then out of the front door and down the steps, with no idea of where he was going, only that he needed space. And air. And room to breathe.

He was halfway towards the lake when it started to rain. Big, fat drops that had him soaked in half a minute. Not that it helped cool him down. His internal engine was running at maximum speed, his thoughts spinning too fast to catch, bursts of adrenaline pumping through him.

For he knew. Big time. He knew that he'd just screwed up the way he knew when a campaign hit that sweet spot where colour, tagline and key image all came into perfect sync.

But he didn't feel himself, his emotions slipping about inside him, unable to find purchase, his head too foggy to figure out why.

He'd only been trying to help. To tell Lucinda she deserved better. The best. She and Sonny. Because her kid was great and she was an amazing mother—loving, honest and fierce. She was also a brilliant administrator. And a loyal friend.

Fitz had been dead right. If anyone deserved love, Valentine hearts and eternal happiness, it was Luc.

She'd looked so sad when talking about the band of idiots she'd allowed into her life, he'd have done anything to help her lose the doe eyes. They made him ache. And growl.

And want to kiss everything better.

To place one hand against the wall right by her neck, trapping her in place. To run the other down the length of the delicate green strap barely holding her dress in place. The same dress she'd worn to the damn Christmas party a year and a half ago, when she'd appeared on the other side of the crowd looking like temptation in heels.

He pictured her face tilting up to his, those warm brown eyes melting as he showed her just how heart-stopping he thought she was...

Angus's feet squelched to a stop as he balled his hands into fists.

He had to stop. Stop thinking about her that way.

But he couldn't, not since he'd seen her standing in the restaurant wearing that dress. In an instant, tension had coiled around him like a spring. When she'd slid to the floor behind their tree, and wrapped her legs over his, his entire body had felt trapped in a vice. As though he'd implode if he couldn't touch her, feel her, be with her.

The rain really began to bucket down, the noise thunderous. He tugged his suit jacket over his head, preparing to head for a nearby copse of conifer trees, before he gave up, held his arms out and let it lash him. Cleanse him. Beat down against his skin until the strange, frenetic heat pulsing through him abated.

Finally, after a few minutes, he felt as if he could hear himself again.

When the rain made no sign of slowing, he turned and headed back towards the hotel at a walk, tipping an imaginary hat towards the doorman, who batted not an eyelid at his bedraggled form.

He'd finished the conference rebrand before dinner. He'd called in help from the graphics team back home, getting in touch with a couple who were always happy for overtime and sending them photos of his ideas. He'd worked hard, and it felt good. Like sorbet for the mind.

With that clarity it was time to get the real work done. To look back over the Remède rebrand with new-found knowledge of the industry, through the eyes of long-time consumers, lapsed consumers and competitors.

He just needed one idea. One lightbulb. One—

Angus came to a sliding halt when he saw Charlie and Fitz walking through Reception. Charlie looked just as soaked as he was, while Fitz was bone-dry and sporting enough matched luggage to be heading off on the Orient Express.

"Angus!" Fitz spotted him, holding his arms out as if for a hug.

"What the ever-loving hell are you doing here?"

Fitz did his best super-hero impression, even flicking out a pretend cape. "We're here to save you from yourself!"

Angus growled.

"Oh, put your claws away, sunshine," Fitz scoffed. "I was bored, and Charlie was sitting next to me while I was bored, so I convinced him to keep me company on the drive here. We've booked into this conference of yours too, to see what all the fuss is about."

"All that's left is the awards night and a final speech over breakfast."

"Perfection! Speaking of perfection, where's Lucinda?"

His jaw clenched before he admitted, "With Cat. And Sonny."

"Cat. And Sonny. They gate-crashed too? Well, the gang really is all here!"

"Go home, Fitz. Take Charlie with you before you lose him."

"And miss the big party?"

"Awards dinner."

"Awards dinner? Never! We're not going to miss that. Are we, Charlie?"

Charlie glanced away from the TV over the bar off to the right of the front desk. He'd somehow made them change it to the business channel.

"Come on, cuz." Fitz flung an arm around Angus's neck. "Let's show these ladies of lipstick how it's done."

The awards dinner was long over, the after party in full swing. The DJ played "Celebrate" for the seventh time and Fitz stood on stage, singing his heart out. Charlie had lost his shoes and shirt and was dancing with Ms Black Heels, Ms Henna and about a half dozen other women.

While Angus sat at a table by the doors, checking his watch or checking the hall in case Lucinda came looking for him, now Sonny would be down. If she'd cooled off.

Elena took the seat beside Angus. "Darling boy."

"Elena."

"Why so glum? This is a party. And a great one. Thanks in no small part to you and your friends."

"Not glum," said Angus. "Designated driver. It's my fault they are here so it's on me to get the boys back to their rooms in one piece."

"Mmm... And the lovely Lucinda?"

"Her son is here and her sister. She's spending some time with them."

"Her son? So, she's married, then? I thought—"

"Not married. Very much single." Angus shook

his head, wondering why he'd felt the need to be so vociferous.

"I see. Then I'd be remiss in not saying the two of you complement one another very well." With that cryptic comment, Elena looked out over the happy crowd. Her crowd. "I don't know what I did to deserve you, Angus Wolfe, but it must have been spectacular. Even without all the amazing work you have done for us this weekend, this party is going down in history. Half those here have already paid deposits for the next conference and that is unheard of. Please tell me you'll come?"

Angus went to shake his head, before realising it wasn't a hard no. He'd had a good time this weekend. Broadened his horizons. Looking up and out suited him. "I'll sign up to the mailing list. Then we'll see."

Elena reached out and put her hands over his. Her skin was paper-soft. "I know how busy you are. You're a darling for even pretending. This isn't my first rodeo. I looked you up five minutes after we met. I'm well aware how lucky we have been to have you. I know you've been talking to a lot of the other girls about Remède. How is old Louis? Is he well?"

Angus coughed out a laugh at the thought of anyone daring to call Louis "old". "Ah, he's... keeping on."

"I'm glad. What a dear man. My first job was

working one of his counters in David Jones back in the day. The lushest, loveliest product I've worked with then or since. The kind that makes every woman feel special, despite their scars, their worn-off edges."

Angus stilled as a small flame flickered to life in that place inside where ideas were born.

Elena went to take back her hand before Angus turned his over and captured it. "Special? How?"

Elena blinked. Thought. Then said, "My favourite lipstick—back when I was young and married, a zillion lifetimes ago—was a coral gloss by Remède. I'd wear it day and night, even while washing the dishes, knowing that when my husband came home from a long day at work I'd feel pretty for him. After he passed, I continued to put on that lipstick every time I washed the dishes as it reminded me of all the good. I know it sounds very old-fashioned but it's a rare product that can make queens and housewives alike feel like royalty. Then again, Louis Fournier is a rare man."

She squeezed his hand before letting go, then glanced over her shoulder to the double doors. "Why don't you head off? I'll make sure your boys get home safe."

Angus didn't need to be told twice. He kissed Elena on the cheek before taking off.

His mind was like a wildfire of ideas, burning up everything in its path.

He needed Lucinda.

He needed her with her cheap pencil, her fancy notebook and the way she understood what he meant. Her ability to put his thoughts into words the world would understand.

Something Elena had said tugged at a loose thread inside him and, the more it tugged, the more the way he'd been thinking about Remède's rebrand unravelled.

They'd gone high-concept. Crisp, aspirational glamour. Because Remède was a quality brand. Celebrity endorsements. A string of lean, tanned, beautiful social media influencers all lined up at the ready.

He'd gone for big when he should have been going *in*. Tapping into how to make every woman feel beautiful. Honest. Special.

But how could he do that if he hadn't been able even to convince Lucinda of the same?

Suddenly it was of supreme importance that he did so. That he made Lucinda understand what he'd been trying to say, badly, behind their tree. How special *she* was. And not just on occasions when she allowed herself to wear her mother's perfume.

If he could make Lucinda see it, and believe him, then maybe the rest of the world would too.

Lucinda woke with a start.

Feeling disoriented in the strange, dark room, she glanced at the clock to find it was a little after ten. After saying her goodnights to Sonny and Cat, who'd been tucked in watching *Jurassic Park*, she must have come back to her room and fallen asleep. Fully dressed.

Pulling herself to a sitting position with a groan, she ran a hand over her hair to find it knotted on one side. She gave her face a good stretch, as if shaking off a mask she'd been holding in place for months.

But couldn't find the wherewithal to get up. Get changed.

Had Angus made it to the awards night? Probably. Despite all the whammy errors of judgement, thought and deed he'd made over the past weekend, he was a big one for keeping his word.

"Gah!" she yelled, and fell back on the bed.

What would it take for her to remain angry with the guy? Right now, she could really do with a good head of steam where he was concerned. Some deep-rooted, stomach-churning loathing would be great.

What a rotten thing to think.

Angus Wolfe had never let her down. He'd given her opportunity, support, kindness and space, galvanising her need to work into creating a career she could be proud of. One she was mighty good at.

Just thinking about the man—the way he'd looked her in the eye and said he'd followed her to the hotel because he was worried about Sonny—

made her feel as if her insides were on the outside, as if her nerves were exposed. Every movement scraped. Every feeling ached.

Lucinda turned her head towards the door, thinking she'd heard a gentle knock. Nothing. Even her ears were playing tricks on her.

It sounded again.

"Cat?" she muttered, rolling off the bed and trudging over to the door.

When she whipped it open, she found Angus standing in the hall.

His eyes were preternaturally bright, his hair tightly curled as if it had recently been wet. His tie was skew-whiff.

He opened his mouth to say something before his gaze dropped to her dress. And something seemed to come over him. A kind of mental fugue that made his eyes go dark and his jaw clench.

"Angus," she snapped. "What's going on? Why aren't you at the awards dinner?"

He shook his head. "May I come in?"

Like a vampire; unable to enter without explicit invitation. And just as dangerous. Especially when she was feeling so wobbly. But if they were going to move beyond this weekend, if things had a hope of going back to normal come Monday, it had to start some time.

So, with a sweeping arm, she invited her boss into her hotel bedroom.

"What's so important it couldn't wait until tomorrow?" she asked, closing the door and padding over to the couch in the corner where she'd flung a bra. She tossed it into her open suitcase which she then shut with a toe.

When she looked back, it was to find Angus standing at the end of her bed, staring at the mussed-up blankets on which she'd been sleeping.

"Angus? What's going on?"

His gaze swept to hers, before sliding back to her dress. "I wish you hadn't worn that dress."

"This dress?" Why on earth not? "It's a gorgeous dress. And I look mighty fine in it, thank you very much."

Something in his eyes told her he agreed. And yet he looked pained.

She went to him. "Angus, are you okay? You look unwell. Have you been drinking?"

"Not a drop."

"Okay then, how about you fill me in on whatever was so important you had to come to my room at ten o'clock at night."

"Is it that late?"

"It's that late."

His mobile rang. He ignored it. He didn't even glance at it to see who it was.

"Angus, your phone."

"They can wait."

"It's okay."

He looked into her eyes, believed her, then with a nod grabbed his phone out of his pocket and answered it with, "Fitz, are you bleeding? Have you been arrested? Then don't call me. I'm otherwise engaged." With that he turned off the phone. All the way off. His eyes on her the whole time.

Feeling like she was having some kind of out of body experience, Lucinda said, "If Fitz needs you, take the call."

"He can wait," Angus said. "I'm here with you."

Lucinda curled her feet into the carpet in an effort not to sway straight into the man's arms.

Good gravy, are you so hard up for a man who'll stick, you're getting all woozy over crumbs?

But even as she thought it, she knew it wasn't that.

Despite the times she'd had to leave at the drop of a hat for Sonny. Despite the tough first months when her need to be liked had clashed with his need for personal space. Despite the fact that she stood up to him on a regular basis, refusing to back down when he was in a bolshie mood. Or when he was flat-out wrong.

Angus had stood by her through thick and thin. *He'd never left.*

In fact, he'd done the opposite. He'd followed her here. Not for some small-fry conference with a tenuous link to a favourite client. Not because he feared for Sonny's mental health.

He'd followed *her*. She knew it. Right deep down in that most feminine place inside.

The question was, why?

Slowly she uncurled her toes from their grip on the carpet.

"Angus, what's going on?"

"What's going on? Fitz thought I should know that Charlie is currently leading a conga line at the party downstairs."

"I'm sorry, *what*? Why the heck are *they* here? Did you invite them?"

His left eyebrow notched. "Fitz claims they're here because he's bored and never met a conference he didn't love."

"Why are they really here?"

"I think it's to stop me from doing anything stupid."

"Such as?"

He wouldn't say.

But she knew. Deep within a moment of true clarity, she knew.

For he was looking at her in a way that told her he'd like to tear her clothes off and have his way with her then and there. It was the look she'd been waiting for her whole life. Untempered, unmitigated and all kinds of trouble.

"Why are you really here, Angus?" Her mouth was so dry it was a miracle she found words at all.

He glanced towards the door, as if trying to remember himself. "Remède. Back at the party—the dinner —I'd had a breakthrough about Remède."

"Not here, to my room. But to the hotel." She took a step his way. His gaze dropped to her bare feet. When she took another step, he slid his phone into his pocket and waited.

"What really sent you to the hotel website? And don't tell me it was Sonny because, while I know you love my kid, you know I'd never do anything that wasn't in his best interests."

"I may have had other reasons." His eyes slowly lifted back to hers.

"Such as?"

"Fear."

Well, that was not what she'd expected him to say. "Of *what*?"

"Of Dr Jameson What's-His-Name-Smythe. Of the way he looked at you in a picture Fitz found on Facebook. That he'd marry you and have three more kids."

"Oh."

"And—" He cut himself off.

Lucinda took another two steps his way. "And?"

"Your priorities would change. And you'd… leave me."

She couldn't help it. She laughed. The thought of her *ever* leaving him was ridiculous.

Angus's face grew stony. Some instinct had her reaching out and taking his hand.

"I wasn't laughing at you, Angus. I promise. The thought of ever leaving you is laughable. You know how much I love my job. How important the Big Picture Group and the motley crew who run it are to me." She swallowed. Then said, "How important you are to me."

He took a step her way.

Not expecting it, she rocked back, but he reached out, slid an arm around her waist and hauled her against him. It took everything she had not to swoon.

She waited for him to let her go. But he didn't.

Instead, his voice came to her, rough and low, as he said, "How important?"

She lifted a hand and held her forefinger and thumb an inch apart. "This important."

"Well, that's something." His eyes, dark now, not a glint of light within to be seen, moved slowly between hers. "Did I ever tell you how much I like this dress of yours?"

"That would be a no."

"Enough that I'm especially glad Dr Whatever-the-Hell-His-Name-Was never got the chance to see you in it."

Lucinda breathed out hard as Angus did more than nudge at the line between them. "Angus," she warned, "It's okay. I know I had a moment there, behind our tree, when I was feeling a little sorry for myself, but I'm tough. I don't need you to be extra nice to me."

He reached up and ran a finger over one twisting strap, his finger sliding beneath it as he traced it over her shoulder and down the blade. "The last thing I'm feeling right now is nice."

The line blurred a whole lot more.

And then he went ahead and obliterated it when he said, "The night of the Christmas party, I was hiding at the edge of the makeshift dance floor as Dean Martin crooned about a winter wonderland, while outside in downtown Melbourne it had been a sweltering thirty-five degrees Celsius. I'd been waiting a good half an hour for you to arrive so you could save me from all the small talk when the crowd cleared and there you were. Looking like you'd stepped out of a flower patch. All glowing and fresh and bright as a star. The feeling that came over me—I'd never felt anything like it before. A heaviness in my limbs. A hollowness behind my ribs."

Lucinda knew how that felt, for she was feeling that way right now. "You say that to all the girls."

"Never," he claimed. "They'd laugh in my face."

"Are you kidding? They'd quiver in their heels."

His gaze warmed and his touch moved south, his palm sweeping down her back, sending goose bumps in its wake. "Is that what's happening to you right now, Lucinda?"

Somehow she managed to say, "I'm not wearing heels."

He laughed, the rumble travelling through him into her. And pulled her closer still.

Feeling reckless, she said, "You wore your navy suit that night, the one with the fine pinstripe. No tie. I remember thinking, *wow, Mr Casual even has his top button undone*."

He cocked his head. "It was a party, after all."

"True. But it's not the suit I remember most from that night so much as the—"

"Mistletoe," they said at the same time.

Lucinda felt herself transported back to that moment. Coming out of the store room with a roll of paper towel to mop up a spill, right as Angus had come in. They'd both ended up in the doorframe. Toe to toe. His hands at her elbows. Laughing at the near-collision.

Then someone—a disembodied voice—had headed past them in the hall and shouted, "Mistletoe!"

And they'd looked up.

When Lucinda had dared look down, dared make eye contact with Angus again, he'd already been watching her, chest rising and falling as if he needed more air. The fingers holding her by the elbows had tightened. Just enough to tell her she wasn't alone.

"So," he'd said, eyes flickering to the offending greenery above that was holding them both to ransom, before dropping back to hers, so dark and saying so much without saying a word.

"So," she'd said, her voice cracking, her heady gaze dropping to his decadent mouth.

She remembered thinking, maybe she could do this. Maybe this would be her only chance to see what he tasted like. What those lips would feel like on hers. To slide her hands into his dark curls and kiss the man till they both forgot who they were to one another.

Whether she'd lifted onto her toes, or he'd done it for her, she remembered how they'd edged closer, the air heating, shimmering, the sounds of the party dropping away.

Until the roll of paper towel she'd been holding had fallen out of her hands and rolled down the hall, breaking the spell. Reminding them both of who they were. What they were meant to be doing. And not doing.

"I'd better go clean up the mess," she'd said before all but bolting out into the hall.

It turned out many people had hooked up that night. So many, Fitz had put out a memo saying he hoped they'd all had fun and let off some steam but now it was time to get back to work.

There'd been no recriminations. No complaints. It was the kind of work place where respect, work ethic and good nature prevailed. A couple of short-term relationships had been born before fizzling out, and a couple of long-term ones were still going strong.

While Lucinda and Angus had pretended that their "moment" had never happened.

"I thought you'd forgotten," she said. "Or I'd dreamed it. There had been a fair lot of bubbly thrown around that night. Did I? Dream it?" Her voice was soft, husky.

Angus breathed in deep. "If not for that roll of paper towel, I'd have kissed you then and there."

Lucinda's chest hurt as so many feelings rushed through her body. Good and bad. Dangerous and hopeful. The ache of wasted time. The feeling that the future was concertinaing too fast for her to keep up.

"You never said," she said. "Never even a hint. The rest of the night you were impossible to catch, then come Monday it was business as usual."

"You didn't mention it either. So I deferred to you."

He'd wanted her, but he'd deferred to her. What a heady thought. To actually have a *say* in the affairs of her heart rather than feeling like flotsam tossed about on a great stormy sea.

She lifted a hand to rest against his heart only to find it thunderous, erratic. As if he was fighting some mighty, invisible, internal battle behind his cool facade.

And his hand swept the stray swathe of hair behind her ear, his palm resting against the edge of her jaw. "I didn't want things to change between us."

"I didn't want things to change between us, either," she said, noting they'd both used past tense.

For deep down inside it was what she wanted more than anything else in the world. When she blew out candles on her birthday cake, when people asked what she wanted for Christmas, in her head she always said the same thing.

She wanted to be cherished. She wanted to be seen. She wanted to be important to someone. More than anything, she wanted all that from Angus.

Their friendship, their working relationship, had survived so much already.

He'd seen her premenstrual more times that she could count. He'd forgiven her short temper after a week of little sleep when Sonny had had the croup. She'd seen him quietly distraught when he'd lost his grandfather's watch. Heartbreakingly stoic when he'd lost his mother.

But never, in all the years she'd known him, had she felt this close to the man. This close to doing something truly reckless. Like leaning her cheek against his shoulder. Tipping up onto her toes and kissing the edge of his chin. The glasses dent at the top of his nose. Bussing her lips against his.

And, as her heart sent blood around her body before drawing it back again, she knew—knew right, deep down in places primal and eternal—that she wasn't alone.

Angus's eyes were so dark they were now devoid of colour. His jaw so tight she could make out the shape of every muscle under the skin. If he tucked her hair behind her ear again, she'd jump him. Then and there.

Six and a half years of working for the guy be damned.

She'd find another job. Agencies tried to head-hunt her all the time.

But she didn't want to walk into another job. She wanted *her* job. The thought of not going to the Big Picture Group every day made her heart hurt. She'd helped build that place—created connections with amazing businesses, grown a network of favours, been instrumental in helping the clients leave better off than when they'd arrived.

But it felt as though all of that was happening in another dimension as she melted in his arms. Caught as she was in the maelstrom in his eyes. Mesmerised by his thumb caressing her cheek. By the supremely male evidence he could not hide.

The only reason they'd gone no further was because he was stronger than she was. He'd practically spelled it out for her. He would never make the first move.

For he deferred to her.

Knowing she was about to leap into unchartered territory without a map, a guide or an escape plan, Lucinda wrapped her hand around the knot of his tie and pulled him towards her.

"By something stupid," she said when his face was near level with hers, "do you think Fitz meant this?"

She lifted up onto her toes and placed a light

kiss on his cheek. His skin was warm, if unexpectedly rough. He smelled like heaven.

Then she moved to the other cheek, her touch almost reverent, the grip on his tie strong.

When she moved back to her flat feet she looked into his eyes. They burned like a long-dormant volcano rumbling back to life. As if he was barely holding himself together.

"Don't do that unless you mean it, Luc," he said again, his voice coming from somewhere deep and private, making her feel as if she were trespassing some place in which another living soul had never been. A place she ought to think very carefully about trespassing on now.

"Never," she said.

"Luc..." he said, his voice fuelled with warning, even as he pulled her up against him so she was in no doubt how tempted he was. The way he said her name—the longing, the history, the regret—tipped her over the edge.

With an outshot of breath, like a sigh she'd been holding onto for several years, Lucinda grabbed Angus harder by the tie, pulled him down to her level and kissed him.

She felt him still, as if he were holding the entire universe at bay, before he wrapped both arms tightly about her and kissed her like a man starved.

It was crazy. Wild. As if they'd both been clinging to civility for so long that now it had been stripped away, they were left stark, bare.

He tasted of heat. And cinnamon. Of tenderness and chance. And she couldn't get enough. Needing more, needing to climb inside the man's very skin, she leapt into his arms, wrapping her legs around his hips.

He laughed against her mouth.

"Luc," he said, his hands trying to get purchase on the layers of tulle as he held her to him, "are you trying to give me a heart attack?"

"Yes," she deadpanned. "Now that I finally have you where I want you, what I really want is to put you into decommission."

"Now?" he said, pulling back far enough to look deep into her eyes. "Now that you finally have me?"

What could she possibly say bar, "Angus, I've wanted this for longer than I can remember. And if you didn't know that already then you're not half as smart as you think you are."

At that he said nothing. At that he leaned into her and kissed her again. Slowly this time. Achingly slowly. Sweetly, deeply. Till her lungs collapsed and her bones dissolved and she no longer cared if she came back together in one piece again.

She was only half-aware of the jolt as his knees hit the bed. As he laid her carefully on the soft mattress. There he took his time, swiping her hair from her face, first one side then the other. She ducked her cheek into his hand. Her eyes closed as she all but purred.

When her eyes opened it was to find his roving over her hair, her cheeks, her mouth, as if he was committing every angle, every freckle, every smile-line to memory.

She lifted a hand, only to find it shaking, and pressed it against his cheek. The scrape of his stubble sent shivers through her. The reverberations, she was sure, would never quite go away.

"Finally," he said.

It was like coming home.

Only to a home she'd never known. One of ease and bliss and the sweet ache of longing.

"Don't stop," she said, eons later, breathless, no longer herself. "Don't you dare stop."

"I won't," he promised. "Not for all the world."

And he didn't. Not until later again when, replete to their very marrows, neither of them could move, talk or fathom how it had come to pass.

Or how it hadn't happened sooner.

CHAPTER NINE

Lucinda lay on her side, the sheets pulled up to her chin, the blissful, cool, soft cotton of the hotel pillow against her cheek. She couldn't keep the smile from her face even if she wanted to.

For after the bed there'd been the shower. Angus had joined her there and… *Oh, my.*

Once he'd dried her off with a big, white fluffy towel, the friction making havoc with her already overloaded senses, he'd found an old T-shirt in her suitcase—as if he knew the black, lacy ribbon thing wasn't really her, and helped her into it. Then he'd proceeded to lift her onto the bathroom bench and… *Oh, wow.*

Lucinda felt the side of the bed depress as Angus sat beside her. Barely able to keep her eyes open, she managed a, "Mmm…?"

She waited for him to kiss her on the shoulder before making a stealthy exit. She'd always imagined that would very much be Angus's MO: no sleepovers, no false expectations. But all her imaginings so far had not even come close to the reality.

Instead, he lifted the sheet, tucked himself in behind her, bare bar his black boxer shorts, slid his arm over her and pulled her close.

She was spooning. With Angus. And she decided then and there that reality was far better than fantasy.

"Angus?" she said, her voice hoarse.

"Hmm," he hummed against the back of her neck.

"Why did you come here last night? There was something you were in an all-fired rush to tell me—"

"Right. It was Remède," he said. "I'd forgotten... Distracted as I was by other things."

"Really. I hadn't noticed."

He nipped the tendon between her neck and shoulder, and when she cried out, he kissed the spot till she was purring once more.

"I'd had a breakthrough," he murmured.

"Tell me about it."

"Now?" he asked, and she could hear the smile in his voice.

She turned onto her back so she could look him in the eye. "I'd like to know."

He nuzzled his nose into her hair before lifting up onto his elbow, his head resting in his palm. That face, she thought, her heart stuttering at the sight of him. His nearness. The unusual ease of his expression, the full glory of the man behind the mask.

"Elena, of all people, said something that reminded me of something you'd said," he murmured, his finger now tracing the edge of her arm, the curve of her shoulder, the rise of her neck. "The Japanese pottery tradition where they use gold dust to highlight the repairs, not conceal them?"

"Kintsukuroi." She loved that fact. It had helped her through so many of the mistakes, the bad times, the regrets—imagining the mental scars healing with rivers of gold.

"Taking Remède back to its core construct, that's what it's all about. It isn't about covering up a woman's flaws. Hiding them behind a 'dewy glow' or fancy 'protein bond repeating serums'."

Wow, he really had been paying attention at the conference.

"So what is Remède about?"

"You."

"Me?"

"You and your mother's perfume. It's about making a woman feel special while also feeling very much herself. Whether by way of a scent that sweeps her back to sweeter times, or a lip colour that makes her feel loved, makes her remember to smile. Remède—with its tastefulness, its poignancy, its longevity—is the gold dust, the through line, that holds their best memories together."

It was a wonder that this big, quiet, self-possessed giant of a man could think that way. It took tenderness. It took heart.

Lucinda reached up and slid her hand behind his neck, pulled him down to kiss her.

Goodness knew how much later, voice croaky, he murmured against her mouth, "I take it that means you think I'm on the right track?"

"You, Angus Wolfe, are a wonder. When, hundreds of years from now, you finally depart this mortal coil that brain of yours ought to be bronzed. Or, better yet, studied. No, replicated. For the betterment of mankind."

"Only my brain?"

"Well, I can think of some other parts of you that are pretty good too."

Angus settled himself over her, his gaze boring into hers, his expression so sincere it took all her power not to burst into tears.

Then he said, "I'm not sure what I did in a past life to deserve you, Lucinda Starling, but whatever it was I'm very glad I did it."

And then he kissed her, and held her, and cherished her. And when she finally fell asleep she didn't dream. She didn't need to.

Angus shut the door to Lucinda's hotel room with a soft click. Then he closed his eyes and leaned back against the door.

The hall was thankfully quiet, the guests no

doubt all enjoying a Sunday morning lie-in, as dawn only just peeked over the hills beyond.

Watching Lucinda as he'd dressed, the pre-dawn light shining softly golden over the familiar curves of her face, the urge to wake her with a kiss, a touch, a caress—to make love to her again, or simply to see that look in her eyes when she saw him there—had been so strong he'd had to breathe his way through it.

Strong feelings were not his forte. Not when it came to his private life. They confused, they encouraged bad decisions. So, he'd left her be.

Leaning against the door he took a few moments to think. To plan out what steps to take next. For there was no map for where he'd just been. No tried and true strategy to fall back on.

Only, his mind remained blank. Empty. He felt light, washed clean. The kind of clean that meant he could smell flowers from a mile away. Could see colours he'd never seen before. Like the world after a storm.

Lucinda's *I've wanted this for longer than I can remember* ran on a loop inside his head. She'd wanted it. Wanted *him*. Said if he didn't know it already he wasn't as smart as he thought he was.

What he hadn't said was, "Right back at you."

From the very first moment he'd seen her waiting to interview at the Big Picture Group offices, he'd known she was different from anyone he'd ever met. Her light had been bewitching. He'd felt he had no choice but to invite her into his life.

But even as their friendship had deepened, even as she'd become intrinsic to his life, he'd held back that one last part of himself. Broken, burned and unwilling to burden anyone with his scars, he'd held back—especially from someone as light and lovely as Lucinda.

Until last night, seeing her walk towards him in that dress, he'd given in. Given up. Given over to her.

A shiver rolled down his back, landing with a hot thrum of energy in his gut, as he imagined a life in which he'd resisted. In which he'd never known the taste of her, the feel of her, the sounds she made when she was really happy.

Then he heard a noise somewhere down the hall.

Within a second he recognised the pair of people hunched over against the wall several doors down.

Cat—hair wild, barefoot, wearing what looked like a onesie—was down on her haunches, her hands resting on Sonny's knees as he sat leaning against the wall. Crying.

Without thinking, Angus jogged their way, calling out, "Cat?"

Cat stood, groaning as her knees cracked.

Sonny shot Angus a wet glance before wiping his eyes with a sleeve.

"Everything okay?" he asked Cat as he neared, keeping his voice down.

"He took off out of the room while I was in the bathroom," Cat said, looking chagrined. "Bad dream. Not like him. Could be something he ate. The strange room. Or the dinosaur movie marathon we watched last night."

Angus shot her a look.

Cat shrugged. "Either or."

"Mmm… Hey, bud," Angus said, crouching down but glancing past the kid, trying to look as casual as all get-out. For he'd hated being fussed over when he had been upset at that age. It had only made him feel as if he was under a spotlight. As if showing how he felt had been wrong somehow.

Sonny sniffed.

"Bit early for a hike, don't you think?"

A quick glance saw Sonny's mouth doing its best to turn down. "I wasn't hiking. I was looking for Mum."

"She's asleep, bud. But you know she'll come see you the minute she's awake."

He glanced up at Cat to find she was glaring down the hall in the direction whence he'd come. She then gave him a swift once over, no doubt taking in the crumpled suit, the time of day. Her eyes narrowed as she put the pieces together with ease.

Then she crooked a finger at him and took a

few paces away, tapping a foot on the floor till he joined her.

Her voice lowered to a hiss. "Please tell me I did not just catch you on a walk of shame…from my sister's room."

He slid his hands into his suit pockets. "Not sure that's any of your business."

Even while he could honestly have said *no*. For he felt no shame. No regret.

"What the hell were you thinking?" Cat asked, her voice rising.

"Cat," he warned. "Not the time or place." Angus looked to Sonny, whose tears had dried up and who was watching them carefully over the tops of his knees.

But Cat, who looked as if she'd had about as much sleep as Sonny, wasn't having it. "And I thought you were smarter than this. Well, I hoped, and prayed and begged whatever gods might be listening that even if she drank the Angus Wolfe Kool-Aid, you were experienced enough to make sure nothing ever happened. Why couldn't you have just left her the hell alone this weekend?"

Wasn't the first time Angus had been told point blank he wasn't good enough, but it was the first time in a long time, and the inviolable walls that usually buffeted such assaults, had been put away for the night.

Glaring at Cat, he kept his voice low. "Because she deserves better than some schmuck who cancels dates, spends half his time on the phone and says 'fine' when she tells him she might have to work instead of go away with him!"

"And you think that you can do better?"

Angus ran a hand through his hair.

"That you can be there for her, heart and soul, one hundred percent?" Catriona laughed, the sound completely lacking in humour. "Luc is your assistant. And that's it. Weird crush dynamic you've had going on for years notwithstanding. Her real life is with us. Me and the kid. The people she can count on to be there for her. Always. Unless you can promise me right here and now that you're in it for the long haul, for better or worse, putting her first, before the job, then cut your losses and move on now."

Angus's gut churned at Catriona's demands. And, while his usual method would be to rock back, to make it clear how little he cared, how little he could be impacted by the whims of other people, this time he leaned in.

"Luc means the world to me, Cat. Her happiness, Sonny's happiness, are more important to me than my own. And you know it."

Cat's eyes flared. Surprisingly in triumph.

But he was too riled to make sense of it. "She's the closest thing I have to family. I can't lose her. I won't. It would do me in. What I've achieved, what I've earned, what I've learned…without her none of it would be worthwhile."

The world was quiet for a beat, before Catriona coughed out a laugh. Then she crossed her arms and said, "Well, it's about time."

While Angus tried to figure out why Cat was looking so bloody smug, Lucinda's voice floated towards them. "What on earth's going on out here?"

Angus turned to find Lucinda padding down the hall, wrapping herself in an old, tasselled, dark-green pashmina that fell below her knees. He'd seen her wearing it more than a dozen times before when they'd shared suites at conferences. After she'd taken him in when he'd been sick. In hospital when they'd thought Sonny might have had pneumonia.

He'd thought seeing her in her magical green dress for the first time had been a watershed moment. But this…watching her walk towards him in that ancient wrap, looking flustered, soft and well-ravished—by him—made looking at her in that dress feel like a walk in the park.

He felt himself smiling from way down deep inside. If only she'd look his way, she'd know it. She'd feel it. That everything had changed. And it was all okay.

But, before Cat or Angus could fashion a sane answer to her reasonable question, Sonny was on his feet, bolting into her arms.

Lucinda held the kid tight, running her hands over his head and down his back, before leaning down and lifting his face to hers. Checking with her special mother powers to make sure he was in one piece before planting a big kiss on his hair.

Then she looked up at the grown-ups and mouthed, *"What happened?"*

Cat moved towards Lucinda and Sonny, putting a hand on the kid's shoulder. "Sonny came looking for you. I went looking for him. And found Angus. Skulking down the hall."

Lucinda's brow furrowed, her hands moving to cover Sonny's ears. But she still wouldn't look Angus's way.

"You okay, buddy?" she asked, attention back on her son. "Did you want something? Or did you just miss me? You know if you wanted me you only had to ask Auntie Cat to call and I'd have come to you in a heartbeat."

"I had a bad dream. That friend of yours, the one who was meant to come away with you, was chasing me and tried to eat me."

Lucinda's eyes were wide as she looked at Cat, who bit at a fingernail.

"He asked. When you told him you were going away for the weekend, he asked why he couldn't come too. I told him you had a friend staying with you."

"Cat. Seriously?

"I panicked!"

Lucinda held Sonny tighter. "My friend Jameson doesn't eat meat, so you're perfectly safe."

"I don't want him to be my new dad."

"Oh, honey bunny. That's just fine because he won't be. Is that what you thought was happening this weekend?"

Sonny nodded, fresh tears pouring down his sweet face. "If I have to have a new dad, why can't it be Angus?"

All three adults held their breath as Sonny's bombshell landed with what felt like a sonic boom.

"Angus?" said Lucinda, recovering quickest. "Sweetie, Angus can't be your dad."

"But why not?" Sonny begged, his bottom lip quivering as he looked to Angus with eyes filled with wishes and tears.

Angus had long since had a zillion reasons lined up as to why he would never be a father, for not a single "father" who'd waltzed in and out of his life had made the job seem appealing, but in that moment he couldn't think of one. Not when the urge came over him simply to step in, wrap them both up tightly and vow to protect them from anyone who made them sad. Anyone who dared make either one of them cry.

But it was not Angus's place to have a say. Angus who was now pulling his leg hairs through the pockets of his suit pants to keep from doing something or saying something. It was Lucinda's job. Only Lucinda's. If he'd learnt anything from being in Sonny's shoes, it was that.

"Why?" Lucinda repeated, her face collapsing as she saw the earnest plea in Sonny's expression. "Because he's Angus. He, um… He doesn't cook, for one thing, and a dad needs to be able to cook."

"*You* don't cook."

"I do! Just not very well. I'd bet the house that Angus can't boil an egg. And he…ah…he certainly doesn't clean. And you know how much cleaning I have to do. A dad would have to help me with that. What else? Angus never buys his own groceries. Or answers his own phone. He's too busy to coach your footy team. Or read to you every night. Angus can't be your dad, hon, because he's practically a big kid himself."

Angus knew Lucinda was trying to soften things for Sonny, to bring him down from the ledge, yet with every reason she gave it felt like death by a thousand cuts. Everything she said was true. To a point. But the fact that the litany of reasons why he could never take on that role in their lives had been on the tip of her tongue spoke volumes.

Sonny sniffed. "But you tell me all the time the most important ingredient in making a family is love. And you love Angus. And I love him. And Cat loves him."

Cat snorted.

"We do, hon," Lucinda said, flicking her sister a look. But not Angus. If only she'd look at him. Just for a beat. Her smile could include him, temper her words. Maybe this was salvageable. But no. Her attention went right back to her son. "Angus is one of our very best friends. But it takes more than tickles and bad jokes and a mad footy boot to be a dad. It takes patience and compatibility and commitment. He would have to want it more than anything else in the world. And you know how much Angus loves his job and his nice clean apartment and his me-time. Besides, Uncle Angus has to learn how to take care of himself before he can be entrusted to take care of anyone else."

Even Cat flinched at that last twist of the knife.

While Lucinda smiled down at Sonny as if delighted at having navigated a potential disaster.

"Come on, kid," said Cat, holding out a hand to Sonny before leading him down the hall to their room. "Let's order something gross and sugary from room service. Mum will be along in a minute."

And soon it was just the two of them. Angus and Lucinda. And finally, she looked his way. Her eyes heavy. Her mouth soft. The weight of the night before once more wrapped itself around him like a siren song.

"I'm so sorry about all that," she said, twisting and untwisting a corner of her wrap.

"You have nothing to apologise for," he said, his voice sounding as if it was coming from someone else.

"Yeah, I do. I ought to have seen that coming. And I never wanted you to feel uncomfortable, or beholden, or put in a position where—"

"I didn't. I don't. He's a great kid, and I… I love him right on back." The moment the words left his mouth, Angus felt light-headed, as if he'd been blowing up a balloon for too long. But he was still grounded enough to see Lucinda startle.

"I know," she said. "I know you do."

But when she smiled he saw only flashes of the Lucinda from the night before. Heat and desire and such sweetness it made his skin hurt. And the deeper feelings they'd both secretly held onto for years.

But there was a resoluteness there now as well. Her mind was with her son now, or it very much wanted to be.

Her son. Her number one priority. From day one she'd made that clear. And it was one of the reasons he was so taken with her.

Long-ago promises he'd made to himself and to his own mother kicked in, and instead of hauling Lucinda into his arms and attempting to unravel all that he was feeling, sensing and experiencing that morning he did what he'd always done.

He deferred to her.

He slid his hands into his pockets and causally leaned against the hallway wall. "You're okay for a lift home?" he said.

He hated himself when she flinched. When she

finally seemed to pick up on the coolness in his voice.

"I drove, remember?" she said. "Cast aside last minute, as I was, by my date."

He nodded. "Head off early, if you'd like. I can finish up here. Sonny looks like he needs you."

"Right. Thanks. No reason to stick around any longer now, I guess."

No, he thought, with chagrin, *none at all. Not the fact you admitted that you've wanted me for a long time. Not the fact that we just spent all night in one another's arms. And not the fact that it's taking every single ion of power I have not to haul you into my arms and beg you to stay.*

But no one would be any the wiser. For he was an expert at concealment. At hiding such strong feelings. It was safer that way. Easier for all.

"I'll leave you to it, then, shall I?"

She swallowed, her eyes bright, conflicted and beautiful.

They could get past this. They were friends. They were practical. They were too enmeshed in one another's lives for it to be any other way.

"See you tomorrow?" she said.

"Tomorrow," he returned, then he pushed away from the wall and strolled away.

CHAPTER TEN

ANGUS COULDN'T GET his head straight on this, the day he needed to more than ever before.

He'd been back at work for a couple of days, every second spent implementing the complete about turn on the Remède rebranding.

Louis Fournier and his team were due at the Big Picture Group offices in less than two hours. And he had to convince them to throw out the ideas they'd okayed a week before.

He knew he was right, his instincts on song. The *kintsukuroi* method was a perfect fit for the Remède ethos, as well as following the current trend in beauty being all about wellness and authenticity. It had real potential to turn the company around.

It was just every other single aspect of his life that felt jagged, ill-fitting and wrong.

And if he couldn't focus, couldn't demonstrate absolute certainty, couldn't be the man in whom Louis had seen all that potential and convince them that they were right to put their faith in him, to trust him, it could yet all go up in smoke.

The phone rang on the other side of the smoky glass and his gaze was drawn that way as it had been a hundred times a day since he and Lucinda had come back to work a few days before.

Who was he kidding? His gaze had always been drawn that way. He'd convinced himself it was because Lucinda was his good-luck charm, his guard at the gate, his anchor.

When the truth was, she *was* all that and so much more.

Lucinda was also strong, soulful, warm and kind. She was trusting, unsure, loyal and lovely. She was his friend, his confidant, his favourite person on earth.

And when she'd taken him by the tie, pulled him in and kissed him every fibre of his being had cried out in relief.

This, a voice had whispered inside his head. *This is everything you have worked towards. Everything you've ever wanted. Being the kind of man Lucinda Starling could want.*

Then Lucinda had taken such pains to explain to Sonny why Angus was her friend, her confidant and one of her favourite people on earth and why he could never, ever be more.

He'd had no armour to protect himself. He'd felt the slice of every word—just as he had as a kid, told constantly by his mother's line-up of deadbeat boyfriends that he didn't matter, that no one would care if he'd never been born. That he wasn't enough.

And now she was out there, smelling of that damn Someday perfume that made his head spin. Wearing that skirt that fit so right it looked as if it had been sewn on. Her hair was tucked over one shoulder, sleek and dark and tempting. He remembered how it had felt sliding through his fingers...

Damn it.

Angus sat forward, sinking his face into his palms, then he gouged his finger through his hair, tugging hard enough to hurt.

This was why he'd resisted all these years. This ache. Deep. Physical. Knowing her, being with her, opened up in him wants and desires he'd never let himself entertain. Hopes of a future, a partnership, a family—managing to carve out a life his own parents had never been able to.

He'd followed her to the damn resort for fear of losing her and somehow it felt as though it was happening anyway. Leaving him brimming with a kind of psychic pain he couldn't control. Or name. And sure as hell didn't want.

Well, enough was enough.

"Lucinda!" he shouted, forcing himself out of his chair.

He saw her shoulders square. She took a moment before slowly pressing her chair back and making her way through the smoky glass door between her world and his.

Without saying a word, she stood there with her fancy notebook and her cheap pencil, chin tilted, knees locked. She appeared cool. Unmoved.

And utterly lovely.

But, the closer he looked, he could see how her ankle jiggled. How she nibbled at the inside of her lip. The smudges under her eyes.

If he was disoriented in this new landscape, then so was she.

The only way forward, as he could see it, was the one that had got him where he was today. Disengagement.

His strength was in his ability to compartmentalise. It had helped him through the very worst parts of his childhood. And it had helped him deal with the temptation of having this woman sitting just outside his office for the past six-and-a-half years.

It had to help now.

"Angus?" she said. "Did you actually want me, or were you shouting my name for the fun of it?"

"I wanted you," he said.

Some strong emotion fluttered across her deep, brown eyes.

But she pulled herself together, moved to the pink velvet chair he'd bought her as a gift, sat on the edge, crossed one ankle over the other and held her pencil over her notebook. "Shoot."

Angus moved more slowly to the front of his desk, his feet knowing what his mind refused to admit—that more than anything, more than having things back to the way they were, he wanted to be near her. Needed to be. And he always had.

She looked up, her brown eyes wary. And beautiful. And sad.

It was the sadness that finally got him—as if she too was battling with the knowledge that a seismic shift had happened this past weekend. It shook him. Made him buck up and damn well pull himself together.

"Remède," he said, his voice so gruff he barely recognised it himself.

She lifted her chin. "The boardroom is set. Food is on its way. Champagne is chilling. The IT team are working on the last layout changes to the website. It'll be close but they'll get it done in time. They have tickets to Comicon riding on it."

"Great."

"How about you?" she asked. "Are you ready?"

And despite the fact they'd tiptoed around one another for days, far more clumsily than after the Christmas party, the care in her voice—honest, real and clear as day—shone through.

And Angus's heart dropped into his chest as if it had fallen into a well.

"I am," he said. "You?"

She blinked. "Me? Ready to flirt and charm and flitter about? Always."

"You do more than that, Luc."

Her face crumpled at his use of her nickname. "I know," she said, voice soft. "I was kidding."

"No. You weren't."

She swallowed. A conversation like this would have felt different a week before. Full of banter, sass and good-natured ribbing that would have left them both feeling as if they were floating an inch off the ground.

Now every word had weight. Now every word mattered. Stacking up against him, building a wall so large soon neither would be able to see past it.

Before he could kick the damn thing down, Lucinda was already on her feet, heading back towards her door.

If this was the way things were going to be from now on it would be untenable.

"Luc," he said, stopping to clear his throat. "Lucinda."

She stopped, turned. "Mmm?"

I want you. I adore you. I need you. I can't lose you. You are a part of me. The best part of me. You took a shell of a human being and made him whole.

Some deep, undamaged part of himself, some sliver of light and good, took him by the throat and gave it a squeeze. Made him check himself. To be truly sure. For Cat was right—there was no lower scum on earth than a man who would mess with a single mother unless he was in it for the long haul.

"You know I couldn't do any of this without you," he said.

Lucinda looked at him, right at him, her warm brown eyes like a laser.

"I know you say that, Angus, and some part of you might even believe it," she said, with a flicker of a humourless smile. "But the truth is, you always could."

Lucinda stood looking down at her desk, at the tub of sharpened pencils, the pile of pretty notebooks.

The joy that it had given her—the sense of ownership, of purpose, of self-respect—felt like something that had happened in a movie she'd once watched.

It was ruined. She'd ruined it. Making love with Angus, telling him she'd wanted him for the longest time…

He looked so pained every time they made eye contact now, as if he was choking on something. It had to be regret.

Not that *she* knew what to say. Whether to apologise or make light. To tell him she was struggling too. To agree to pretend it had never happened. They'd made it past the Christmas party near-kiss and managed to work together just fine. If anything, the sexual tension had upped their game.

So long as they'd stayed either side of the immovable, inviolable line they'd kept between them, she'd been allowed to exist in a kind of perfect balance between working with Angus in a job that fulfilled her more than she ever would have thought possible and basking in the presence of the smart, sharp, talented, determined man she adored.

Only it hadn't been balanced. It had been emotional purgatory.

And now the line was gone, obliterated, she was totally untethered, her feelings all over the place.

Maybe she should just look Angus in the eye and tell him she'd thought herself a little bit in love with him before and now she was drowning in it.

Every time she looked at him, she saw not her boss, or the man she'd had a secret crush on for years, but his bare chest as he'd hovered over her, the dark heat in his eyes as they'd made love. She felt again the tenderness in his touch, the way he'd relaxed in a way she'd never seen in him when he'd cradled her as she'd fallen asleep. As though protecting her was his happy place. As though something that had kept him chained all these years had finally broken free.

Then she'd woken up. Alone. In every possible way that could mean.

Reaching out and finding him gone, her heart had stuttered in her chest. She'd told herself it was okay. That he hadn't said goodbye before leaving her room because it wasn't goodbye. That they'd be together again at breakfast. And beyond.

Only to slowly begin to panic about what came next. Would they head into work on Monday holding hands, gazing into one another's eyes over the boardroom table, co-signing Fitz's form that people had to sign when they started seeing one another at work?

Then, with all that piling up in her head, when she'd found Sonny in the hall and been forced to answer why Angus couldn't be her boy's dad…

He'd been so good to Sonny, and for Sonny. If Angus was keen and ready and wanted it too, he'd be a wonderful father. Kind and fun with solid boundaries and strong arms.

But he'd made it so clear over the years that fatherhood was not for him. That he believed no man should come close to that job without a medical, a police check, a licence and a wide-open heart.

So she'd brought out every lame thing Cat had accused him of in order to distract Sonny from the idea. She'd gone into pure self-defence mode.

But then, so had he.

Leaning against the wall in the hall, the very picture of causal indifference, offering her an early mark. Pushing her away. The wall that kept him separate from the world all but rebuilding before her very eyes.

She'd had Angus but she couldn't *have* him.

He was too flawed, thorny, demanding and damaged. She'd spent too long making sure other people were happy, as if doing so was the only way to make them stay.

But what if staying wasn't always the right answer? What if sticking, depending on her roots, believing in for ever, was the problem rather than the solution?

Before she was fully aware of where she was going, Lucinda walked down the hall, feeling as though she was on her way to her own execution. Yet at the lift she didn't even hesitate before pressing the button to head up to the HR floor.

Fitz's office was a mirror of Angus's only it was plush and brash and noisy and messy, where Angus's was spare and neat and still.

Lucinda gave Velma a wave. Velma nodded, letting her know she could head right on in.

Fitz glanced up, serious face on, as Lucinda entered his office. It softened when he saw it was her.

Taking off a pair of red tip-tilted glasses he'd clearly borrowed from Velma, he leant back in his chair. "You coming in or are you just going to stand there all day?"

"Stand here?"

"Sit," he insisted clicking his fingers. "Now."

Her feet dragged as she took the last few leaden

steps towards the chair by Fitz's desk. When she sat, her breath left in a sad little whoosh.

"I was wondering when you might show up."

She blinked at him.

"You, Lucinda Starling, are a mighty oak, putting up with that fool of a boss of yours for as long as you have. And coming back to work, being your usual amazing self after what happened over the weekend…"

She leant forward, her head dropping to her knees. "You know? How do you know?"

"Sweetheart. It's my job to know. Besides, I was there. I was stumbling back to my room the morning after the party—boy can those women dance—right as Angus was checking out. Looking like a big, broken bear with a storm cloud over his head."

Lucinda lifted her head. The thought of Angus, broken, made her heart hurt. The thought he might feel that way because of her? How had she let things get so out of hand?

Because you love him, you goose!

Well, she thought miserably, there was that.

Fitz checked his nails as he went on. "I bugged him till he told me why. No details, unfortunately. Just the bare bones. But I'd figured it out. There's only one person in the whole world who can bring out that kind of emotion in our boy."

He pointed a finger Lucinda's way.

"I can't," she said, barely able to string more

than two words together. "I can't do it any more, Fitz."

Fitz stopped fussing and looked at her. Then he hopped out from behind his grand desk, came over to her, lifted her out of the chair and pulled her into a hug.

"Of course you can. You're in love with the guy. Anyone with two eyes and a brain like a steel trap could see it."

Something in the back of her head, some last remaining thread of a survival instinct, told her to baulk, to scoff, to poo-poo Fitz's suggestion. But, sounding and feeling like a kicked puppy, she murmured, "Does he know?"

"My cousin?" Fitz snorted. "Smartest guy I know, bar Charlie, who doesn't count because he's not human. But when it comes to the workings of the heart, Angus is as clueless as they come."

"It's not his fault."

Fitz laughed softly. "Only a woman in love would look at Angus Wolfe and believe the reason he hasn't settled down with a good woman— or a bad woman, for that matter—isn't entirely his fault."

With a groan, her face fell against Fitz's chest, her neck no longer able to hold up her head. She felt as if she had the flu. The love flu. The *unrequited love* flu. The Angus Wolfe strain.

"How did you two finally crack?" Fitz asked, his voice lacking its usual bolshie tone.

She knew what he meant. And she knew the answer. "He looked at me."

"Hmm," said Fitz in mock seriousness. "He has a way of doing that. What the hell does that even mean?"

She laughed, despite herself. The Angus Wolfe love flu was making her light-headed. "You know—the *look*. The kind that makes you see exactly what's going on in the other person's head and it's enough to make your kneecaps melt clean away."

"Ah, that look."

Lucinda lifted her head.

"He'd given me the look once before, you know? At that crazy work Christmas party a couple of years back. All that bubbly and dancing and mistletoe, someone was always going to do the walk of shame that night."

"Right," Fitz agreed, shifting from foot to foot, making Lucinda wonder for a moment who *he'd* walked from that night.

"The look that night—it was hot. And lingering. And brimming with the promise of sweaty limbs and torn clothing and regret." Lucinda laughed, though it felt more like a whimper, and stepped out of Fitz's hug. "And why am I telling you any of this?"

"Because you need to let it out or you'll implode. And you know there's not a single thing you can say that will change how deeply I adore you."

She nodded. He was right. She looked down at her hands. "Nothing happened between us at that party. Nothing anyone else would think was inappropriate. HR, for instance."

Fitz breathed out. Hard. "But last weekend? Sweaty limbs, torn clothing…"

"And regret."

"Luc. Honey."

"It's okay. I'm a grown-up. I knew what I was doing. And I knew no good would come of it. At the very least I'll be able to live off it for a long, long time. Perhaps even until I'm old and grey, and Cat and I are still living together in my sweet little cottage, watching Netflix and bickering."

"Sounds like a plan." Fitz reached out and put a hand on her shoulder as if he could tell she might well collapse to the floor otherwise. "So, I'm assuming you didn't come up here because you knew I have no filter and would happily listen to any details you might impart as to your dirty weekend with my stupid cousin?"

"I can't believe I'm about to say this out loud, but I need you to tell me what to do so that I can officially resign."

Fitz didn't even stiffen, as if he'd seen this coming a long time before she had.

She'd be fine financially. Her little cottage was all hers, Sonny was in a great public school and she'd get another job with a single phone call. She knew the kind of money she'd get offered from other firms.

But she'd miss this. She'd miss *him*. The thought of turning up to work for anyone but Angus made her feel physically ill.

She'd seen the man nearly every day for the past six-and-a-half years and had loved him for almost as long.

"He loves you too," said Fitz, as if he'd read her mind. He went to his desk to sort out the required paperwork. "In his own way."

"I know," Lucinda said. "But if he taught me anything these past few years it's that I'm worth more than that. Angus's way of loving just isn't enough."

And there it was. The truth she'd steadfastly avoided admitting to herself. For it meant no longer having a crush on her boss to keep her safe from truly opening herself up to the possibility of the kind of love her parents had. The kind of love she'd feared she'd never find if she ever really went looking.

She knew Angus would be side-swiped. For all that he'd shut her out over the past few days, he wasn't lying when he said he didn't want to lose her.

"Don't tell him," she said. "Remède will be here in an hour. And there's nothing more important to him than that."

"Nothing?" Fitz said, looking at her over the red sparkly glasses.

Then, muttering to himself about how he should have been a shrink or a psychic, Fitz printed out the necessary forms.

Lucinda stood outside her little cottage looking over the duck-egg-blue front door, the cream eaves, the gardenia bushes that had bloomed for the first time ever last spring.

Trying to reconcile herself with the fact that she was home. At two in the afternoon. Not because she'd had to pick up Sonny sick from school but because she no longer worked for Angus Wolfe.

She'd somehow made it back to her office after she'd finished hashing out her exit with Fitz. Then waited in the ladies' bathroom until the last possible moment before slipping into the back of the room for the Remède pitch.

Angus had sat at the top of the room beside Louis Fournier, foot resting casually on the other knee, finger playing lightly over the seam of his mouth. A picture of cool ease, when she knew how important it was to him that this meeting went well.

Angus hadn't looked her way, but he'd known she was there. She'd seen it in the way he shifted on his seat, the way his other hand clenched, as it had been doing all week.

She'd spent the meeting feeling as if she was on the other side of a mirror as his band of dashing, clever, talented marketing and graphics geniuses had played their symphony of social media spots and print ads and the complete overhaul of the website relaunch of the Remède brand.

It had been all she could do not to blub when Angus had explained the theory of *kintsuku-roi*, not even pausing before crediting it to her. How Remède was a celebration of women—of mothers, daughters, sisters, friends—at every stage of life.

She hadn't been even the slightest bit surprised when Louis had pulled Angus into a bear hug, muttering praise and thanks into his ear while he shed a tear.

The Big Picture Group team had been on a total high after all the last-minute work they'd put in, yet the moment the meeting was done Lucinda had slipped out through the door—only to hear Angus's footsteps meet hers as he'd jogged to catch up.

"Hey," he'd said, his voice a little rough. "Hey, slow down. What's the big rush?"

"Stuff to do."

"So that was wild in there."

"It was amazing. You were amazing." Her voice had caught as she'd said, "I'm so proud of you, Angus. Not many would have gone to the lengths you went to in order to get that so right."

Lucinda had picked up her pace. Or she'd tried to, until Angus's hand had clamped around her arm.

She'd stopped and turned to find herself toe to toe with her boss. Her brilliant, impossible boss. Close enough to catch the scent of his soap, the fresh cotton of his shirt, to see the thread unspooling from a button hole. She made a mental note to remind him not to buy that brand again, before remembering that wouldn't be her job any more.

"Lucinda," Angus had murmured, his voice scraping her insides in a way that had her curling her toes into her shoes so as not to shiver.

Pulling together every ounce of self-protection she'd had at her disposal, she'd dragged in a short, sharp breath and looked up into his eyes. Warm, hazel and far too astute for comfort.

"What's going on?" he'd asked.

She remembered looking down the hall to see who might be watching. Who might note them standing closer than two work mates ought to stand. But everyone was busy chatting, laughing and moving in and out of one another's offices, the hive all a flutter after the successful meeting.

Then she'd moved to Angus's office, pushed open the door and crooked a finger his way.

A smile had hooked at the corner of his mouth. A smile so cocky, familiar, so beloved, she'd felt it as an ache deep down inside. Then he'd sauntered after her.

Expecting…something better than what he was about to receive.

But Lucinda had known, if she hadn't done it then and there she might not have done it at all.

So she'd pulled a single sheet of white paper out of her notebook and held it out to Angus—

The front door of the cottage swung open and Lucinda near leapt out of her skin.

Catriona poked her head around the door, a piece of toast poking out of her mouth. Then she glanced at her watch. "I thought I heard a funny noise out here. What are you doing home so early?"

Lucinda found her feet and walked up onto the porch. Swinging past her sister, she said, "I quit."

"You *what*?" Cat cried, then stopped to choke on a crumb she'd inhaled.

Lucinda had time to unwrap her scarf and hang it on the hall stand before Cat came hustling inside, her socks shuffling on the wooden floor. "Please tell me you're kidding."

"I thought you'd be happy."

"Why the hell would you think that?"

"Because it means I won't be working with Angus any more."

Cat flapped her hands, her eyes near bugging out of her head. "Why would that make me happy?"

Lucinda turned to face her sister. "You don't like him. You've never liked him."

"First, that's not true!" Cat cried out. "And second, when did you suddenly care about that?"

"So, you *like* Angus?"

"He's a freaking gem! No other boss would pay you as much as he does. Or give you the time off you need."

Lucinda stood wearing one high heel as she'd already kicked off the other shoeoff. And she breathed deep. "Can you just…not. Today. Or ever again. I'm not in the mood for games."

"Luc, I'm not playing. I promise. I'm too shocked. Seriously. I feel as if there's been a tear in the space-time continuum. You can't quit Angus."

"I didn't quit Angus. I quit my job."

"Same thing."

Lucinda glanced at her sister to find her standing in the middle of the hall looking…lost. "Come on, Cat."

"I mean it. I'm worried right now. I'm the quitter. I've quit a million jobs, a million men, but you? You're the 'for ever' girl. It's probably why I've never been able to hate Angus, even though he's so annoyingly good-looking and confident and brilliant. Because from day one he knew you were the for ever girl too. Just like he's a for ever guy."

Lucinda closed her eyes against the memory of that final moment. He'd refused to take the piece of paper, so she'd opened it up and read it out loud.

"Stop," he'd said, his voice rough when she was about half way through.

She'd looked up, expecting refusal, an argument, maybe even some kind of revelation. But she'd never seen him look so empty, so cold.

"I don't need notice," he'd said.

"What do you mean?"

"Go." He'd cocked his head towards the office door. "If you don't want to work here any more, just go."

She'd recoiled physically, taking a step back. "You don't mean that."

"When have you ever heard me say something I don't mean?"

And so, without another word to the man she'd worked alongside for the past several years, she'd walked out of his office on boneless legs, cleared out her desk, packed her meagre possessions into her big handbag and left. Nobody had noticed. Everyone had been too high, celebrating the Remède success.

Lucinda tuned to her sister. "If he's a for ever guy, Cat, then why did he let me go?"

Cat took her by the hand, wrapping it up tightly between hers. "He's hurt."

"*He's* hurt? I'm the one who's had to deal with his moods all week. With the fact he could barely even look at me. As if I'd done something unforgivable. We were both there that night." Oh, wondrous night.

Cat snorted. "I'd put money on him looking at you. The man can barely stop looking at you. If you guys weren't both equally mad about one another, it would be creepy how much the man looks at you."

Lucinda's lungs started to tighten with the effort of trying to hold in the words that were so desperate to come out. "What do you mean, he looks at me?"

"Are you kidding? The man could be the poster boy for longing."

Lucinda slowly kicked off her other shoe and leaned against the hallway wall.

"And don't get me started on how he looks at you when you're with Sonny. It's heart-breaking. Like watching a little homeless kid standing outside a candy shop window."

"Why would he do that? He's not a family kind of guy. You know his background. You know how hard he had it as a kid. His dad leaving, his mum and her string of appalling boyfriends. Family to him is a four-letter word."

Cat crossed her arms, no longer looking lost so much as mad. "Are you telling me, seriously, that you don't consider Angus family? That you'd let anyone else come into this house, sick, when your boy is here?"

"Well, no."

"Is there anyone else you'd text before watching a new episode of *Warlock Academy*?"

"Never."

"Has he seen you cry? Snort-laugh? Trip over? Swear? Has he seen you without make-up? In that God-awful green pashmina wrap thing? Has he ever played a board game with you, seen what a bad loser you are and come back for more?"

Lucinda nodded.

"And yet, with all that evidence to the contrary, he looks at you as if he's stumbled on a fairy princess in a secret, magical glen."

Lucinda leant harder against the wall and slowly slid down to the floor, letting her bare legs kick out in front of her.

Cat, her annoying, clever, difficult, stubborn, wonderful sister, slid down next to her.

"That's not normal, is it?"

"For a mere boss and employee? Ah, no. Have you ever seen any of my editors over here? Have they ever followed me away on a holiday weekend?"

"Why didn't you ever point this stuff out to me before?" Lucinda asked.

"I did. In my way. I say the grass is blue, you agree, saying it can look bluish in the right light. I say night is day, and you agree it can seem that way when the moon is bright. But, when I even think about saying something against Angus, you bite my head off and proceed to wax lyrical about how amazing the man is. I picked on him because I hoped you'd one day notice that the only time you stop trying to please everyone and simply tell your truth is when you're defending him." Cat nudged her with her shoulder. "I could stick a mirror up to your face, but what can I do if you refuse to open your eyes?"

Lucinda thought about it. Really thought.

Watching him struggle over the Remède account had changed things for her. The man had created a shiny, incisive, clean, fresh rebrand over which any company would salivate. It would have won awards, no doubt. But he'd known it wasn't right, had known it had missed the heart of the business. The soul. So he'd gone deeper, pushed himself outside his comfort zone, talked to people on the ground level, immersed himself in the product—learned the difference between lipstick and lip-gloss, for goodness' sake—to make it right.

Throughout, there had been no hiding the fact that beneath the Angus Wolfe mask was a man with a heart of gold. Not gold powder, or veins of gold, but the pure, twenty-four-carat good stuff.

Yet, so afraid of being left was she, she'd made a habit of pushing, of making it impossible for most men to bother. All men, bar Angus. He'd refused to budge. Refused to be disappointed. Refused to let her down.

And, the more she'd grown to care about the man, the more terrified she'd become of losing him. Losing him as she'd lost so many of those she'd cared about most.

When she'd felt things turning, changing, when a chance to find out what might actually be possible between them had presented itself, she'd pushed him away. Telling herself she was protecting her son when really she'd just been using his love as a shield.

"I was eighteen when I met Joe, can you believe that?" Lucinda heard herself say. "Mum and Dad had died not that long before. You were living overseas and I was at home. Alone. When Joe came on the scene, I saw him as my out. A chance to not be the good girl, to run away, to quit being me for a while. I think I was so happy when I found out I was pregnant, not because it was Joe's baby, but because it was mine. Because there'd be someone to love who would love me best."

Lucinda didn't realise she was crying until she tasted a tear on her bottom lip.

Thinking of Sonny, she wanted to crawl into his bed and gather up his toy fish, donkey and the headless rabbit. How long had it been since *he'd* even cuddled those toys? He was more into more grown up toys now. Transformers. Superheroes of his own.

She could learn from that. From Sonny. The way he loved. And forgave. Forgave Cat when her patience ran thin. Forgave Lucinda when she ran late from work. Forgave Angus when he forgot the name of a Pokémon.

Lucinda dropped her head into her hands.

The fact that Angus Wolfe knew the name of even one Pokémon should have been a sign. One of those huge, flashing road signs you can practically see from space.

He loved her. Angus *loved* her. And he'd done so for a very long time.

"But I've quit," she said, tears now flowing freely as it fully hit her what she'd done.

"So, un-quit."

"I'm not sure I can. I'm not sure I should. I'm not sure he'd take me back. You're right. I hurt him. The one person he knew he could count on walked out, right when he was enjoying the biggest high of his career. I should have talked to him. Told him how I feel. Instead I treated him as if his opinion about us didn't matter. I let him down so very badly."

"Fitz is right. You two doofuses deserve each other, you really do."

"Fitz?" Lucinda said, the weirdness of that statement somehow making its way through the fog. "When have you been talking to Fitz?"

Cat looked down at her toes, wriggling them back and forth. "We…may have hooked up at that Christmas party of yours a year or so ago. And a handful of times since."

Lucinda gawped, then realised she didn't have the energy to care.

"Come here, you," Cat said, holding out an arm.

And Lucinda leaned over and rested in her sister's embrace.

Tomorrow she'd deal with tomorrow.

CHAPTER ELEVEN

"Whoa, hold up, there, cowboy."

Angus pulled up outside Fitz's office when Velma positioned herself bodily between him and the glass door.

If she'd been anyone else he'd have feinted left and cut round her, but rumour had it Velma had wrestled in her youth, and even in the heightened state he was in his self-protective instinct kicked in just in time.

"I need to speak to him," Angus gritted out. "Now."

"Honey, what you need to do is take a breath. Calm down. And remember that boy in there is family. He loves you. And he only has your best interests at heart."

All Angus knew right then was that he was wound so tight he could feel his blood stuttering through his veins. "Fine," he managed. "I'll give him a head start."

Velma's cheek twitched before she knocked on the door and called out, "He's here."

"I can see that," Fitz's voice called back. "Send him in."

Velma moved aside and slowly opened the door for Angus, who burst through it like water through a crack in a dam.

Fitz sat behind his desk, feet up on the table, ridiculous red glasses on the end of his nose. "Sit," he said.

"I'm not going to bloody well sit."

"Sit. Or I'll get Velma to escort you from the room."

"She can try."

"Whatever."

Fitz dropped his feet to the floor then came out from behind the desk. The man clearly had a death wish.

"I'm assuming you're here about the lovely Lucinda," said Fitz as he sat on the edge of his desk, crossed his arms and glared at Angus.

"She quit."

"Yes."

"And you let her."

"What are you suggesting I should have done? Tied her to the chair? Blackmailed her? Stuck my fingers in my ears and said 'la-la-la-la-la' till she gave up and went back to work?"

"You could have called me. Let me know what she was thinking of doing."

"And what would you have done? Ridden up here on your white steed, thrown her over the saddle and swept her off to the top of a high tower?"

Angus gritted his teeth so hard he swore he heard a crack.

Fitz breathed out, long and slow, then said, "She can't work for you any more, Angus. Not after what happened. Hell, I should have split the two of you up years ago. My reasons were purely selfish, and for that I apologise. Together you guys make the rest of us a ton of money."

"Nothing happened. Before last weekend. Nothing had ever happened."

"Angus, mate, every time the two of you are in the same room something happens. The air crackles and heats up several degrees. A yeti could walk through the middle of the office and you wouldn't notice. Knowing that, I should have moved her to another department, if only because it would have given you both one less reason not to go for it."

Angus went to say, *"Go for what?"* but he knew. It seemed everyone but him had been aware of it for a long time. He slowly lowered himself into Fitz's spare chair, his head falling into his hands. "Where is she now?"

"My spies told me she left a little while ago."

"Was she okay? When she left?"

"What do you think?"

Angus didn't need to think. Not after the way she'd looked at him when he'd told her to go.

She'd looked as if she'd been slapped.

If he'd been attempting to redraw the line between them—after she'd made it clear at the weekend that despite their night together she didn't see a future between them—he'd gone about it the right way. For he'd turned a fluid line in the sand into the Grand Canyon.

"How about you?" Fitz asked. "Are you okay?"

Angus rubbed his hands over his face. "I don't know. I truly don't. I can't imagine going back down there and doing what I do without her beside me."

Neither could he imagine looking up and seeing someone else sitting in her chair. Or going a day without talking to her, hearing her stories about Cat and Sonny. Without watching her work a phone, or seeing her smile.

Life without Lucinda was a life he truly couldn't fathom.

Angus grabbed hold of his hair and tugged, the pain barely registering.

But life with her, really *with* her…

Lucinda had told Sonny that he wasn't ready for fatherhood. That he couldn't take care of anyone else until he learned how to take care of himself.

But he'd been playing father to Sonny for years.

He'd been ready for Sonny. But the truth was, he hadn't been ready for *her*. That was why he'd deferred to her. Why he'd never put his own needs first where they were concerned.

But that didn't mean Angus didn't *know* what he needed.

He needed for his work to be satisfying.

He *needed* Sonny. For he loved that kid as if he was his own.

And he needed Lucinda. He needed her like he needed air. It wasn't the dodgy, supernatural teen TV shows on Netflix he loved so much, it was having an excuse to talk to her late into the night. She sustained him. She challenged him. She had taught him how to live, how to laugh and how to love.

And, as if the wheels and cogs of the universe that had ground harshly and noisily around him his entire life were finally slipping into their rightful place, silencing the constant burr in his head and dissolving the shackles around his heart, Angus knew what he had to do.

He stood. The wheels and cogs were now spinning in the opposite direction and spinning fast. "Her letter of resignation. It was addressed to me. Not to Big Picture. Meaning, while she no longer works for me, she could still work for the company."

Fitz scoffed. "Um, yeah. I might have taken longer than I ought to split the two of you up, but you don't think I was stupid enough to let her leave altogether? Oh, Angus, you might be the star of this operation—the Dorothy, if you will—but I am the great and powerful Oz."

Angus let Fitz's waffle slide. He was already

too deep inside a plan. A plan to fix things. Fix everything. By pulling off the most important re-branding of his life. His own.

"Where have you put her?" His voice dropped to a growl. "She's not working for you."

"You kidding? Velma would curl up and die if she didn't see my gorgeous face every day. We hadn't hashed anything out yet. I told her to come back tomorrow and we'd work it out."

"Good. Because I have an idea."

"Do I need to write this down? I feel like I need a notebook and a pencil. I know I won't look nearly as gorgeous as Lucinda in one of those skirts she likes to wear, but I'll try."

Angus shot him a glare, but it was barely half-strength. He was too charged to pretend to be of-fended. In fact, he was done pretending altogether. Any more pretending, he'd get a stomach ulcer.

Holding back his feelings as a kid, when he'd been scared or lonely or worried about his mum, had meant those hurting him had left him alone. It had helped him get through the rough.

But he wasn't in the rough any more. He was in the prime of his life.

He'd achieved everything he could ever have dreamed of.

Only to realise he'd not been dreaming big enough.

"Get that pencil and notebook," he commanded. "I'm ready."

* * *

"You ready?" Fitz asked after rapping noisily on Angus's glass door.

"Ten seconds," Angus said, holding up a hand as he went over the plan in his head, double checking he hadn't missed anything, so used was he to having Lucinda there to fill in the blanks.

It felt like months since he'd seen her, not days. Months in which he'd had to answer his own phone and schmooze his own clients. Call IT for help when he couldn't open his email.

He would hire another assistant, but right now he needed the clarity of remembering what it was he loved about his work. The rush of being in the trenches.

And now it was Lucinda's first day back. She'd taken a week off. Time owed, Fitz had said. Time to think about the offer he'd made regarding a new position in the company.

A promotion, actually. A big one. She was taking over Charlie's job as Manager of Financial Affairs.

Charlie was brilliant, and a big part of their success, but the guy couldn't lead. When Fitz and Angus had discussed the idea with Charlie, he'd near wept with relief. He and Kumar would continue to pound away at their calculators, making money for their clients and the Big Picture Group, while Lucinda would be the new face of the department. And the boss.

Angus's gut had hurt when Fitz had told him her first question before accepting had been to make sure Angus would be okay with it. He wished he'd seen her face when Fitz had told her it was all Angus's idea.

"Now or never," Fitz said.

Yeah, that was what he feared.

Angus stood, looking around him for what he might need to take to a staff meeting.

"Come on! Hurry up! No resting on your Remède laurels, mate. Boardroom. Now." With that, Fitz strode away.

Angus left through the small door that took him past Lucinda's old desk. It looked eerily tidy. There was no paper, no pencils. The back of the chair sat perfectly parallel with the desk.

He opened a drawer and found it empty too. Until, when he closed it, there came a tell-tale sound just before a cheap 2B pencil rolled towards the front.

He picked it up and ran a thumb over the black and red stripes along its length.

A smile stretched across his face. Knowing how much she liked pretty notebooks, one of the first gifts he'd ever bought her was a very expensive pen. It had sat in the back of the same drawer for years while she'd continued to use her discount store pencils instead.

No airs. No graces. She was who she was. Thank the gods for that.

Holding the pencil tight, like some kind of talisman, Angus made his way down the hall towards the boardroom.

When he arrived, Fitz was talking with Velma, who tried to look stern but couldn't contain the flicker at the corner of her mouth.

Charlie and Kumar sat against the wall, watching a video on Kumar's phone—no doubt a stock fluctuation. Or a UFO sighting. Hell, maybe it was a kitten lost down a well.

Angus moved to his seat at the far end of the table and sat, feeling as though fireworks were going off in his belly.

"Sorry!"

Angus stilled as Lucinda hustled breathlessly into the room, tucking a stray strand of dark hair behind her ear. The same stray strand that never stayed put.

He sat taller in his seat, his nerves un-pinching, his muscles relaxing, his bones yielding.

It had been a week since he'd seen her. A week more than he ever wanted to go without seeing her again.

"Sorry. I couldn't find…a thing. Sorry."

She shot Fitz a chagrined smile. He gave her a big thumbs-up.

Then she moved over to Charlie and tapped him on the knee. She looked nervous, as if he might be upset that she was now his boss. But, Charlie being Charlie, he grinned his sweet grin and gave her a hug.

After which Lucinda looked around before picking out a new chair. Her chair. At the table. Where she deserved to be.

As she fussed, fixing her skirt, cricking her neck, trying to get comfortable in her seat while she chatted with Fitz, Angus sat forward, leaning his chin on his hand.

He couldn't have recounted afterwards exactly what it was that she was wearing, only that she was put together in a way that was perfectly Lucinda. Professional, yet whimsical. Neat, yet sassy. Elegant, and as sexy as all get-out.

She glowed. Surely everyone else could see that? Her aura must have been made of spun gold. Or perhaps the sun simply hit her at the exact right angle. Whatever it was, he couldn't take his eyes off her.

"Okay," said Fitz, clapping his hands. "Charlie. Kumar. Save the soft porn for upstairs. Everyone ready?"

"Sorry," Lucinda said again. "I was looking for a pencil and couldn't find the right one… Which sounds ridiculous. Because a pencil is a pencil is a pencil, really. Am I right? It's not as if there's only one perfect pencil for me. In fact…anyone got a pen?"

Angus cleared his throat.

He saw her brace herself, as if she recognised

the noise as his. Just as he'd recognise her scent in a crowd. Her laugh among a million others. Her sad smile from her tipsy smile from the smile she saved for those for whom she cared most.

As if the world was in slow motion, Lucinda looked his way. Not smiling. Not a bit. Her mouth was pursed. Her cute little frown lines entrenched above her nose.

When her eyes snagged on his—those gorgeous, big, warm, clever, brown doe-eyes—he felt as if he'd been sucker-punched.

In fact, the entire table seemed to hold its breath, waiting to see what either one of them might do and say.

Then Angus slowly held up the pencil he'd found in her drawer.

Her old drawer. Her ex-drawer. For she no longer worked there, just outside his office where he could look up and see her all day every day. Where he caught the occasional burst of her laughter through the thick glass, which made the world feel brighter, lighter, no matter how much work was on his plate. Where he saw her head bent over her work and knew she was on his side.

Louis Fournier might have been the first man who'd looked at him as though he wasn't some punk kid, but Lucinda Starling was the first woman who'd looked at him and seen him for who he was.

Not a meal ticket or a good time. Not a party invite or a business opportunity. Not someone to ignore, or use or degrade. But a man in his own right. Flawed, damaged, stuck back together a little wrong but stronger for it. A man who saw the world not as it was but as it could be.

And she saw him as hers.

For he was her guy. And she was his girl.

"Oh, for Pete's sake!" Velma cried out, her strong voice booming across the room. "Stop mooning over the man and take the damn pencil so we can get on with this farce. The rest of you may feel as if time is on your side, but I have work to do."

Angus came to and found Lucinda staring at him, her cheeks pink, her eyes wide, unable to hide the cocktail of feelings he now realised he'd seen there before. Many times. For years, in fact.

He'd ignored them in the past—no, he'd *denied* them—fearful that if he'd claimed those emotions she'd spook, or deny, or eventually see that he was not worth it and he'd end up losing the most important person in his life.

He placed the pencil on the table and rolled it her way. She watched, a kick catching at the corner of her mouth as the pencil came to a stop right in front of her, before she blinked, caught herself, slowly gathered up the pencil, and looked down at her notebook.

Fitz clapped his hands. "Hear that everyone?

My Velma has work to do so let's get this meeting under way."

"Meeting," Velma said, scoffing, before she pressed back her chair and lifted her exuberant frame out of the seat with a grunt. "We all know there's no meeting. No minutes to take. No decisions to make. Nothing bar the fact we need to settle the Lucinda-Angus issue once and for all."

"Excuse me?" Lucinda said, perking up. "There is no issue."

"*Pfft.* There's an issue the size of Fitz's ego."

"Huge!" said Fitz, holding his arms out wide.

"Enough," said Angus, silencing the room. *Now who's Dorothy and who's the great and powerful Oz?* he thought. "Velma is right. There is no agenda, bar getting Lucinda in here with me, so the rest of you can vamoose."

Lucinda's eyes couldn't have gone any wider if she'd seen a ghost.

The rest of the team, cool-headed in the face of drama and excitement, happily packed up their stuff and herded chattily from the room.

Once everyone was gone, and it was just the two of them, Lucinda's shoulders slumped and she looked his way.

"Congratulations," he said.

She winced. "It's not why I left—"

"I know. But this is a good thing. The finance team have skated for years. You'll turn our smallest department into a juggernaut in no time."

She smiled and it nearly reached her eyes. "I think you're right. I can't believe it, but I also can't wait. So, thank you. Fitz told me it was your idea. Charlie needs me. While you…" She took a breath. "You don't need anyone, Angus. It's your defining characteristic. It could be written on your tombstone."

For a very long time he'd thought so too. Otherwise everything his mother had done, everything she'd sacrificed, the times she'd left him to his own devices, would have been for nothing.

But none of that mattered now.

The only thing that mattered was sitting far too many chairs away.

He pushed his own chair back and strolled towards her. He wondered if she even realised that she turned her chair to face him, a north to his south.

"You're wrong about one thing," he said.

"What's that?"

"You're wrong about what I need." He stopped a couple of metres away. If he came any closer he'd not be able to resist touching her. And first there were things to say. "I have something for you, Lucinda. A gift."

She sucked in a breath, her hand going to her neck. And then he saw it: the ladybird necklace he'd bought her all those years ago. And any concern that he was going too fast, that he might be over-reaching, disappeared.

"But it's not my birthday. Or St Patrick's Day. Or Sunday Funday."

"And yet…" Angus glanced through the glass walls of the boardroom and nodded.

Having been given the signal, Louis Fournier entered the room.

Lucinda stood. "Monsieur Fournier. Is everything okay?"

"Everything is wonderful," he said, giving Angus a smile before turning to Lucinda and handing her a small spring-green bag with a white satin ribbon.

She reached out and took it, glancing at Angus.

"Open it," he said, his voice rough.

He saw her hands were shaking, as she did just that, pulling out a small bottle of perfume.

A very special bottle of perfume. For Angus had had Remède's Someday perfume—the perfume her father had bought for her mother every year for her birthday—rebranded as a special edition. It had been a rush job, using glass makers in Venice, printing out of Sydney. It had cost him a personal fortune. And Louis Fournier had been behind him all the way.

The shape of the bottle was the same—a smooth, curving twist. Though the new label was shaped like the leaf of a fiddle-leaf fig, the colour the same spring-green as his favourite dress.

"Someday" was written in the same sweeping

script font, only the words "Every Day" were now written beneath in neat, clean silver.

Lucinda's hand fluttered to her mouth as she sat back in her chair with a thud. When she looked up at Angus, her eyes filled with tears. Then she looked to Louis who was watching her with pure adoration in his eyes. "Monsieur Fournier?"

"Don't look at me, this is all Angus. The design, the colour, the shape, the name. It took some doing, but he can be a very convincing man when he's on a mission. Especially when his mission, dear girl, is you."

Her eyes swung back to Angus's.

No longer able to stay away, he moved in beside her and dropped into a crouch.

"What is it? What's in the bag?" Kumar whispered from the doorway.

It seemed the gang hadn't blithely gone back to work after all.

"Shh!" Velma. "Don't distract him. Kid's finally stepping up."

Angus ignored them. It was easy when Lucinda was looking right into his eyes. "Hey," he said.

"Hey." She sniffed.

"Do you like it?"

"I don't..." She gulped. "I don't even know what to say."

"Usually I can't get you to shut up."

She laughed, then hiccupped. And this time the smile came from her eyes before it lit up the rest of her lovely face. "You really had this made. For me?"

Angus nodded.

"But you told me to go. When I tried to resign. You didn't give me the chance to say why."

"You told Sonny I had no desire to be his father, without giving me the chance to answer that question for myself."

Her mouth dropped open. It would have been funny if Angus wasn't already on emotional overload.

She swallowed, licked her lips then said, "I did do that. And what would your answer have been?"

"That having the both of you in my life is the best part of my life. And that, if you didn't know that already, then I have been remiss. And I will make sure, from this day forward, that not a minute goes by that you don't know how important you are to me. How necessary. How much I love you. And how much I *will* love you. Every day."

"You do?" she asked, her voice like a breeze. Then she hit him. A slap to the chest. After which she gripped her hand into his shirt. "So why didn't you say something? Why didn't you haul me up, tell me off? Tell the truth?"

"I deferred to you. Sweetheart, I've always deferred to you. But I'm not going to do so any more. Now it's my turn to take what I want."

With that he reached out, cupped her face in his hands and kissed her.

"I'm not sure that's appropriate," said Velma from the doorway.

"She doesn't work for him any more," said Fitz, waggling his eyebrows.

Velma scowled. "I meant to be kissing in front of a client."

The CEO of Remède waved an elegant hand in their direction. "I am French. Let them kiss."

And kiss they did. Until Lucinda dropped from the chair onto her knees so that she was flush against him. He tasted her heat, her desire. When he tasted her tears, he moved to kiss them away, each and every one.

She pulled away suddenly and blurted, "I love you too. You know that, right?"

"I do."

"You said it, and I said nothing when I should have said—I love you, Angus. I've loved you for years. For ever. I was happy loving you in silence. But I can already tell I'm going to be a whole lot happier loving you out loud. You're my pencil," she said on a burst of laughter. "The one and only pencil for me."

"What did she say?" Fitz asked.

Louis shook his head. "Something about a pencil?"

"Staff meetings here sure aren't like staff meetings at my old job," said Kumar. "They had donuts, for one."

"Enough," said Fitz, reaching round them to

take hold of the door. "Get back to work, the lot of you."

When the door shut with a snick, Angus breathed out.

Finally. Finally, it was just Lucinda and him.

He disentangled himself from the delicious warmth of her arms, stood and held out a hand.

"You ready for this?" he said when she stood by him, toe to toe.

She grinned. "I was born ready. You?"

"You'd better believe it."

EPILOGUE

LUCINDA CAREFULLY HELD three coffees in paper cups high over her head as she edged her way past the multiple sets of knees, shivering to fend off the Melbourne winter chill, before taking a seat on a cold wooden bench behind the boundary fence at the local AFL field.

Tilda and Francine—mums to kids on Sonny's footy team—made room for her to sit then gratefully took the hot drinks.

"What did I miss?" Lucinda asked, backside slightly lifted off the seat as she spotted Sonny running down the left wing, calling for the ball.

"Much running in circles by most of them," said Tilda.

"Bastian spent quite some time staring at the clouds."

"One did look like Iron Man, so can't blame the kid."

Lucinda laughed as she planted her backside and took a moment to notice just how much her life had changed over the past few months.

Who knew that simply deciding not to be scared any more would make room for so much other stuff? Good stuff. Amazing stuff.

Taking on the position of Manager of Financial Affairs had given her far better hours at work, giving her the chance to do some school drop-offs, and pick-ups. Giving her the chance to make mum-friends—women who struggled with mothers' guilt while trying to forge a life for themselves, just as she did.

The extra time at home had given Cat more breathing space too. She was in London now, writing for an airline magazine, and ignoring Fitz's irregular pleas to come home because he was bored without her.

And Sonny had never been happier. Half a football field away, she could *feel* how utterly joyful he was.

It didn't take long for her gaze to seek out another figure on the field.

For Sonny's coach was hot stuff. Backwards cap, track pants that did nothing to hide the glorious male form beneath. Long-sleeved T-shirt rolled up at the elbow and covered with a lime-green coach's smock.

Arms outstretched, Coach Angus—*her* Angus—herded the boisterous bunch of under-nines into free space and reminded them to call for the ball, to look out for their team mates, then waited patiently for one of the girls to take her kick.

Step, step, drop the ball and thwack. It actually hit the kid's boot, which earned a clap from the crowd. Then the funny-shaped ball spun off sideways before rolling towards Sonny. And, boy, if the kid didn't swoop on it, keeping his feet in a move taught by none other than the coach himself while playing in the back yard every afternoon after school.

Sonny burst down the centre, heading straight for the open goal. Then he stopped and passed the ball to another team mate, who ran in and kicked a goal.

"Woo-woo-woo!" called Tilda. "Go, Bridget!"

Francine glanced up from her phone. "Oh, no. Did my girl do something good?"

"Ripper goal. With an excellent assist from super Sonny." Lucinda's heart, thumping in her chest, swelled with pride. And hope. And relief. And all things good, warm and wholesome.

Then the half-time buzzer rang out and the kids came running over to the fence line in their long shirts and falling down socks, sweat dripping from their hair, hands reaching for their water bottles.

After having a quick chat to the fifteen-year-old referee, Angus came jogging after them, the sharp wintry sun catching on the angles of his face as he loped their way.

Tilda and Francine let go of a tandem sigh.

"Have we ever thanked you properly?" Tilda asked.

"For?" Lucinda asked, her voice a little dreamy.

"Him," Francine answered. "Last year's coach was an absolute dud in comparison."

Tilda leaned around Lucinda to hit Francine on the arm. "Your husband is a doll."

Lucinda lifted her coffee and squeezed out from between them. "I'm outta here before this turns ugly. And you're welcome."

The women laughed and watched as Lucinda edged her way along the fence line to where the team sat in a circle, eating orange quarters.

"Hey, bud," she said, holding a hand to her eyes to block out the sun.

Sonny turned to find her, an orange peel stuck behind his lips to look like a big tooth. He pulled it out and the grin remained. "Did you see that?"

"Did I ever! Awesome team playing."

A shadow fell over her, blocking the sunlight. She dropped her hand and looked up into Angus's face. A halo of sunshine trimmed his gorgeous form.

"Hey, coach," she said.

"Hey, yourself."

He leaned over and kissed her, a devastating mix of heat and chill, yet somehow totally PG.

"Ew!" Bridget called out, and soon a chorus of "Ew!" and "Yuck!" followed.

Angus's lips smiled against hers before he pulled away.

"Having fun out there?" she asked.

He grinned, all beaming teeth and hot hazel eyes. "Yeah, actually. It's such a kick to see them improving. Did you see Sonny's assist?"

"I saw."

"That kid," he said, shaking his head in amazement. "The way he handed that off. He kills me. Comes down to some kick-ass parenting."

"Coach said 'ass'!" Milla cried.

Angus laughed. "That I did. And when you're as big as me you can decide if it's a word you want to say—or not. Till then, let's see who can think of the best word ever invented. Like…"

"Bubble gum!" Milla said.

"Chocolate!" said Bastian.

Angus grinned down at his team, his gaze lingering on Sonny. Lucinda saw the hitch in his chest and felt her own hitch in response.

She tipped up onto her toes, reached over the fence and wrapped her arms around Angus's neck, her hand landing on his chest. She whispered, "Thank you for loving my Sonny."

"Thank you for letting me."

How could she not? "Did I tell you today how much I love you?"

"Once or twice," he murmured. His hand lifted to close around hers, his thumb running up and down the sensitive middle of her palm.

She snuggled closer until her entire body seemed to sigh from an overload of pure bliss.

"Now you're just showing off!" That was Francine.

Lucinda buried her face in Angus's neck. "You have a fan club, you know?"

"Yeah," said Angus. "At training they threatened to bring placards. I told them to bring orange quarters instead."

"It worked."

"I'm very convincing."

"So I've heard."

He turned his head just enough to smile into her eyes, then gave her a quick kiss on the nose.

With a sigh, Lucinda let him go.

Now she had him for real, she found it all too hard not to hold tight. Only the belief that he would indeed love her for ever made her able move away. To stand alone.

Angus clicked his fingers. "And I've had thoughts on how with a few tweaks the club could make some serious dosh."

"Sponsorship deal?"

Angus looked at her in wonder. "You. Me. It's like we have one brain."

"Two brains," she said as he backed away to join his team, now squeezing their water bottles at one another. "It's more fun that way."

A haze came over Angus's eyes and she knew he was trying to figure out a client for whom the line might work as a strap line. For, while his hours had also cut right back, ever since he'd moved in and they'd begun working on adding a second floor to her little cottage the guy never switched off.

As she made her way back up to the stands, her phone rang.

"Lucinda, pick up," crooned the ringtone of her phone in a deep, sexy voice, delivering a message that told her exactly what he'd like to do her when a certain someone was asleep that night.

She quickly pressed the button to hang up the call before it went further than PG. Then, grinning and blushing, she looked over her shoulder to find Angus with his phone to his ear.

She gave him a quick thumbs-up, a "yes, please" to every plan he had, before sliding her phone into the back pocket of her jeans.

While it was the kind of ringtone that would get her sideways looks at the supermarket, she might keep it for a while.

Maybe she'd keep it for ever. She was a for ever girl, after all.

* * * * *

Shattered

Sarah N. Harvey

orca soundings

ORCA BOOK PUBLISHERS

Copyright © 2011 Sarah N. Harvey

Library and Archives Canada Cataloguing in Publication

Harvey, Sarah N., 1950-
Shattered / Sarah N. Harvey.
(Orca soundings)

Issued also in electronic format.
ISBN 978-1-55469-846-2 (bound).--ISBN 978-1-55469-845-5 (pbk.)

I. Title. II. Series: Orca soundings
PS8615.A764S53 2011   JC813'.6   C2011-903352-6

First published in the United States, 2011
Library of Congress Control Number: 2011929277

Summary: After March shoves her boyfriend and he ends up in a coma, she
tries to figure out what it means to have a perfect life.

*Orca Book Publishers is dedicated to preserving the environment and has
printed this book on paper certified by the Forest Stewardship Council®.*

Orca Book Publishers gratefully acknowledges the support for its publishing
programs provided by the following agencies: the Government of Canada
through the Canada Book Fund and the Canada Council for the Arts, and
the Province of British Columbia through the BC Arts Council and
the Book Publishing Tax Credit.

Cover photography by maXx images

ORCA BOOK PUBLISHERS
PO Box 5626, Stn. B
Victoria, BC Canada
V8R 6S4

ORCA BOOK PUBLISHERS
PO Box 468
Custer, WA USA
98240-0468

www.orcabook.com
Printed and bound in Canada.

14 13 12 11 • 4 3 2 1

To Maggie

Chapter One

It was close to midnight by the time I got to the end-of-the-year party at Brad Bingham's place. I had to work late. And then Mom and I argued about me using her car. I won, but barely. She wanted me to promise not to drink. I negotiated her down to a single beer. Like she'd ever know. From down the block I could see the multicolored Christmas lights the Binghams leave up year-round to light up the backyard and deck. A mindless techno dance mix was blasting out of huge speakers balanced on the living-room windowsills. It was warm for June—hurray for global warming. Most of the guys, and some of the girls, would no doubt already be topless. Brad's parents weren't home. If they had been, they would have been out with the dancers on the lawn. Forming a conga line and passing around a doobie. All of us envy Brad his parents.

I slipped in the side gate and onto the back deck, where the hot tub is. Tyler loves the hot tub. So do I. I had my bikini on under my sundress. I pulled the dress over my head, kicked off my flip-flops and stepped into the light. That's when I saw a slutty tenth grader named Kayla writhing on my boyfriend's lap in the hot tub. She was naked and so was he. His red board shorts were in a damp heap on the deck, next to her string bikini and an empty vodka bottle. The lights—red, green, yellow, blue—shone on their wet skin. Tyler's eyes were closed, his neck arched. A small moan escaped his parted lips. Kayla's back was to me. I always thought it was bullshit when people said they got weak in the knees. I was wrong. I wasn't just weak in the knees. It felt as if every joint in my body had turned to water. I put a hand out and steadied myself against the fence. I considered picking up the bottle and smacking Kayla upside the head with it. Instead, I took a deep breath, perched on the edge of the hot tub and said, "Hey, guys. Having fun?"

Tyler's eyes flew open, and he shoved Kayla off his lap. She disappeared for a moment under the hot tub's foaming bubbles. For a second, I thought about holding her under. Not long enough to kill her. I'm not insane. When she surfaced, she tried, without success, to cover her breasts and hairless crotch with her small hands. Her nail polish was silver. Tyler, ever the gentleman, tossed her a towel. As she wrapped it around herself, she turned to me and snarled, "So much for your perfect life, bitch," before she ran, dripping, toward the house. She cheats with my boyfriend and I'm the bitch? I picked up the bottle and threw it after her, but she was already inside. The bottle exploded when it hit the back door.

Tyler made a grab for his shorts, but I was way ahead of him. I picked them up and tossed them over the fence into the next yard.

"Not cool," I said. My hands were shaking and my feet felt numb. "Not cool at all. We're done, Tyler. Don't call. Don't text. Don't come to my house."

Tyler crouched in the hot tub, begging. "Don't go, March, baby. Let's talk about it."

I shook my head. I wanted to leave, but I couldn't move. Tyler climbed out of the hot tub and wrapped a towel around his waist. I noticed that his nipples were erect. I thought about how the last tongue on those nipples had not been mine. The sushi I had snacked on at work rose in my throat. I swallowed hard as he took a step toward me, whining, "She brought vodka. You know what vodka does to me, babe. It didn't mean anything."

I kept shaking my head. Tyler and I had been friends since third grade and going out since we were thirteen. Four years. Neither of us has had sex with anyone else. Or so I thought. Now our relationship was as shattered as the bottle I had thrown at Kayla.

I put my hands up in front of me as Tyler approached. Isn't raising your hands, palms out, the universal symbol for "back off"? He should have stopped. But he didn't. Suddenly I wasn't frozen anymore. I felt strong. And angry. Angrier than I've ever been. His bare, wet chest collided with my palms, and I shoved him—hard. He staggered and fell backward. All one hundred and seventy pounds of him. It was like felling a redwood with a steak knife.

"Timber!" I yelled as he crashed against the hot tub. I waited for him to get up, but he lay perfectly still. I nudged him with my bare toe. Nothing. Nothing at all. I froze up again, I'm not sure for how long. Could have been one minute. Could have been ten. It was just Tyler and me, in a bubble of colored light. I'm not proud of what I did next. I knelt down and made sure he still had a pulse. I'm not sure what I would have done if he hadn't, but he did. I stood up, put on my dress and flip-flops and used my cell to call for an ambulance. I didn't give my name, and I didn't wait for the ambulance to come.

I walked down the rotting wooden steps, shut the gate behind me and got into Mom's Honda. It smelled like her: Trident cinnamon gum and Dove body wash. I love that smell.

I turned the key in the ignition and drove off. I heard the siren. Then the ambulance passed me, its lights blurred by my tears.

Chapter Two

When I got home, I did what I always do when I'm upset: I emailed my brother Augie. He was probably awake, playing online Scrabble or writing an essay. When he first went away to university a year ago, he told me he liked getting my emails. He refuses to text or use Facebook. So I tell him about my life, and he says

I make him laugh. It's not like writing for school. I do as little of that as I can get away with and still get good grades. Good enough to keep Mom and Dad off my case anyway. Augie's the smart one. I'm the fun one. All my report cards, since grade one, have said pretty much the same thing. *March is very social, and it affects her grades in a negative way.* Augie's report cards said sort of the opposite. So now he has a few really close friends and a massive scholarship. I have three fake IDs, a closet full of designer clothes, and a hot boyfriend. Make that a hot ex-boyfriend.

Hey Augie,

Tonight I caught Tyler banging a chick named Kayla in Brad Bingham's hot tub. I broke up with him. I don't get it. Kayla is a total ho. You know what she said to me? She said, "So much for your perfect life, bitch." For some reason that made me feel like shit, but I'm not sure why. Is it my fault that he cheated on me? Did I deserve it? What did she mean? I feel like I'm going crazy.

March

I couldn't bring myself to tell Augie about shoving Tyler, or about leaving before the ambulance came. Usually I tell Augie everything. This was the first time I had kept a secret from him. It didn't feel good. I shut my laptop and crawled into bed. My bedroom is huge and painted sky blue with shiny white trim. It's on the top floor under a gable, at the opposite end of the house from Mom and Dad's room on the main floor. You get to my room up a narrow twisting staircase off the kitchen. Augie's bedroom is two doors down, waiting for him to come home for a visit. In between is the guest bedroom. The bathroom across the hall, complete with claw-foot tub, is cold, even in summer. Mom keeps promising to have it renovated, but she's always too busy.

My bed is tucked into a south-facing nook that is lit at night by the lighthouse near the golf course. There are blackout curtains, but I never use them. The green light washes over me as I sleep. I find it comforting, as if I am being stroked by a friendly alien. When I was little, I used to tell people that when I grew up I was going to be the lighthouse keeper. The lighthouse is automated now, so that career is out. So far, I haven't thought of another one.

I love it when it's foggy and the foghorn sounds every sixty seconds. Mom hates the sound of the foghorn. So mournful, she says. But to me it's like the light from the lighthouse. Reassuring. My best friend, Natalie, hates the light and the foghorn. She always stays in the guest bedroom if we have a sleepover, even though I have a king-size bed. If it's foggy, she uses earplugs.

After I wrote to Augie, I lay in bed and counted the seconds in between the flashes of light. One-two-three-four-five. It never changes. It was a clear night, so there was no foghorn. Soon the light lulled me to sleep.

When I woke up the next morning, I was happy. For about twenty seconds. Maybe less. However long it took my brain to provide me with a vivid playback of Tyler and Kayla in the hot tub. Someday I'd have to ask Mom or Dad what goes on in your brain right after you wake up. Not today though. Showing interest in their work is dangerous at the best of times. Once they get started, they can't shut up. It's best not to encourage them. My parents, Dr. Richard Moser and

Dr. Yvette Kleinman, are psychologists.
Research psychologists, not therapists.
They don't listen to people's problems.
They study their brains. I won't bore
you with the technical details. Basically
they study how memories are formed
in the brain. They don't care too much
about the memories themselves.

For example, most of my friends have
great memories of going to Disneyland.
My parents don't believe in those kinds
of vacations. It's all camping or culture
for the Kleinman-Moser clan. Vacation
as education. Augie loved the Grand
Canyon, the Galapagos Islands, Machu
Picchu, the Louvre. But I wanted the
Pirates of the Caribbean, Toad's Wild
Ride, Indiana Jones. Still do.

"You can go on your own dime,"
Mom said when I whined about it.
"I'm not paying for all that fake Disney
claptrap. Where are you going to want
to go next? Las Vegas? Climb the fake

Eiffel Tower? Go on a gondola ride down a manmade canal in an artificial Venice?" She was smiling, but I knew better than to argue with her. I have the memories my parents want me to have. Up until now.

I dragged myself out of bed and opened my laptop. There was a new message from Augie in my inbox.

Dear March,

You're not crazy.

It's not your fault.

Nobody's life is perfect. Perfect is boring.

This really is something you have to work out on your own. It's about time. I always said you were a smart girl. Gotta go, March. Give my love to Richard and Yvette. Keep me posted.

August

"Thanks a lot, Augie," I muttered as I shut the laptop and got back into bed.

I was exhausted and sad. I wanted to sleep forever. Figuring out my life would have to wait.

Chapter Three

Mom and Dad were sitting at the kitchen table when I went downstairs a few hours later to get something to eat. Last winter Mom painted the kitchen a yellow that is actually called Good Morning Sunshine. Even if it's raining, the room feels flooded with sunlight. The oak table is one they got when they were first married and totally broke. They stripped off about five layers of paint and sanded it until it was as soft as silk. Augie and I argue about who's going to get the table after Mom and Dad die. Mom let us use it for anything when we were growing up: eating, arm wrestling, playing Uno, doing science projects, studying, painting, building Lego cities. She says that all the marks we've made on the table over the years add character to it. She's never tried to sand any of them away.

"Augie sends his love," I said.

"Augie?" My dad looked around the room as if expecting Augie to pop up.

It's a joke in our house that Dad studies memory for a living but doesn't seem to have one himself. Augie and I are named for the months we were born in so my dad would be less likely to forget our birthdays. He still forgets.

"You know. Your son. The one who's in Ontario. The one who's reading Hitler's autobiography for credit."

Nothing bugs my mom like being reminded that her genius-IQ son is working on a degree in German. She acts like fluency in German makes him a Nazi or something. Her family is French and Jewish, which explains a lot, I guess.

In the end, she couldn't stop him going, because he got a full scholarship, including room and board. He's at the top of all his classes, and he's already presenting papers at conferences. In the fall, he'll be studying in Germany as part of an exchange program. I don't know why she can't just be proud of him.

"You came in early last night," she said as I squinted into the fridge.

"Yeah. Lame party. *Plus ça change...*" Mom loves it when I speak French.

She thinks we are bonding. If Augie had chosen to do a degree in French, she would have been over the moon. "Are there any eggs?"

"*Oui,*" she replied. "Scrambled or fried?"

"Uh, fried?"

"Bacon?"

I turned away from the fridge and stared at her. She never cooks breakfast. She never even eats breakfast. She thinks bacon is cut directly from the devil's ass. Not that she believes in the devil. Something was up. I glanced over at Dad, who was hiding behind the newspaper. No help there.

"What's up, guys?" I asked.

"Sit down, honey," said my dad, lowering the paper. "Your mother and I have something to tell you."

My first thought was, Oh, shit. They're getting a divorce. My second thought was, Who's going to get the house?

Natalie's dad lives in a shithole down-town, and Nat has to spend every second weekend there. She hates it. My third thought was, Maybe Mom's pregnant. But she couldn't be. She had a glass of wine at dinner a few nights ago. No way she'd drink if she was pregnant. And she's too old. I think.

I poured myself a glass of grapefruit juice and sat down across from Dad. "What's up?" I repeated.

"You tell her," Mom said, squeezing Dad's hand.

Dad reached across the table and took my hand. If we'd been god-fearing folk, I would have thought we were about to pray.

"Tyler's mother just called. I've got some bad news, sweetie."

I thought fast. No one knows what happened, I told myself. No one. Not even that ho, Kayla. I pushed away the image of Tyler and Kayla in the hot tub.

If I thought about it, I'd go crazy. "It's okay," I said. "I already know. Nat just called me. Tyler got wasted and hit his head last night at the party, but it's not that serious. A concussion, Nat said. Tyler's had them before from playing hockey." I took a sip of my juice. My hand was steady. I've had a lot of practice lying to Mom and Dad. Without it, I'd never get to do anything. If lying to your parents was a school subject, I'd get an A+.

I could almost see Mom's brain sorting through the available information: *Tyler is hurt. March isn't concerned. She came home early last night. Therefore something is going on.* They'd find out sooner or later, so I said, "We broke up last night. Before he got hurt. Obviously."

Mom nodded slowly and sat down beside me at the table. "I'm so sorry, March. Do you want to talk about it?"

I shook my head, knowing she wouldn't push it. She's good that way. "As you wish," she said. "Do you want to know what Mrs. McKenna said?" When I nodded, she continued. "It's worse than they originally thought. Because he's had concussions before, he's at higher risk for serious complications."

"Complications?" I stood up too quickly and almost toppled over. Mom caught me and pulled me back down onto the chair. How could there be complications? Tyler was young and healthy. And I hadn't pushed him that hard. Had I? I put my head on the table and tried to breathe slowly. Green spots floated in front of my eyes. Mom stroked my hair. I started to cry. I cried until the placemat was slimy with snot and my nose was plugged and my eyes were swollen shut. And then I cried some more. She didn't say anything other than "Shhh, shhh, shhh." At one point,

I shook so hard my teeth rattled. Then Dad put his arms around me and held me tight, as if I was a six-year-old who'd fallen off the monkey bars.

Eventually my sobs became sniffles, and then hiccups. I went to the bathroom to pee and wash my face. When I looked in the mirror, I didn't recognize the bloated face that stared back at me. Ugly. So ugly. A hit-and-run kind of girl. The real me. "So much for your perfect life, bitch," I said to the mirror.

When I came out of the bathroom, Mom said, "Why don't you go back to bed, March. Try and sleep. I'll bring you something to eat in a little while."

"Not hungry, Mom," I said. I ached all over, as if I was coming down with the flu.

"We'll see, *cherie*," she said. "Get some rest now."

Chapter Four

I woke up as the sun was setting. I had slept all day, but I still felt leaden and dull and hideous. I could hear music playing downstairs. Some old rocker that Dad likes. Tom Petty, I think. Dad was singing along: *"I wanna free fall, out into nothin'. Gonna leave this world for a while. Oh, I'm free, free fallin'."* I felt like I was already in a free fall, but not the cool kind the song was talking about. I wondered how Tyler was doing, whether he'd phone me soon. Whether I would answer. As the light faded from the sky, Dad brought me a tray. Buttered toast soldiers and a soft-boiled egg in an egg cup shaped like a pink chicken. A pot of Mom's raspberry jam. A cup of weak tea with milk and sugar. Food for an invalid. Not a killer.

"Thanks, Dad," I said, sitting up in bed and pulling the duvet up under my chin. He put the tray in my lap and sat down on the end of my bed. Dad's not much for idle chitchat, so I knew he must have something important to say. I lopped the top off my egg and dipped a toast soldier into the yolk. Perfect. Dad sat and watched me eat.

"We heard from Mrs. McKenna again," he said after a while.

I looked up, a piece of toast halfway to my mouth. "And?"

"And Tyler's still in a coma. He might have what's called an acute subdural hematoma."

"In English, Dad," I said, shoving the tray onto my bedside table. The sight of the food suddenly made me want to puke.

"It's serious, March. If he's bleeding into his brain, something has to be done to relieve the pressure. Before his brain is damaged. The procedure is called a craniotomy, which involves drilling—"

I barely made it to the bathroom before the toast soldiers marched up my throat. When I got back to my room, Dad was gone, along with the tray. I pulled the blackout curtains over the windows and lay in the dark, thinking about drills going into skulls, about blood, about pain. Mom crept into my room at some point. I pretended to be asleep.

"Dear heart," she whispered. "It's going to be okay."

She didn't know that. No one did.

I thought about the McKennas, sitting in a hospital waiting room, praying it was going to be okay. Wondering why this had happened to their beautiful boy. I thought about Tyler, his head shaved, motionless under cold, bright lights. The right thing to do was to confess, to sit up and tell my mother that I had shoved Tyler into the hot tub and run away. But I didn't. I couldn't. I was selfish. I know that. All I could think about was how disappointed in me she would be. How horrified that a child she had raised could be so weak, so cowardly, so lacking in common decency. If Tyler died, I would be a murderer. And my perfect life would be gone. Just like Kayla said. I deserved to be punished, but I still couldn't tell my mother. Or my father. I couldn't even tell Augie. I curled myself into a ball and cried myself to sleep.

When I woke up, it was pitch-black in my room, and for a moment I had no idea where I was. I pulled the curtains back and let the green light wash over me. The house moaned as a gust of wind hit it. My windows rattled, and I wished I could climb into bed with my parents and listen to my mother sing a French lullaby I used to love. I hummed the tune, but it wasn't the same. I switched on the light, got my laptop, climbed back into bed and wrote to Augie.

Hey,

It's the middle of the night here. Tyler is in the hospital. The doctors might have to drill a hole in his head. I don't know what to do. I think I should go and see him. Even tho we broke up. Am I right?

I miss you.

March

I put the laptop on my night table so I could hear it *ping* when Augie wrote back.

Then I sat and waited for the dawn. When it was finally light enough to see, I got dressed in jeans and my old gray hoodie. I let myself out the back door without waking my parents. I'm good at that.

I climbed the hill behind our house and slid through the hole in the chain-link fence to get to my favorite place in the world. Blueberry Hill. Where there are no blueberries. Not that I've ever seen, and I've explored pretty much every square inch of the park. Blueberries grow in bogs (I looked it up online). Blueberry Hill is all rock and Garry oaks and Scotch broom. Augie and Natalie and I used to play *Buffy the Vampire Slayer* on the hill. We all took turns being Buffy, even Augie.

I scrambled down the far side of the hill and tucked myself into a spot Augie and I had discovered years ago. Moss-covered boulders sheltered me from the wind off the sea and hid me from other visitors to the park. Augie and I used to come here—alone or together—to get away from our parents. To read, to stare at the distant mountains, to smoke weed, to drink, to argue, to laugh. I ran away to this spot when I was nine and Mom wouldn't let me have a Barbie. The first time Tyler and I had sex was up here, the summer I turned fourteen. The last time Augie visited, at Christmastime, we came up here and talked. About his courses, about his latest boyfriend, about how crazy Mom and Dad are. It was freezing, but we didn't care. Now I leaned my head against the rock wall behind me, lifting my face to the rising sun and closing my eyes.

Chapter Five

I must have sat there for three hours, trying to figure out what to do next. By the time I had the outline of a plan, my ass was sore and my back ached. I didn't get up. I knew I deserved the pain. I stared out at the ocean and poked small holes in my palms with a thorn from a gorse bush. I could hear Augie's voice in my head: *You're a smart girl, March.* He was always telling me that. I remembered him reading to me when I was about four. *Hop on Pop.* As he read, he pointed at the words with a grubby finger. "This is how you learn to read, March," he said. "It's easy." At six, he could already read harder books than *Hop on Pop,* but it was my favorite. He read it to me every night for a year. Then he stopped. "Read it yourself, March," he said. So I read it to him, slowly and carefully, and he told me I was the smartest girl in the world. I wondered if he'd still think that when I told him my plan. Maybe it would be better not to tell him. Not to tell anyone. Let my actions speak for me.

I was still arguing with myself when I heard voices. A man's and a woman's, calling, "Bonnie! Bonnie! Here, girl." I hated sharing the hill. I burrowed deeper into my rock cocoon. Out of nowhere, a tiny brown dog hurtled into my lap.

It lay still for a second, panting. I wondered if it was hurt, but then it leaped up and licked my face. I picked it up and held it in front of me as it squirmed. "You're a cutie-pie, aren't you?" I said.

And suddenly I am three, sitting on my mother's lap in a bright garden. Augie is running a tiny red metal car up my chubby leg and saying "Vroom, vroom." The car tickles. My mother is laughing. I wiggle my bare toes in the sunlight. A man leans over and picks me up, holding me in front of his face. I squirm, and he says, "What a cutie-pie. Gonna be a heartbreaker, this one." The man's face is a blur, but it's not my father's voice. My father has never uttered the words *cutie-pie*. And I'm the one with the broken heart.

My dad's not much interested in what he calls "surfaces." What you look like, what you wear, where you live, how much money you make. All wasted on my dad. The fact that I'm considered the hottest girl at my school means nothing to him. I'm sure he'd prefer it if I was the smartest or most socially responsible girl, but he's never said so. Neither has Mom, who's totally gorgeous but doesn't seem to care. Augie's the only one who ever suggests that I might want to think about something other than clothes and parties. Well, Augie, I thought as I put the dog down and stood up, be careful what you wish for.

By the time I got home, Mom and Dad had left for work. There was a note on the counter. *Sorry we won't be home for dinner. Leftover lasagna in the fridge.* I toasted a bagel and called my boss, Jeremy, at the restaurant where I'm a server. He was less than thrilled when I told him I was quitting.

"Two weeks' notice would have been nice, March," he said. "Even a week. Who's gonna cover your shifts?"

"I'm sorry," I said. "I mean, it's not my fault. My parents enrolled me in this environmental camp for the summer. It's in, like, Tofino." It felt bad, lying to Jeremy. But I knew he wouldn't have any trouble replacing me. Dozens of hot girls dropped off résumés every day. Lots of them had more experience than me. I would be replaced before the day was over.

"You sure about this?" Jeremy asked. He was a good guy. A good boss. No groping the girls' asses in the kitchen, no gross comments or obvious drooling. Devoted to his wife and kids. He deserved better than this.

"Yup," I said. "Can you mail me my last check?"

"No problem," he said. "And March?"

"Yeah?"

"Good luck."

I hung up and opened my laptop. I couldn't afford to worry about Jeremy. Not if my plan was going to work. My Facebook wall was jam-packed with stuff about Tyler. Stuff I hadn't read and didn't want to read. Ever. I deleted my Facebook profile. Not deactivated. Deleted. Completely. One giant un-friending. No more liking, poking or commenting. No more posting my latest profile pictures and having everyone tell me how awesome I looked. Those days were gone.

I set up a new Gmail account and deleted my old one. I sent Augie my new info with a short message promising an explanation soon. If I told him what I was doing, I was afraid he'd try to stop me. And I was afraid I might listen. Augie's so rational. And what I was doing was the exact opposite of rational. I turned off my cell phone and tossed it in a drawer. Natalie had called, texted and left messages. I didn't read them or listen to them. No way she'd understand what I was about to do. I was going to miss her.

It only took about ten minutes of searching on Craigslist to find the kind of job I wanted. A really shitty one. A tacky gift shop downtown was looking for a cashier, five days a week, including weekends. The kind of place that sells toxic made-in-China souvenirs. Minimum wage. No benefits. No tips. Perfect.

Chapter Six

When I got up the next day, I threw my contact lenses in the trash. They'd be as dry as cornflakes soon. My old red plastic glasses were still in my night-table drawer. I started wearing contacts at thirteen. No one but my family ever sees me wear the red glasses. Not even Tyler. Especially not Tyler. As I slid them on, the earpieces pinched my head like lobster claws. The nose pads hurt too. I'd have marks from them soon. Perfect.

I checked to make sure Mom and Dad had left for work. Then I went to their bathroom and found a box of her hair dye. It was hidden under the sink, behind the toilet-bowl cleaner. She thinks no one knows she colors her hair, but she's been going gray for years. No one would ever describe my mom as vain, but I guess we all have our weaknesses. The color she uses is called Medium Golden Brown, which is a pretty accurate description of her real hair color. Pretty, but kind of boring. She's all about looking natural. Not me. Like Mom, I was blond when I was little. If I didn't fork over a big chunk of change every six weeks or so, I'd prob-ably be Medium Golden Brown as well. Not that I'd ever planned on finding out. Until now.

Back in the upstairs bathroom, I stood in front of the mirror, squinting at myself through my ugly glasses. My hair lay on my shoulders, smooth and straight. I took a deep breath and picked up the shears I had found in the kitchen junk drawer. My hand shook as I made the first cut, near my jaw. The scissors were dull, and the cut was jagged. Good. I slashed and snipped until I was left with a sink full of blond hair and a lopsided chin-length bob. And bangs. Very crooked bangs. I wouldn't recommend this method to anyone who wants to look even remotely attractive, but that wasn't my goal.

An hour later, my hair was brown. Muddy Gross Brown. Just the way I wanted it. When I looked in the bathroom mirror, I saw a stranger. A brown-haired, short-sighted stranger with a bad haircut. No eye liner, no lip gloss, no mascara. Someone the old March wouldn't even notice, let alone hang out with. I couldn't do anything about the fact that I have great skin and perfect teeth, but I planned on stuffing myself with sugar and fat. Bring on the zits and the cavities.

I cleaned up the bathroom and then changed into a pair of Mom's pleat-front khaki pants and one of her pastel golf shirts. Her shoes didn't fit me, so I wore my old running shoes. The ones I wear when Mom forces me to go for a nature walk with her, or Dad insists I help in the garden. I stopped in front of the full-length mirror in my bedroom. For a moment I felt faint. Short of breath. Sweaty. Sick to my stomach. Was I crazy? Should I call my hairdresser? Buy new contacts? Get my old job back? Change into my own clothes? Put on makeup? I looked at the girl in the mirror and shook my shorn head. "No," I said as I shut my bedroom door. "No," I said as I left the house. "No," I said as I walked to the bus stop. As long as Tyler couldn't live a perfect life, neither would I.

I hate taking the bus. It makes me itchy. All those sweaty hands and whiny kids and people with god-knows-what diseases. Coughing, sneezing, resting their greasy hair on the seatbacks. The loser cruiser. I hadn't ridden the bus for years. Before I was able to drive, there was always someone around to take me where I needed to go. A parent, an older sibling, a boyfriend. My boyfriend. Who never complained when I asked him to pick me up from work or drive me to the gym. My boyfriend, who had screwed another girl. My boyfriend, who was in a coma because of me.

I blinked away my tears as the bus wheezed up to the curb. I wasn't even sure how much it cost to ride the bus. As I fumbled around in my purse for the correct change, a guy sitting in the seat behind the driver looked at me and muttered, "You retarded or something, bitch?" He was balancing a filthy black pack on his lap, and when he opened his mouth, I could see he was missing some teeth. He also smelled like a sewer. I considered flipping him off, but decided against it. Who would defend the dumb girl with the bad clothes and the ugly glasses? All the other passengers were staring out the window or listening to their iPods. The bus driver had already pulled into traffic. I stuffed the correct change into the fare box and lurched to the back of the bus. No one else spoke to me. I might as well have been invisible. It was the weirdest feeling, but not unwelcome. It meant my plan was working.

The closest bus stop to the souvenir shop was outside a 7-Eleven and across the street from a McDonald's. Tough choice. I'd never eaten anything from a 7-Eleven, so I went in and bought the grossest thing I could find—a Corn Dog Roller—and an Invincible Orange Slurpee. Probably about 3,000 calories. Enough to put some flab on my ass.

As I was crossing the street, a voice said, "Poems for sale." At least that's what I thought I heard. It could have been "Porn for sale," given the kind of people who hang around the 7-Eleven. But I was alone at the light. No one beside me. No one behind me. Could stress make you hear voices? "Poems for sale." There it was again. A girl's voice. Soft and low.

I whirled around and dropped my Corn Dog Roller. A hand reached out and grabbed it just before it hit the sidewalk.

"This stuff is crap, you know," the person attached to the hand said. No wonder I hadn't noticed her. A girl about my age was sitting on a folded blanket in an alcove next to the bank on the corner. In front of her was a cardboard sign that read *Poems for Sale*. Weird, I thought. But at least I'm not hearing things. A small gray cat, wearing a tiny harness and leash, slept in the girl's lap.

The girl held the corn dog out to me. She was obviously a nail-biter and her hands were grimy.

"Keep it," I said.

She shrugged and took a bite. "Usually I prefer organic, grass-fed meat, but my chef is on vacation."

My eyes must have bugged out a bit, because she laughed and said, "Kidding. Wanna poem? Fair trade, I promise." The cat mewed, and she fed it a bit of the corn dog.

I shook my head and mumbled something about my job interview as I hurried away from her. I tossed the Slurpee in the garbage before I got to the gift shop. It was too sweet and the orange flavor tasted like piss. Or what I imagined piss tasted like. I could already feel my teeth rotting.

Chapter Seven

"My last girl, Katie, was with me a long time." Mr. Hardcastle, the manager of Castle Gifts, frowned at me over his smudged glasses. As if his employment problems were my fault. I'm not good at guessing people's ages. Everyone between thirty and fifty looks the same to me. Mr. Hardcastle wasn't fifty yet, but he wasn't under thirty either.

He was wearing faded jeans and a wrinkled plaid shirt. His shoes were scuffed black lace-ups. Not exactly business casual. His hair was on the long side and greasy. "She went back to Saskatchewan to look after her mother—breast cancer," he added. "You know how to work a cash register?"

I nodded. "A year at Starbucks. It's on my résumé."

"Thursdays and Fridays off. You're sure you don't mind working weekends?"

"Weekends are good," I said.

"I open the store every morning, and I come back at the end of the day to cash out and close up. And to make sure you're not robbing me blind." He gave a little snort that might have been a laugh. Or post-nasal drip. "The rest of the time you'll be working alone. You can lock the door and put up a sign when you need to take a bathroom break. But you should bring a lunch and eat it in back."

He pointed to a tiny room behind the counter. "And keep an eye out for shoplifters. Kids are the worst. If you actually see them pocket something, you can ask them to turn out their pockets or empty their bags. Or you can call the cops." Another snort. "Not that they do anything."

"Okay," I said.

"If it isn't busy, you can stock the shelves or tidy. I'd rather you didn't read, or talk on your cell or text when there are customers in the store. But I can't do much about that, can I?"

"I like tidying," I said. "And I don't have a cell. And I hate reading."

"Excellent." Mr. Hardcastle folded my résumé and stuffed it in a drawer. "See you tomorrow at ten then. Don't be late. Payday is the first and the fifteenth. We're open every day but Christmas and New Year's." He stuck out his hand and we shook. His hand was cold and damp, like a dead jellyfish. It was all I could do not to pull away and wipe my hand on my pants. "Welcome to the Castle Gifts family," he said.

"Thanks," I said. He turned his back on me and went into the back room. As I left the store, I picked up a little pencil-top eraser in the shape of a Mountie and slipped it into my pocket. I didn't need it, but it felt good in my hand. Something else the old March wouldn't do—steal something useless.

Poetry Girl and her cat were gone when I passed the corner. I wondered where she slept. Were there shelters that allowed pets, or did she sleep in a doorway or in the park? Did she sell enough poems to buy food for herself and the cat? And how did you sell a poem anyway?

I thought about that all the way to the hospital. How different our lives were, but also how messed up. By the time I got to the hospital it was close to 6:00 PM. I was counting on Tyler's mom and dad being at home with his younger brothers and sisters. All five of them. Tyler's parents are Catholics. Devout Catholics. Which explains the big family. They were probably at home saying grace, holding hands around the kitchen table. Praying for Tyler.

Eating together is a big deal in Tyler's house. Nobody eats standing up at the sink. Nobody nukes a pizza pop and eats it in the car on the way to hockey or piano lessons or choir practice. Tyler's mom makes dinner, and they all sit down together. Every single night. It's kind of miraculous. I used to love going there for Sunday dinner. The praying didn't bother me. I just shut my eyes and held hands with Tyler on one side and his youngest sister Tamara on the other. His hand was always cool and dry; hers was always hot and sticky. The words flowed over me like a summer breeze. I always said "Amen" with everybody else. I was going to miss those dinners.

Now, as I approached the hospital's front doors, I realized that I had no idea whether Tyler was even allowed to have visitors.

"Four-oh-four," the woman at the information desk said when I asked for his room number. "North Wing. You family? He's only allowed family."

"Cousin," I said. "I'm his cousin. From Regina. I came as soon as I could. He's, like, my favorite cousin."

The woman frowned at me. She'd probably heard the "cousin" story a million times. Her phone rang and while she answered it, I walked away. The elevator to the fourth floor smelled bad—like sweat and antiseptic and maybe blood. I pressed the button 4 with my elbow and used the hand sanitizer before I went into the ward.

A young nurse pushing a meds cart smiled at me. Her nametag said *Rosa, R.N.* "You look a bit lost," she said. "Who are you looking for?"

"Tyler McKenna. Room four-oh-four," I said. "I'm his cousin."

"Oh, too bad. You just missed his folks." She pointed down the hall. "Last room on the right."

"Thanks," I said.

She put a hand on my arm. "Brace yourself. It's a bit of a shock. Lots of tubes. A respirator. But he's doing well. And he's getting great care. The best."

"Thanks," I said again. I wondered how someone in a coma could be doing well, but I didn't ask. Rosa, R.N. gave me a jaunty wave as I headed down the hall.

Tyler was in a private room. I wasn't surprised. His dad has donated a lot of money to the hospital. Money he made running an online travel agency called Pilgrims' Progress that specializes in

Catholic pilgrimages. He's a multimil-
lionaire. A great dad. If you want to go
to Lourdes for a miracle, he's your man.
I was sure he'd airlift Tyler there if he
didn't wake up soon.

Chapter Eight

The door to Tyler's room was closed, which for some reason struck me as funny. I mean, he was in a coma. It's not like he'd care about noise or whether people could see him as they walked by. Even so, I closed the door behind me when I went in. I did care about privacy, even if he didn't. The room was filled with light and flowers. Tons and tons of flowers. I giggled and then clamped my hand over my mouth. Tyler doesn't know a rose from a daisy. He thinks cut flowers are stupid and a waste of money because they die after a few days. He always gave me chocolate roses on Valentine's Day. Now he was lying perfectly still under a sheet. Tyler, who was always in motion, even in his sleep. Nurse Rosa was right. It was shocking. Lots of tubes. And lots of machines with lime-green lights.

But he was still Tyler. I pulled a chair up to the bed and took his hand in mine. Cool and dry, like always. We sat like that for a few minutes. Silent. Connected. I noticed his lips were a bit chapped. Tyler was always smiling, laughing. Now his lips looked like those wax lips you can get at Halloween. I tried not to think about those lips kissing Kayla. It hurt too much.

I got up and put the little Mountie eraser on his bedside table so he would see it when he woke up. If he woke up. "I'm sorry, T," I whispered. "Get better. See you soon." I closed the door on my way out. Nurse Rosa wasn't around to see me cry.

I dozed off on the bus ride home and almost missed my stop. When I got to my house, both cars were in the driveway. I hadn't thought too much about what my parents were going to say about what I'd done. As I opened the front door and called out "I'm home," I caught a glimpse of myself in the hall mirror. The new me. Red glasses halfway down my nose. Creases on one cheek from sleeping on the bus. I ran my fingers through what was left of my hair. Nothing much I could do now.

Mom was in the living room, curled up on the couch with a glass of wine. Her eyes were closed and she was humming along to the Beatles. *Isn't it good. Norwegian wood.* Creepy song. Another full glass of wine sat on the coffee table, an open bottle beside it. I could hear the shower running upstairs. Sorry, guys, I thought. Relaxing with a glass of wine and an old Beatles album is off the table.

"Mom?"

She opened her eyes and blinked. Once. Twice. Her mouth opened slightly and a tiny gasp snuck past her lips. A bit of wine slopped onto her shirt as she reached over to put the wineglass on the coffee table. I could almost hear her thoughts. *March has been traumatized, first by the breakup and now by Tyler's coma. She's obviously very confused. Possibly having some sort of breakdown. We need to be supportive, not critical.* My parents may not be therapists, but they've picked up a few tricks along the way.

"That color looks good on you," she said. I looked down at my wrinkled pink shirt. Her pink shirt. Tyler once told me he loved my mom because she was always so calm. So rational. His mom was always shrieking, he said. Shrieking at his dad, shrieking at her kids. I bet she shrieked extra loud when she found out he was in a coma. But he wouldn't have heard her. I almost wished my mom would shriek. Then I could shriek back and stomp off to my room like a normal teenager. End of discussion. But that's not the way it works in my house.

"I'm not sure about the haircut though," Mom continued, frowning slightly. "It's certainly a different look for you. Very punk. Or is it Goth?"

"Neither," I said. "I did it myself. I quit the restaurant and got another job. Downtown, at a gift shop."

"So many changes," Mom murmured. "Do you want to talk about it?"

"Not really. I'm okay. Just tired."

"Did you eat? I could heat up the lasagna."

"No, thanks. I ate." I started up the stairs to my room. Her voice floated up after me.

"We'll talk later, March. With your dad."

Not if I can help it, I thought.

Hey Augie.

Heads up! Mom and Dad will probably be calling you soon. Here's the deal. I cut my hair and dyed it brown. I'd send you a pic, but I don't wanna scare you! I'm not wearing my contacts anymore. I got a new job too. I'm not crazy. Just trying to figure out what it means to have a perfect life. That's what you told me to do, right? I went to see T in the hospital. So messed up. Him. And me. And him and me. Don't tell Mom and Dad, okay? About me visiting T. They'd tell T's parents, and then there'd be a scene. Like the one that's about to happen. I can hear Mom and Dad outside my door. Time to face the music, I guess. As long as it's not opera! LOL.

March

PS. I met this girl. She sells poems on a street corner downtown. Maybe I'll buy a sonnet tomorrow.

Time to face the music, March. Augie always said that to me when I was in trouble. And I always said, *As long as it's not opera.* Or bluegrass. Or Celine Dion. It always made him laugh. I wondered if he'd laugh when he read my email. I shut the laptop, got out of bed and opened my door. Dad was leaning against the wall in the hall, sipping from his glass of wine. Waiting.

"You can come in," I said, peering down the hall. "Where's your tag-team buddy?"

"She's having a bath. It's been a long day. Problems at work and now…"

Now your beautiful, popular daughter has been replaced by a troll, I thought. Just like in one of those fairy tales Mom used to read to me.

"We're both worried, March. But we didn't want you to feel ganged up on."

"Very considerate," I said. "But I'm okay. I just needed a change. That's all."

"A new look. A new job. These are big decisions." He stood at the end of my bed and eyed me over the edge of his wineglass. "What's going on, March? We understand that you're upset—by the breakup and Tyler's accident. But this?" He waved his arm in my direction. "This is an extreme reaction. Quite extreme. If you need some help—"

I cut him off. "I don't need any help. I haven't had a breakdown, just a haircut."

"It looks like more than a haircut to me, March," he said. "It looks like—I don't know—a statement of some sort." He lifted an eyebrow.

"I'm tired, Dad," I said as I crawled under my duvet and turned my back on him. "That's my statement."

Chapter Nine

When I got up the next morning, there was a message from Augie.

Hey Sis,

In the immortal words of Miss Piggy, "Beauty is in the eye of the beholder, and it may be necessary from time to time to give a stupid or misinformed beholder a black eye." I always loved those red glasses. So retro.

Ask the poetry chick for a sextina. And good luck avoiding the stupid and the misinformed.

Love,

Bro

I laughed. Then I felt guilty for laughing. There's nothing funny about this, March, I reminded myself. No matter what Augie says. But when I caught a glimpse of myself in the bathroom mirror, the red glasses looked less hideous than they had the day before. My hair, however, was still a disaster. I frowned at my reflection. The glasses looked ugly again. Weird. Maybe I was one of the stupid and misinformed.

Mom and Dad had already left for work. A note on the table said, *Have a great day at work, honey. Pad Thai for dinner. XO Mom PS. English muffins in fridge.* She knows I love English muffins. Well-toasted, with tons of butter and strawberry jam. I poured myself a bowl of Dad's All-Bran and covered it in skim milk. It tasted like wet sawdust. But at least I'd be regular.

I left early to catch the bus to work. I wanted to find Poetry Girl and ask her to sell me a sextina. Whatever that was. I could have googled it, but I wanted to be surprised. It sounded kinda dirty, which could be interesting. More interesting than the poetry I'd had to read for school anyway.

It felt strange to be walking through my neighborhood at eight thirty in the morning. Lots of sprinkler systems pumping precious water onto ridiculously green front lawns. I paid enough attention in my environmental studies class to know that watering lawns was insane.

Mrs. Lombardi, our next-door neighbor, looked up from picking up her paper and glared at me. She's known me since we moved here when I was six. She always calls me Bella. Beautiful.

Now I looked like a stranger to her. An ugly stranger.

"Hi, Mrs. Lombardi," I called out. "Lovely morning."

She did a double take. Staggered backward and dropped the paper, a hand to her heart, her wig askew. I would have laughed, if it hadn't been so sad.

Stupid and misinformed, I thought as I walked on to the bus stop.

I stopped at the McDonald's to buy Poetry Girl an Egg McMuffin and a large coffee. I filled my pockets with sugar packages, creamers, stir sticks and napkins. When I got to her corner, she greeted me with a smile even before I handed her the paper bag of food.

"You again," she said.

"Yup. I'm in the market for a sextina. You got any for sale?"

"A sextina," she said after she had taken a few bites of the Egg McMuffin and shared some of it with her cat. She added six sugars and fours creamers to the coffee and stirred it dreamily, staring across the street at a guy pulling cans out of a garbage can. "A sextina. Yeah, I think I've got one. Just give me a minute."

She closed her eyes and lowered her head. The cat batted her face with a soft gray paw. I checked my watch: *9:15*. I didn't want to be late for my first day at work.

At 9:17, she raised her head, opened her eyes and started to speak.

Turns out, a sextina is pretty long. It took two minutes from start to finish— I checked my watch. And it wasn't dirty, not in any way. It started with "September rain falls on the house" and ended with "the child draws another inscrutable house." In between there was a line that went, "Time to plant tears, says the almanac." There was a woodstove, a grandmother and a man with buttons like tears. When she stopped speaking, I was crying. I'm not sure why. Maybe it was her voice—low and tender, for my ears only. Maybe it was the image of the child and the grandmother and the iron kettle on the woodstove.

"*Time to plant tears*," I repeated.

She nodded. "Very complicated structure, the sextina. That one's by Elizabeth Bishop. Great poet."

"How much do I owe you?" I asked.

"You already paid," she said, gesturing at the empty McDonald's wrapper, the coffee cup.

I shook my head and put two dollars in the hat on the sidewalk. "That poem—the sextina—it's too beautiful to be bought with some shitty food. Way too beautiful."

"You may be right," she said. "But we all gotta eat. Even if it's crap."

Suddenly my choice of All-Bran over an English muffin seemed pretty dumb.

Way to make a statement, March, I thought.

"Thanks though," she added. "For both—the crappy food and the money. Not much of a market for poems these days."

"People are stupid and misinformed," I said. "My brother, Augie, was the one who suggested I ask you for a sextina. I'd never even heard of it before."

She looked up at me and I noticed her eyes were the same shade of gray as her cat's fur. "Not everyone is stupid and misinformed then," she said. "Not your brother. Not you."

"Especially me," I said. "My name's March, by the way." I stuck out my hand and instead of shaking it, she took it in both of hers and held on for a second.

"I'm Hazel," she said. "Pleased to meet you."

Chapter Ten

When I got to work, Mr. Hardcastle was already there, even though I was fifteen minutes early. The door was locked, and when I tapped on the glass, he looked up from where he was counting cash at the counter. He smiled and held up a finger for me to wait. When he opened the door, the smile was still there. It made him look almost young. But he also looked rumpled and tired, as if he'd slept in his clothes. There was a stain on the shoulder of his shirt. His hands shook slightly as he shut the cash drawer.

"Gotta run," he said. "Here's my number. For emergencies only." He handed me a smudged business card. "I'll see you at six."

I nodded as he ran out the door. What would constitute a Castle Gifts emergency, I wondered. A biblical-style flood? A robbery at gunpoint? The need for a roll of dimes? I settled myself behind the counter on a high stool and thought about the poem Hazel had recited. From memory. Amazing. I could barely remember the words to "Mary Had a Little Lamb."

The day was filled with non-emergencies: Why was the bathroom light switch under the front counter? Where was the toilet paper? How do you say "Do you want a bag?" in Japanese?

When Mr. Hardcastle returned just before six, he wasn't smiling anymore. He had a serious case of five o'clock shadow. A bad smell—sour and burnt, like when you let milk boil over on the stove—wafted off him as he waved me out the door.

"See you tomorrow," I said. "Everything went well. No emergencies. Unless you count the occasional snowstorm." I pointed at the snow globes, which I had lined up and dusted. I hoped he wouldn't notice that one small snow globe was missing. I couldn't resist. It had three zombies in it. Zombies in top hats. Tyler loved zombies.

Mr. Hardcastle grunted and locked the door behind me. Maybe he was a morning person.

I went to the library on my way to catch the bus to the hospital. It's not somewhere I usually hang out. Mom used to bring Augie and me here every

Saturday afternoon for story time. I remember being so proud of having my own white kiddie card. It pissed me off that that kids could only take out ten books at a time though. It never seemed like enough. But I hadn't been to the library in years. Dad bought me an ereader last Christmas, but I still don't read much. I'm not sure why, exactly. Maybe it's because everyone else in my family is a hardcore bookworm. Piles of books everywhere. Even in the bathroom. My parents gave up on bedside tables years ago. They just have huge stacks of books next to the bed. The last book I read that wasn't for school was *The Secret Garden*. My bedside table is home to a Little Mermaid lamp and my phone charger. And now my red glasses.

It took me a while to figure out that weird library numbering system and find *Elizabeth Bishop: The Complete Poems 1927–1979*. But there it was on the shelf: call number 819.15, right where it was supposed to be. And there was "Sestina." Elizabeth clearly wasn't one for fancy titles. And I guess there's more than one way to spell *sextina*. I considered getting a library card and checking the book out, but it seemed like too much trouble. Instead, I made a copy of the poem and tried to memorize it on the way to the hospital.

When I got to Tyler's room, he looked exactly the same as he had the day before. No surgery after all. I managed to recite the first stanza of "Sestina" from memory. The rest I had to read from the copy I'd made. I cried when I was finished. Tyler didn't.

"I got you something," I said. I shook the snow globe in front of Tyler's face. The zombies' top hats wobbled slightly in the flurry. "Zombies from *The Corpse Bride*. In a snow globe."

Silence.

"I'll put it next to the Mountie, okay? Maybe the zombies will attack Dudley Do-Right."

More silence as I placed the snow globe next to the pencil-topper on the bedside table. Beside a vase of yellow roses was a lamp made from a figurine of the Virgin Mary. The light formed a halo around Mary's head. Mary wore her usual sky-blue robe, with a black-and-gold rosary draped over her clean white feet.

"Hail Mary, full of grace," I mumbled. Then I giggled. "Hey, Tyler. Remember when you told your mom you'd done a great Hail Mary pass at a game? And she sent you to confession. And grounded you for a week for blasphemy."

No response.

I got out my lip balm and ran it over his cracked lips. The scent of strawberries filled the room. I stroked his face—his cheekbones felt like blades and he needed a shave. His nails were growing too. That must be a good sign. A sign of life. I'd bring some clippers next time. Give him a mani-pedi. Maybe a shiatsu massage. Or a seaweed wrap. I giggled again. Tyler wouldn't be caught dead at a spa. Even thinking the word *dead* made my heart pound. He couldn't die. I wouldn't let him. We weren't done yet. I had things to tell him. If there was ever a time for a Hail Mary pass, this was it. An act made in desperation with only a small chance of success.

I picked up the rosary and ran it through my fingers. The glass beads were warm, as if someone had been touching them only moments before. I repeated the last stanza of the poem as I counted the fifty-nine beads with my fingers. *"Time to plant tears, says the almanac. / The grandmother sings to the marvelous stove / and the child draws another inscrutable house."* Over and over. Fifty-nine times. I knew I would never forget this poem. I wondered if this was how Hazel memorized her poems. Saying them over and over and over until they were seared into her brain. When I kissed Tyler goodbye, I imagined that his lips moved against mine. I poked my tongue into his mouth, past his parted teeth. I tasted something metallic and medicinal. But when I pulled away, I knew he hadn't moved. Not even an eyelash.

Chapter Eleven

"Natalie called me at work today," Mom said over dinner. "She's very confused and upset."

Welcome to the club, I thought.

"Shutting people out isn't helping, March," Dad said. "We're all concerned about you, Natalie included. She's your best friend. Call her. Tell her what's going on."

"She wouldn't understand." I put my fork down and pushed my plate away from me. It hit my water glass, which Mom caught before it flooded the table.

"Frankly, March, neither do we," Mom said. "It's all so...extreme. And you're not being fair to Nat. Or to us."

"How so?" I asked, standing up and dropping my dishes in the sink. "How am I not being fair? By dyeing my hair? Changing my job? Wearing glasses? Is it fair that Tyler cheated on me? Is it fair that he's in a coma?" My hands gripped the back of Mom's chair. "Maybe I like looking like shit, being invisible, selling Chinese crap to Japanese tourists. Maybe I deserve it. Maybe it's just more...honest."

"You may be right," Dad said. "But we're less interested in what you're doing than in why you're doing it."

"And what do you mean—maybe you deserve it? And is that why you broke up? Tyler cheated on you?" Mom turned in her chair and looked up at me. There was no anger on her face, no judgment. Just love. And worry. For a moment, I considered telling her everything. The party, Kayla, shoving Tyler, visiting the hospital. But I didn't want the look on her face to change from love to disgust. Even though I probably deserved it.

"Nothing," I said. "I didn't mean anything."

I spent my days off on Blueberry Hill. Crying. Pacing. Pounding the rocks with my fists until the pain in my heart seemed almost bearable. I only went home to sleep. Mom and Dad left me alone. By Friday night, I knew what I needed to do.

On the bus to work on Saturday, the driver smiled and said hello to me.

A woman in a nurse's uniform pulled a toddler onto her lap so I could sit down. I played pat-a-cake with the kid all the way downtown while the mother dozed, her head resting against the window. I got off the bus a few blocks from downtown and went to a café I sometimes go to with my dad. Funky wooden booths with benches lined the walls. The burnt smell of roasting coffee hung in the air. A guy in a faded Led Zeppelin T-shirt sold me two breakfast bagels: one with bacon, one without. I bought a large coffee, loaded it up with sugar and cream and walked into town. Hazel was on her corner, the cat in her lap. When I crouched down beside her, the cat hissed at me.

"No, Basho," she whispered. Her voice sounded different, and when she raised her head, I could see that her lip was split and there was a bruise on her cheekbone.

"What happened?" I asked, putting the coffee and bagels on the blanket beside her.

"Nothing." She unwrapped the bacon bagel. Her eyes widened. "Wow. This is a step up from McDonald's."

"Do you need to go to a clinic?"

She shook her head and took a small bite, wincing as the food brushed the cut on her lip. "I'm okay."

"You don't look okay."

"Thanks." She laughed. A short, sharp, not-very-happy laugh.

I sat on the blanket beside her and ate the other bagel. The cat butted my hand, and I fed him some egg. "What's his name?"

"Basho," she said. "After a Japanese poet."

I dug in my bag for some change and held it out to her. Three dollars and change. "Is this enough?"

"For what?"

"One of Basho's poems."

"More than enough," she replied. "Most of them are only seventeen syllables long." She peered at the money in my hand. "That's about twenty cents a syllable. Sure you can afford it?"

I nodded. Seventeen syllables. Even I could probably memorize that.

Clouds appear and bring to men a chance to rest from looking at the moon.

She wasn't kidding. Seventeen syllables is a short poem. A very short poem. Not even five seconds long.

I asked her to repeat the poem. Her voice was so beautiful, even with the slight lisp from her split lip. When she was finished, I recited it back to her, trying to pause in the right places.

My voice sounded rough and raw after hers. She clapped softly when I got it right. As I walked away, she was feeding Basho the rest of her bagel.

At work that day, I stole a shot glass with a moose's butt on it. When I got to the hospital after my shift, I added it to the collection on Tyler's bedside table. As far as I could tell, nobody had moved anything except the rosary, which was now draped over Mary's clasped hands.

"I have a new friend," I said to Tyler. "Her name's Hazel. She has a cat named after a Japanese poet." I pulled the rosary out of Mary's praying hands and lay down beside Tyler on the bed. It was like lying beside a warm log on the beach. I recited the haiku. Fifty-nine times. The beads felt like shelled peas in my fingers. When I was finished, I put my hand on Tyler's chest and closed my eyes. Up and down. Up and down.

"Wake up," I whispered. "Wake up, Sleeping Beauty."

The next thing I knew, Nurse Rosa was standing over the bed, a smile on her face.

"He opened his eyes a while ago," she said. "Just for a second."

I sat up suddenly and felt the room shift slightly. Nurse Rosa reached out a hand to steady me.

"Who was here?" I asked. "Who saw it?"

"Just me. But I've called his mother. She was pretty happy, as you can imagine. So are the doctors."

I nodded and gazed down at Tyler. His eyelids were still and slightly purple.

"What does it mean?" I asked. "Is he going to wake up soon?"

"It's usually a good sign," Nurse Rosa said. "All we can do is watch and wait and keep him comfortable." She looked at the rosary in my hands. "You a Catholic too?"

I shook my head. "Nah. Just desperate."

She laughed. "I know how that feels. You need to go now, hon. Visiting hours are over and I need to get some things done here."

I leaned over to kiss Tyler goodbye. No tongue tonight, not with Rosa in the room. "See you tomorrow," I said to Rosa, "and thanks for telling me about his eyes."

"No problem," she said as I left the room. "Nice shot glass, by the way. With any luck, he'll be sipping orange juice from it soon."

Chapter Twelve

I didn't know what I was going to do when Tyler woke up. I just wanted him to wake up. That was as far ahead as I could think.

When I got home from the hospital, I wrote to Augie.

Hey Augie,

Tyler opened his eyes today. I wasn't there, but a nurse told me about it. Nobody can say when or if he'll wake up, but I'm sure he will.

The poetry girl's name is Hazel. I asked her for a sextina (or sestina, in case you didn't know). She recited one by a poet name Elizabeth Bishop. You should look it up. "Time to plant tears, says the almanac." I feel like that's been my life lately. Planting tears. Today she recited a haiku by a poet named Basho. That one I have memorized. Seventeen syllables about how clouds give you a chance to rest from looking at the moon. Maybe that's what I'm doing—resting from looking at the moon.

I wonder what Hazel's story is. Today she had a split lip and a bruise on her face. I wanted her to go to a clinic but she said no. I bring her food, but it doesn't seem like enough. Maybe I'll ask Mom if I can bring her home. Her and her cat, Basho. Two strays. Mom loves strays, right?

Gotta sleep now. Love you,

March

The next morning when I arrived at Hazel's corner, she wasn't there. In her place, a young guy with filthy jeans and matted dreads sat on a flattened cardboard box. The sign in front of him said *I'm hungry. Please help.* I stood in front of him, coffee in one hand, a bag of breakfast bagels in the other.

"Where's Hazel?" I asked.

"Who?"

"Hazel. The girl who sits here. The one with the cat. The one who sells poems."

"Hazel." He turns the name over in his mouth as if it's a hard candy. "That's her name?"

"Yeah. Do you know where she is?"

"Dunno. You gonna eat that?" I shook my head and handed him the bag and the coffee.

"Hope you like cream and sugar," I said. "Hazel likes her coffee sweet."

He took a sip and grimaced. "No shit. Good coffee though. Thanks. Are you March?"

When I nodded, he stuck his hand deep into the pocket of his grimy gray hoodie and pulled out a crumpled sheet of lined yellow paper. "She said to give this to you if I saw you."

I took the paper and smoothed it out.

Dear March,
   I thought you might need this sonnet.

Written below in small neat printing was "Sonnet 29" by Shakespeare. The one that starts *"When in disgrace with fortune and men's eyes..."* We studied it in my lit class last year. The only thing I remembered is that bootless doesn't mean that you have no boots. It meant futile or useless. As I read the sonnet again on the street corner, I wondered how Hazel had figured out that I was in disgrace. Outcast, cursing my fate. At the end of the poem, Hazel had written: *Some things are forgivable, others aren't. Figure out the difference. Be kind to yourself. Your friend, Hazel.*

When I looked up, I was alone on the corner.

When I got to Castle Gifts, Mr. Hardcastle came to the door with a finger to his lips.

"Shhh. They're sleeping." He pointed to the twin stroller parked in front of the counter. Inside, two babies slept under matching blue blankets.

"Peter and Mark," he whispered as he filled the cash drawer. "Identical twins. My mom usually looks after them, but she's hurt her back."

"Where's their mom?"

"Dead," he said flatly. "Car accident six months ago, when the twins were two months old. She went to the store for diapers. Drunk driver hit her." The cash drawer clicked into place, and he straightened his shoulders.

"I'm sorry," I said. "That's terrible."

"Yes," he said. "It was. It is. My mom is great, but she's not so young anymore. The boys tire her out. Hell, they tire me out."

As if on cue, one of the babies woke up. Mr. Hardcastle sighed and rummaged in his jacket pocket and pulled out a grubby-looking soother.

"How do you tell them apart?" I asked as he wiped the soother on his shirt and popped it in the baby's mouth. The baby spat it out on the floor.

"This is Mark," he said. "Born two minutes before Pete. Mark's the wiggler. And see—he's got a birthmark on his left hand. Birthmark. Mark. We only noticed after we named him."

Mark obligingly waved a tiny fist, and I saw the faint brown smudge near his chubby wrist. I held out my hand to him. He grabbed it and tried to stuff it in his mouth.

"Everything goes in the mouth these days," Mr. Hardcastle said. "And I mean everything. Keys, stones, books, my glasses, sometimes food!" He laughed and squatted in front of the stroller. Mark smiled and drooled and kicked his blanket off. Pete slept on.

Mr. Hardcastle stood up and released the brake on the stroller. "See you at six," he said. As he pushed the stroller toward the door, Pete woke up with a wail. "And so it begins," Mr. Hardcastle said with a grimace.

"I could close up," I said. "I know how to cash out. Then you wouldn't have to come back later. Or open up in the morning. I mean, if you don't mind giving me a key..."

Mr. Hardcastle turned and stared thoughtfully at me. Pete started to cry. "You'd have to make the bank deposit," he said. "And take the float home. Can't leave money on the premises. Too many junkies."

"I'm okay with that. Really."

"Maybe for a day or two then. Until my mom is back on her feet. You sure you don't mind?" He fished a key out of his pocket. "The deposit stuff is in the drawer. The bank's around the corner. Just drop the bag in the after-hours slot."

I nodded and took the key. "It'll be fine," I said.

He rubbed his face with one hand. "Forgot to shave," he said absently. "I stay up at night working on my thesis. Mornings are a bit of a blur. As you can imagine."

"Your thesis?"

"Yeah. Botany. My PhD. I was almost finished when Fran died."

"I'm sorry," I said again.

"What can you do?" he said.

Chapter Thirteen

When I left Castle Gifts that night, I stuffed the bank deposit, the float and a Colonel Flapjack keychain in my backpack. Colonel Flapjack is a beaver in an RCMP hat. I figured he could join Dudley Do-Right in his battle against the snow-globe zombies. I also figured it was wrong to steal from Mr. Hardcastle, so I paid for all the junk I'd taken.

After I made the bank deposit, I checked Hazel's corner, but she wasn't there. Neither was the guy who'd handed me the poem. Maybe tomorrow.

A well-dressed drunk guy sat next to me on the bus, even though there were lots of other empty seats. I met the bus driver's eyes in the rearview mirror, and he raised his eyebrows. I shrugged, and the drunk guy said, "My wife just left me for my brother." He started to cry.

"You'll be okay," I said.

"What do you know?" He got up and staggered to the back of the bus. I could still hear his sobs.

That's a good question, I thought. What do I know? I stared out the window and made a mental list of things I know.

1. Tyler is going to be okay.
2. I need new glasses.
3. I am going to tell Tyler what happened.

4. There are worse things than having a bad haircut.
5. Living an honest life is harder than it sounds.
6. I am going to be okay.
7. I like my new job.
8. Being cheated on really hurts.
9. Tyler shouldn't drink vodka.
10. Kayla is a bitch.
11. I want to talk to Nat.

"Hey, sweetheart. You gonna get off so I can get a coffee?" The bus had pulled up at the hospital. The bus driver was standing over me, grinning. The drunk guy was long gone.

"Sorry, sorry," I said, scrambling out of my seat. "I wasn't paying attention."

"That's what they pay me for," the bus driver said. We walked into the hospital together. Then he saluted me and strolled down the hall toward the Tim Hortons.

Tyler's mother was waiting at the elevators, punching the Up button repeatedly. Her hair, which was usually styled in a sleek blond bob, was pulled back in a messy ponytail. Her roots were showing. Her normally flawless skin was blotchy. When she saw me, she stopped jabbing the button and clutched her gigantic purse to her chest.

"What are you doing here, March?" she said. "I told your parents. No visitors except family. Especially now that he's come out of the coma. The doctors were very clear. Family only until further notice."

"He's out of the coma? For real?" Even though I was kind of faking my surprise, I wasn't faking my happiness. If she'd been anyone else, I would have hugged her. Instead I just grinned at her.

She frowned at me and said, "Your hair is different."

"A lot of things are different, Mrs. McKenna."

She nodded, as if she understood. "The hospital called and I ran out the door. I left Brady in charge." She put a hand to her mouth. Her pale pink nail polish was chipped. "Do you think that's okay?"

The elevator doors opened. "Brady's, what? Thirteen?" I said.

She nodded.

"They'll be fine, Mrs. McKenna." No use telling her Brady was a little jerk. But I wasn't about to offer to babysit. We were on Tyler's ward now, and I could see Nurse Rosa talking to Mr. McKenna outside Tyler's room. Mrs. McKenna stepped away from me. Her back stiffened.

Mr. McKenna stepped forward and took his wife's hand. "Wait here, March," he said to me. "Family only. Doctor's orders."

Before I could protest, he and Mrs. McKenna had stepped into the room and shut the door in my face.

"Aren't you his cousin?" a voice said.

Nurse Rosa was leaning against the wall, arms crossed, smiling.

Living an honest life is harder than it sounds, I thought.

"No," I said. "I'm his girlfriend. Or I was, until right before the accident. Is he okay?"

"Well, he opened his eyes and asked for a Coke, so yeah, I think he's gonna be okay. In the long run."

"What do you mean—in the long run?"

"Coma recovery isn't always straight-forward. It's not like in the movies. Some patients need a lot of help, for a long time."

"But he will get better, right?"

Nurse Rosa patted my arm. "I've already said more than I should. I'm not a doctor. Go and wait in the patient lounge. I'll let you know when his folks leave. If he's still awake, you can have five minutes with him. As far as I'm concerned, you're his cousin from Regina. The one who brings him weird gifts. Now get out of here and let me do my job."

She laughed and gave me a gentle shove toward the lounge.

I sat in a beat-up corduroy recliner in the small, overheated lounge. The TV was on, but the sound was muted. I tried to watch Tom Selleck silently solve a crime in New York City. But not even his awesome 'stache could hold my attention. My thoughts bounced around like Ping-Pong balls in my brain. Bounce to Tyler. Bounce to Hazel. Bounce to Mr. Hardcastle. Bounce back to Tyler. At some point, I discovered the chair had a remote. I fiddled around with that for a while. One button made the whole chair rise up and deposit me on my feet. That was cool, but it didn't stop the bouncing in my brain.

I lay back in the chair and closed my eyes. I must have fallen asleep, because the next thing I knew, Rosa was shaking my shoulder.

"They're gone," she said. "Five minutes."

I wiped the drool from my chin and stood up. At least I wasn't wearing Mom's clothes anymore. I'd found an old pair of black pants and a plain white shirt in the back of my closet. I was still wearing my old runners though. I ran my hands through my hair. Nothing much I could do now. Tyler was going to wake up to a whole new me, whether I liked it or not.

When I opened the door to his room, he looked the same as he had the night before. The machines were gone though. I had kind of expected him to be sitting up, sipping a Coke. Smiling his wicked smile. I stood at the end of the bed and watched him for a few minutes. Was I ready? Time will tell, Mom always said. While I was watching him, his eyes opened. I stepped to the side of the bed. He turned his head toward me and blinked a couple of times. His eyes were unfocussed.

"Hey, Tyler," I said.

"Water," he croaked. I picked up a plastic cup full of ice water from the bedside table and held the straw to his lips.

"Welcome back," I said.

He waved the glass away.

"March?" he said.

"That's me."

"Those glasses suck ass."

Chapter Fourteen

That was all Tyler said. "Those glasses suck ass."

Then he closed his eyes and went back to sleep. So much for my fantasy of a tearful reunion after my big confession. So much for undoing the past.

I left the hospital and went home. My parents had kept dinner hot for me. Veggie meatloaf and peas. Ugh.

They sat with me in silence while I stared at the plate of food.

"Mrs. McKenna called," Mom finally said. "She says you were at the hospital. So you know the good news."

"Yeah."

"You don't seem very excited about it," Dad said.

"It's going to be a long haul," I replied. "His nurse told me that."

Dad nodded. "Brain injuries are tricky things."

"So they tell me," I said. I pushed my plate away. "None of it made any difference, did it?"

"None of what?" Dad asked.

"The hair. The glasses. The job. After all that, I'm still me."

Mom and Dad exchanged a glance that probably meant *This is what we've been waiting for.*

"I'm still the girl who ran away. I'm still a bad person. And I don't know if I can tell him."

There was a pause before Mom said, "You ran away? I'm sorry, March. I don't understand."

"I caught Tyler cheating. I shoved him. He hit his head. I ran away."

Mom and Dad exchanged another glance. This one probably meant *This is worse than we thought*.

I looked away from their concerned faces. "A good person would have stayed with him. A good person wouldn't have lied about what happened."

"So you cut your hair and quit your job because you wanted the outside to match the inside. And you felt ugly inside," Dad said.

I nodded. "But it didn't make any difference, did it?"

"What difference did you want it make?" he asked.

"Jeez, Dad. Could you be a little less psycho-babbly? I wanted to even things out. I guess I wanted to suffer."

"And did you?"

"Not as much as I thought I would. I mean, yeah, the whole Kayla thing was pretty bad. But I kept meeting people who actually *were* suffering. This girl, Hazel. She's homeless. And my new boss has twins and their mom is dead. But they liked me, even with bad hair and ugly glasses. Kids on the bus showed me their toys. The outside didn't matter at all."

"Because they could see who you really are, March," Mom said.

"Didn't you hear me, Mom?" I yelled and slammed my fists on the table. My knife and forked jumped off my plate. "I pushed Tyler. And I left him for dead."

"And you checked his pulse and called nine-one-one. And you tried to—" She paused. "You tried to atone."

"In the Middle Ages, people atoned by wearing hair shirts," Dad said. "Your mom's clothes and that haircut and those glasses are your hair shirt. But the thing about atonement is that it doesn't go on forever. At some point, there has to be some forgiveness. If you're religious, you ask God to forgive you."

"And if you're not," Mom chimed in, "you have to forgive yourself."

"But I want Tyler to forgive me first."

Mom stood up. "Let's get some rest. We'll go to see Tyler tomorrow. Together. I'll clear it with the McKennas. Okay?"

I nodded and went upstairs. There was an email from Augie, sent earlier that day. It was one word: *Congratulations*. Sometimes Augie can be a real pain in the ass.

In the morning I called Nat and told her everything.

She was mad at first. Really mad.

"You should have told me," she yelled. "I could have helped you. I'm your best friend."

"I know," I said. "But I thought you'd hate me. I hate me. I left him, Nat. Lying on the deck."

"Did you check his pulse? Did you call nine-one-one?"

"Yeah, but—"

"You caught him cheating on you. That's, like, temporary insanity right there."

"I know, but—"

"You should have stayed. No question. But you didn't. And he's gonna be okay, right?"

"I think so."

"Then get over yourself and do something useful."

"Like what?"

"I dunno. Maybe Mrs. McKenna could use some help with the kids. Maybe you could drive Tyler to rehab. There's gotta be something."

"What if Tyler hates me? What if I can't forgive him either?"

"Then you deal with that. And you still help out."

I nodded. "Will you come to the hospital with me tomorrow?"

"What time?" Nat said.

After I finished work on Monday, Mom and Dad drove me and Nat to the hospital. Mom said Mr. and Mrs. McKenna were at church. I went in to see Tyler by myself. Mom and Dad went to the patient lounge to play with the recliners.

Nat curled up on a chair in the hall outside Tyler's room. "Shout if you need me," she said, slipping in her earbuds.

Tyler's eyes opened when I walked in. The head of his bed was raised so he was almost sitting up.

"What happened to your hair?" he rasped.

"Cut it. Dyed it."

"Were you here before? I think I remember those glasses."

"I was here last night. You were pretty dopy. But you told me the glasses suck ass."

He laughed. "Well, they do. The hair's okay though."

"Thanks." I sat on the visitor's chair beside the bed and picked up the zombie snow globe. "I was here a few times. No one knows. I brought you this stuff."

I shook the snow globe, and he smiled. His teeth looked gray and a bit fuzzy.

"Zombies. Cool," he said. "Thanks. I wish I could say I remember you being here, but I don't."

"Do you remember anything? How you hurt yourself? How you got here?"

He shrugged. "Not really. I was at the party. And now I'm here. I must have slipped."

I swallowed. It felt as if I had a brick in my throat. He didn't remember. Maybe he never would. Then I took a deep breath and said, "I pushed you."

"What?"

"I caught you screwing Kayla. I was pretty mad. I pushed you, and you hit your head."

"Kayla? I screwed Kayla?"

"You don't remember?"

He shook his head and winced. "I remember drinking a lot of vodka. But I don't remember Kayla being there. Or you. I must have been really hammered. I'm sorry."

"That's it?" I said. "You're sorry?"

"I'm the one who ended up in a coma, March. Not you," he said.

"What happened after you pushed me?"

"I checked to make sure you were alive and then I called nine-one-one."

"And then what?"

"And then I left."

"You left."

The words sat in the air between us, cold and heavy.

"Yes."

"You bitch. I could have died."

"I know. But you're okay now..."

Tyler stared at me, and then said, "Get out."

"Tyler—"

"Get out!" Beads of sweat formed on his forehead. He grabbed a glass of water from the bedside table and threw it at me. I ducked, and it splashed against the wall behind me.

"I'm sorry," I said. "I'm really sorry."

"Get out." He fell back against the pillows and turned his head away from me. I think he was crying.

Nat was waiting for me in the hall.

Behind us, something thumped against the door.

"Zombie snow globe," I said.

"If you say so," Nat said.

Chapter Fifteen

The McKennas banned me from visiting Tyler after that. Mrs. McKenna told my mom that Tyler didn't need "March's toxic drama." But I'm pretty sure he didn't tell them what happened at the party. About a month after my last visit, I got a long rambling text from him. He said he'd started going to church again, and he was trying to forgive me. He was looking forward to going back to school and hoped it wouldn't be awkward. He was sorry for what happened with Kayla, but he thought we'd been heading down a wrong road anyway. The "incident" had been a wake-up call. A game-changer. He wasn't drinking anymore. He wasn't going to be playing contact sports. He sounded like a total stranger. Maybe it was the brain injury. Maybe not. I'd never know for sure.

I spent a couple of days crying after I got that text. All the pain came back. Worse than before. It felt shitty. Really shitty. But in a way, it was like we were even. He hurt me. I hurt him. I was trying to forgive him, and he was trying to forgive me. He was going to be okay. So was I. Maybe I didn't have my perfect life anymore, but I had something different. Something better.

"You've changed," Nat said one day in late August. She was leaning on the counter of Castle Gifts, watching me cash out. "And I don't mean just your hair."

"I like my hair. It's easy."

"Wouldn't hurt to touch up your roots though," Nat said as I locked up. "Maybe get a professional to tidy it up."

"I guess. I'll do it before we go back to school, okay?"

Nat nodded. "At least you're not wearing your mom's clothes anymore." She shuddered. "And the runners…"

I laughed and looked down at my feet. I had bought some new sandals the week before. Comfortable but cute. That was my new motto.

We passed Hazel's corner on our way to Lens Crafters to choose new frames. I hadn't seen her since the day of the haiku. I checked her corner every day on my way to and from work, but it was always empty. As if it was waiting for her.

Someone called my name. I turned and saw a skinny girl with a shaved head and a lot of piercings standing in the alcove where Hazel used to sit.

"I've got something for you," she said.

"You know this chick?" Nat asked.

"Nope," I said.

"I'm a friend of Hazel's," the girl said.

I stepped toward her, and she opened her denim jacket. A small gray head peeked out.

"Basho!" I cried. "Where did you get him? Where's Hazel?"

I reached out and Basho jumped into my arms.

"She's gone," the girl said. "After she got out of rehab, her folks came and got her. Took her back to Alberta."

Rehab. That explained a lot.

"Why didn't she take Basho?" I asked. Basho butted my hand with his head.

The girl shrugged. "Dunno. Allergies, maybe? She told me your name. Where to find you. She said you'd pay me."

"She did?"

"March, it's a scam," Natalie hissed. "Hazel's probably at some crack house waiting for the money."

I ignored her and handed the girl most of my cash. My new glasses could wait.

"Hazel said you'd do the right thing." The girl turned and walked away from us. Basho nibbled my hand.

"You hungry, little guy?" I said.

"Yeah, and probably flea-infested too," Nat said. "But he is kinda cute."

I nodded and buried my face in Basho's fur.

Dear Augie,

I've been memorizing a poem for you. I found it in a book I bought at a secondhand store. It's called "The Waking." It has the best last stanza ever. Even better than "Sestina."

> *This shaking keeps me steady. I should*
>> *know.*
> *What falls away is always. And is near.*
> *I wake to sleep, and take my waking*
>> *slow.*
> *I learn by going where I have to go.*

I recite it to myself every night before I go to sleep. I imagine that somewhere in Alberta Hazel is listening. I'm working on Mom and Dad to let me visit you in Germany. I've already signed up for a German class at school. And it turns out my boss, Jason, knows German too. You'll meet him and the twins when you visit. I can't wait to see you.

Ich liebe dich,
March

Acknowledgments

Many thanks, as always, to Andrew Wooldridge for his unwavering support and his weird sense of humor. Thanks, too, to Robin Stevenson, whose friendship, encouragement and compassion brighten my life.

Sarah N. Harvey is the author of eight books for children and young adults. Some of her books have been translated into Korean, German and Slovenian, none of which she speaks or reads. Her novel, *The Lit Report*, has been optioned for a feature film. She will not be in it. She lives and writes in Victoria, British Columbia, where she is determined to learn how to salsa dance, study Italian and overcome her fear of flying (in no particular order). For more information, visit www.sarahnharvey.com.